A Fatal Affair

FAITH MARTIN

ONE PLACE. MANY STORIES

HQ
An imprint of HarperCollins*Publishers* Ltd
1 London Bridge Street
London SE1 9GF

www.harpercollins.co.uk

HarperCollins*Publishers*
1st Floor, Watermarque Building, Ringsend Road
Dublin 4, Ireland

1
First published in Great Britain by
HQ, an imprint of HarperCollins*Publishers* Ltd 2021

ISBN: 978-0-00-841049-0

MIX
Paper from
responsible sources
FSC˚ C007454

This book is produced from independently certified FSC™ paper
to ensure responsible forest management.

For more information visit: www.harpercollins.co.uk/green

Printed and bound in Great Britain by
CPI Group (UK) Ltd, Croydon CR0 4YY

Prologue

Tuesday 1st May, 1962

No one in the city of dreaming spires on that chilly May Day morning would have been thinking about death. Why would they, when the birds were singing, and everyone was congregating around Magdalen Tower, counting down the moments until it was 6 a.m.; that magical moment when the city began its celebrations in earnest?

Certainly, the excited young choristers clustered at the very top of the college building had no reason to ponder on tragedy. Rather, their minds were firmly fixed on their soon-to-be-given rendition of that lovely piece, '*Te Deum Patrem colimus*', the singing of which had been customary from Magdalen Tower on May Day since 1509.

Even the influx of foreign visitors to the city on that special morning were far more interested in watching, with bemusement and disbelief, the quaint and colourful antics of the Morris Dancers that thronged the city streets, with their jingling bells and clacking sticks, than in contemplating murder.

After all, who in that beautiful and ancient city could believe on such a wonderfully auspicious and bright spring day that anything dark and fatal could be happening anywhere? Weren't the daffodils and tulips, the forsythia bushes and polyanthus, blooming in multi-coloured glory in all the gardens, proclaiming that life itself was good? Little children, perhaps bored with Latin hymns, were laughing and playing and singing their own, far more down-to-earth, songs, every bit as traditional to May Day, and carried on the breeze – 'Now is the Month of Maying' competing with 'Oh the Little Busy Bee' for dominance.

Tourists took photographs. The choristers, flushed with triumph, eventually left the tower. The people in the streets, flushed with having witnessed proper 'English culture' sought out any cafés that might be open so early in the morning in search of that other British stalwart, a hot cup of tea.

And less than seven miles away, in a small country village that had for centuries celebrated May Day almost as assiduously as its nearest city, a plump, middle-aged woman made her bustling way through the quiet lanes and barely stirring cottages, towards the village green.

Margaret Bellham had lived in Middle Fenton for all her life, first attending the village school there, and then marrying a lad who'd grown up four doors from her down the lane, and moving into a tied cottage on one of the farm estates.

In her younger days, she had missed out on being chosen May Queen for the day by the narrowest of margins, and had long since mourned the fact. Still, such disappointments hadn't stopped her from cheerfully ruling the roost on the May Day Committee for the last twenty years.

It was her job to see that the May Day Procession, including all the infants and juniors from the school went like clockwork, with the flower-festooned 'crown' and four lances being allocated to only the most responsible (and strongest) children to carry. It was she who organised the village ladies who would be producing the food for the afternoon picnic, traditionally held around the village duck pond. And, naturally, it was her responsibility to ensure that the village maypole, a permanent structure erected in pride of place on the village green nearly two centuries ago, was ready for the maypole dancing by all the village maidens under the age of eighteen, which would start promptly at noon.

Margaret puffed a bit as she crossed the lane in front of the school, and looked across to check the time on the church clock opposite – barely 7 a.m., so she was well on schedule. Nevertheless, she was mentally making a list of all the things she still needed to do as she turned the corner that would take her past the duck pond and onto the village green proper.

She only hoped, she thought with a scowl, that Sid Fowler had remembered to secure the ribbon-bedecked wooden crown on top of the maypole before it got dark last night. For whilst the stone maypole itself was left in situ to withstand the weather all year round, the wooden piece at the top, with multiple slats carved into it through which the long, colourful 'ribbons' were secured, was always kept stored in the school shed.

Sid wasn't the most reliable of men, though, and she had the spare key to the school shed in her pocket, just in case. She had delegated Rose Simmonds, the barmaid of the village pub, to make sure that all the many ribbons, traditionally the seven colours of the rainbow, had been cleaned and would be bright and sparkling for when the children began their dances.

As a child who had once danced around the maypole herself, weaving and ducking around her fellow schoolmates in order to create the intricate patterns so iconic of the maypole, she knew how much better it all looked when the ribbons were bright and fresh. Spider's Web and Gypsies' Tent were her favourite dances, but the Twister …

At that moment in her reverie, Margaret looked towards the maypole to check all was as it should be, and stopped dead in her tracks. For a second or two, she merely stood and blinked, not really sure that she was seeing what she thought she was seeing.

Falteringly, her brain buzzing like a hive of disturbed bees, she stumbled forward, but as her feet stepped onto the soft green grass of the green, she felt the strength leeching out of her, and she sank awkwardly onto her knees.

She felt her mouth open, but was incapable of making a sound. Instead, she just stared at that year's May Queen.

Nobody had been surprised when Iris Carmody had been chosen. Traditionally, all the village men (in a closed ballot) elected a village girl between the age of sixteen to twenty to be Queen of the May. And Iris, with her long pale fair hair, big blue eyes, heart-shaped face and hourglass figure had been breaking the hearts of local boys since she'd hit puberty. And probably even before then! Now, at the age of seventeen, she had swept all other challengers before her.

As May Queen, she was to rule the village for the day, for tradition had it that the May Queen's every wish had to be met. Of course, in the past, this had led to some jolly japes, with one May Queen famously ordering that all the pigs must be 'painted' green, and all lads must have daisy-chains for belts!

Margaret, for one, had had severe misgivings about giving Iris Carmody, the little minx, so much scope to make mischief, and she didn't believe that she was alone in that. There had been more than one wise matron who had taken her aside and muttered darkly about the village's choice this year.

But looking at Iris now, dressed in a long white gown embroidered with a swathe of tiny colourful flowers and her long, waist-length hair topped by a crown of violets, bluebells, primroses and narcissus, even Margaret had to admit that she epitomised youthful beauty and the spring.

Even the colourful ribbons, hanging from the crown of the maypole, and which were now wrapped tightly around and around her body, holding her fast to the stone edifice, looked pretty.

But underneath the swathe of beautiful fair hair that was

framing her profile, Margaret Bellham could see a string of darkly smudged bruises around Iris's neck, and even more horrifically, the congested, contorted face and lolling blue tongue that made the dead girl look like a grotesque parody of what a May Queen should be.

Finally, the monstrousness of what she was seeing freed Margaret Bellham from her paralysis, and she began to scream, before wailing pitifully.

Chapter 1

It was a week and four days after the murder of Iris Carmody, and DI Harry Jennings was beginning to feel the strain. His officers had been working on the case non-stop, with the press breathing down their necks every inch of the way. He wasn't particularly surprised by this, as a beautiful girl dressed as a May Queen and found strangled and bound to a village maypole was many a newspaper editor's dream.

But it was just one more headache that he didn't really need.

And he knew that another one was about to walk through his office door at any moment. He sighed heavily and leaned back against his chair, feeling the lack of sleep catching up on him. The trouble was, for such a spectacular crime, the investigation of it was turning out to be frustratingly pedestrian.

For a start, nobody had seen the dead girl on the day of her death. The girl's parents had no idea why she'd dressed so early and left the family home when she had such a busy day ahead of her. And nobody in the village had heard anything untoward occurring at the village green, either the night before she was found, or early in the morning – not even those sleeping in the cottages surrounding the crime scene.

And whilst there had been gossip and speculation aplenty within the village about the dead girl – and her love life – there was very little confirmatory *proof* to actually go on. Oh, it quickly became very clear after the PCs had finished interviewing everyone in the small village that everyone and their granny had a lot to say about the dead girl – and not much of it flattering. Or *too* flattering, depending on who was doing the talking. According to most of the women, she was a flighty girl at best, a man-eater at worst, but nobody could actually point the finger with any conviction at the supposedly long list of her potential victims or lovers. And whilst a fair proportion of the men had liked to hint that they knew Iris rather well, on being pushed for times, dates and proof, nobody would actually go so far as to admitting to being the girl's paramour.

Everyone agreed that her 'official' boyfriend of the moment had probably been taken for a fool, but unsubstantiated gossip didn't provide rock-solid motives for murder.

And now, piling tragedy upon tragedy, there had been a second death that was almost certainly connected to the murder of the May Queen. Although this one looked, thankfully, far more straightforward to deal with, and the Inspector had high hopes that it could soon be closed. Especially once his next visitor had been tactfully dealt with.

Well, perhaps …

Here DI Jennings heaved a massive sigh. As he did so, there was a sharp, peremptory rap on his office door, and before he could bid anyone enter, the door was thrust open and a tall, brown-haired man walked in. Dressed in a slightly rumpled, charcoal-grey suit, he was not fat but not particularly lean, and although he was a handsome enough individual, he looked noticeably pale and hollow-eyed. He also looked much older than the fifty-two years that Harry Jennings knew him to be.

As well he might, poor sod, the Inspector thought grimly. Jennings hastily shot to his feet. 'Superintendent Finch, sir,' he barked out awkwardly. 'Er … won't you sit down?'

The Superintendent nodded and sat very carefully and precisely in the chair in front of the Inspector's desk, a clear indication of how rigidly he was controlling himself. The Superintendent had already given his formal statement to Jennings yesterday morning, which had been painfully awkward for both men concerned, but Harry hadn't been surprised to have received the call from Keith Finch late yesterday afternoon asking for another 'informal chat' today.

'Sir, again, I'd like to say how very sorry I am about your son. I assure you, his case is being treated with the utmost care and respect,' Harry said flatly, retaking his own seat.

His superior officer grimaced. 'Yes, I'm sure it is,' he agreed. Then his shoulders slumped slightly. 'Look, let's not beat about the bush, Harry,' he said wearily, suddenly dropping the formality and looking and sounding more like the bereaved father that he was, rather than a still-serving police officer of some rank. 'David's death has left us, my wife and me, I mean ... well ... all at sea, as you can probably imagine.'

Harry cleared his throat helplessly. He was beginning to feel a shade angry and resentful at being put in this position, but he knew it was hardly the Super's fault. Even so, he wished the man would just take some leave and keep well out of things. It would make things so much easier for everyone all around. But he knew, just from looking at the other man's face, that that was not going to happen any time soon.

'Let's put our cards on the table, shall we?' Superintendent Finch said grimly. 'There's no denying that my boy, David, was head over heels about this Carmody girl. He'd not yet brought her home to meet us, even though they'd been stepping out together for some weeks, but we were all well aware that he was well and truly smitten. And I don't mind telling you, his mother was worried about it. Even before her murder, we'd been hearing rumours about her. You know what it's like – women gossip and delight in bringing bad news to your door, and a number of people went out of their way to warn Betty that, well, this girl he was seeing might have been two-timing him.'

'Very distressing for you and your family, sir, I'm sure,' Harry said soothingly.

'Yes, well, his mother was concerned, as I said, but for myself I thought … well, David was a good-looking lad, young, doing well at university … and frankly, Harry, I thought it would all blow over. When I was his age …' He trailed off and shrugged.

Again Harry nodded, wishing that this was all somebody else's headache. But it wasn't. The mess had been dropped well and truly in his lap, and now he had to try and steer a course that kept a superintendent happy, whilst showing no bias or favour in his pursuit of closing the Carmody case.

And the best of British luck with that, he thought sourly. On the one hand, he had his immediate bosses braying at him to close the case, and on the other, he had Superintendent Keith Finch, who was not going to be happy if he solved the case at the expense of his family and his dead son's reputation.

'You thought that he would soon get tired of Iris and find someone more suitable sooner or later.' The Inspector followed his line of thought easily. 'Yes sir, I understand, and who's to say you wouldn't have been proved right?' Harry was careful to keep his voice neutral.

The Superintendent eyed him with another weary smile. 'I realise this isn't exactly an ideal situation for you either, Harry. Especially now. David's death has hit us all hard, but there's no denying …' He paused, took a deep breath and sat up straighter in his chair. 'You know, of course, that they're saying that David killed her? And then killed himself out of guilt?'

Jennings nodded miserably. Three days ago, this man's son had been found hanging in a barn belonging to a close friend of the family. So far, although it was early days, there were no signs to suggest that it had been anything other than suicide. Naturally, the village was aflame with speculation, and the newspapers were only too happy to stoke the fires.

'I find that impossible to believe,' Keith Finch said. Then he held up a placatory hand as the Inspector opened his mouth to respond, adding quickly, 'And yes, I know, how many times have we heard family members of suicide victims or murder suspects say exactly the same thing?' He ran a hand helplessly over his face.

The Inspector, aware that he could put it off no longer, said, 'Sir, I assure you that we're going to conduct a proper investigation into everything, but, obviously, I can't keep you apprised of anything ...'

Luckily, he didn't have to continue. Usually, telling a superintendent things that he didn't want to hear wasn't a smart move for a man with ambitions, and Harry Jennings hadn't been looking forward to doing it. So it was with something of a relief that he stopped speaking as his superior officer again raised a hand.

'Don't worry, Harry, I'm not here to ask you to keep me updated. The Chief Constable has already made it clear that I can't be involved in this thing in any way. Especially with David being a murder suspect in the Carmody case.'

Harry let out a relieved breath. 'Yes sir.' But he was very much aware that he was in a uniquely awkward and unenviable position. He wanted to be able to tell his superiors – and the press – that he'd found the killer of the May Queen; and when a murdered girl's boyfriend hangs himself a few days later, that's usually taken to be as good as a confession. Which meant that, normally, he could be confident of closing the case once they'd been able to collect some evidence cementing the hypothesis that her lover had killed her in a jealous rage.

But when the dead suspect was the son of a superintendent of police, and an old acquaintance, it could hardly be business as usual. Especially when dealing with a man who, before now, could claim to have high-ranking friends in both the police force and society in general.

But Harry was well aware that the Superintendent would not be able to weather this particular storm unscathed. Unfair or not, the chances were that Keith Finch now faced not only a personal loss, but a professional loss too. For surely the powers-that-be were already making plans to pension him off – the usual fate of anyone who caused them such public embarrassment?

Harry had been careful to make sure that there were no newspapers on his desk that morning, but it was impossible that the Finch family wouldn't have read the speculation in the local press. He knew David had had a sister, and he could only guess the hell she was going through right now. He suppressed a shudder and sighed gently.

'The thing is, of course, that I *don't* believe for one moment my son killed her, Harry. Of course, I know you have to consider the possibility that he did, but I have every confidence that you'll find no evidence supporting this. And that you will eventually find out who did,' the Superintendent added hastily, although there was nothing on his face to indicate whether he believed this to be true or not.

Harry swallowed hard, unable to meet his gaze.

'So, to get down to brass tacks. I'm here about the inquest on David. It's set for this Monday, yes?' Superintendent Finch said briskly. Whatever his personal tragedy, he was determined to keep a stiff upper lip, and for that Jennings was grateful. He wasn't sure, given the circumstances, what comfort he could give to a grieving father in imminent peril of breaking down.

'Yes sir. Starting at 10 a.m.'

'And it's the old vulture presiding?'

Inspector Jennings nodded. 'Yes, sir. He's the best, as you know.'

'I agree. I've always rated Dr Ryder very highly – even when he's being the proverbial pain in our necks,' Keith Finch said heavily but with a wry twist of his lips.

Jennings merely grunted. In the past, he'd had to have more to do with Dr Clement Ryder than he'd ever wanted. Why the man couldn't act more like a regular coroner, and just do his job and leave the police to do theirs, he didn't know. But no, he had to stick his nose in – and, even more annoyingly, often come up trumps.

'And that brings me to the purpose of this visit. I've had a word with the Chief Constable, and he's agreed with my proposal.'

At this, Harry Jennings felt his heart rate begin to ratchet up a notch or two, and a slow, sick feeling sidled into his stomach, making him swallow hard. 'Sir?' he asked warily.

'We might turn a blind eye to things, Harry, but that doesn't mean to say that the powers-that-be haven't noticed that that girl of yours and our coroner have developed a habit of, well, shall we say, "supplementing" our more normal lines of inquiry?'

At this point, Harry Jennings got a *really* bad feeling. 'Sir,' he began to object, but wasn't allowed to finish.

'Now, I know we can't expect WPC Loveday and Dr Ryder to help you on the actual Iris Carmody case—'

'No sir, we definitely can't! WPC Loveday has barely completed her probationary period and—'

'But Dr Ryder, as city coroner, has before now done some, shall we say, follow-up inquiries on a number of his inquest cases, isn't that so?'

'Yes sir,' Harry admitted miserably.

'And with some considerable success?'

'Yes sir,' he was again forced to agree.

'Very well then. As I said, the Chief Constable is with me on this, Inspector. After the inquest on my son is over – *no matter what the verdict may be* – you will approach Dr Ryder and ask him to make further discreet inquiries about my son and the circumstances of his death.'

'Superintendent, sir, I don't think that's really wise …'

Keith Finch gave a harsh bark of laughter, and for the first time looked seriously angry. 'It may not be *wise*, Inspector,' he snapped, leaning forward in his chair, 'but everyone's going around saying that my boy – *my boy!* – murdered that girl and then killed himself.' Suddenly he slammed the flat of his palm down on

Jennings's desk so hard and fast, that Jennings nearly went into orbit. The sharp ricochet of sound had the heads of the police officers in the outer room swivelling in their direction.

'*And I'm not having it, Jennings*. Is that clear?' Superintendent Finch said through gritted teeth.

Harry nodded wretchedly. 'Yes sir,' he agreed. Clearly the Super still had some clout with the higher-ups, and he was in no mood to be thwarted.

'Very good. So, continue your investigation into the Carmody case,' the Superintendent said mildly now, standing up and looking as if nothing dramatic had happened. 'Let nothing interfere with that. Continue regarding my son as a suspect if you must. But let that clever girl of yours and the old vulture sniff around my son's case without any impediment. Understood?'

'Yes sir,' Harry said, standing up politely.

It was clear, all right, but that didn't mean to say he had to like it. And, whilst he might have to tread carefully – for now, anyway – that didn't mean he would always have to toe the line. Especially if they finally got some proper evidence as to who had murdered Iris Carmody, and why.

He watched his superior officer leave the room and then slumped back down behind his desk with a groan. Great! As if he didn't have enough troubles already. This was infuriating – another case with his station's annoyingly efficient and pesky lone WPC and the old vulture snooping around in police business.

Just what he needed!

Chapter 2

Dr Clement Ryder, city coroner, was tidying his desk in preparation for leaving for the day. Like his police colleagues he often worked on Saturdays, and although he was not obsessive about neatness, he didn't like dealing with mess at the start of any working day.

Outside, the daylight was beginning to diminish, and he was looking forward to going to home to his attractive Victorian terrace overlooking South Park, and indulging himself in a small cognac. A widower for some time, with two adult children off leading lives of their own, he was content enough to live alone. Nevertheless, he was glad that he'd been able to find a good 'daily' who not only kept his home tidy, but also left a tasty supper warming for him in the oven every evening.

A man just a shade over six feet tall and clean-shaven, he had a head of thick silvery-white hair and slightly watery grey eyes. Although not fat, he was certainly getting a little hefty around the middle, but that was not about to stop him from enjoying his housekeeper's cooking!

He reached for a stack of files, intending to lock them in the bottom deep drawer by his right leg, but as he lifted them off the oak, leather-lined top, he felt his left hand give a quick, involuntary jerk. He had to quickly drop them back onto the desk and then catch the top one before it slid off onto the floor.

He was still scowling angrily at his now slightly trembling hand, when his secretary knocked on the door. Quickly, he thrust his hand down out of sight below the top of the desk, and looked up, careful to put a polite, inquiring smile onto his face.

His secretary, a comfortable-looking, middle-aged woman answered with a polite smile of her own. 'You have a visitor, Dr Ryder. He doesn't have an appointment, but I think you'd prefer to see him. Detective Inspector Jennings?'

Clement Ryder blinked, hoping he didn't look as astonished as he felt. For all the five or so years he'd now been working as a city coroner, he could never remember DI Jennings calling on him voluntarily. Usually, it was he who bearded the policeman in his own den.

'Of course, please show him in,' Clement said, but was very much conscious of the hand trembling in his lap. Surreptitiously, he began to massage his weaker palm with the fingers of his other hand.

Clement had been a surgeon for most of his adult life, but nearly six years ago, he'd noticed a slight tremor in his hand. His worst fears had been confirmed when he'd undertaken a series of tests – abroad and under another name – which had confirmed the onset of Parkinson's disease.

Naturally, he had been obliged to retire at once, not only from surgery, but also from medicine in general, as he could not put any of his patients at risk. It was a decision that had baffled and stunned his friends and professional colleagues alike, as he'd given no real reason for it. But he'd known that he would never be able to keep his condition a secret for long from medically trained, observant people, and being unwilling to endure the pity of others, it was important to him that he kept his illness totally under wraps.

And yet, he'd been unable to retire and do nothing, so he'd

retrained instead as a coroner, studying law and passing the requisite examinations for the position with ease. Here, at least, his medical knowledge and general acumen when it came to observing and understanding human nature wouldn't go to waste. And, he was honest enough to admit to himself, his chosen new career meant that he was still a man of considerable influence and power.

His social circle included presidents of colleges, city councillors, politicians and captains of industry. Over the years he'd not been above using that power, on occasion, to delve further into the cases that sometimes passed through his courtroom. Although a jury of the good old British public could nearly always be relied upon to get things right, in Clement's opinion – which was the only one that really mattered to him – that wasn't *always* the case.

Neither, in his opinion, were the city police infallible! This had led to him investigating one or two deaths that had been attributed to either accident or suicide, but which had proved to be murder instead.

So although he cursed his trembling hand for playing up just when an eagle-eyed member of the constabulary had come to call on him, he was also very much intrigued. Harry Jennings was amongst one of many people who would no doubt be delighted to know of his illness – since it meant it could be used against him to force his retirement – but Clement was confident that the police officer would notice nothing amiss. So far, his illness hadn't progressed to the state when he was slurring his words.

Nevertheless, he leaned back in his chair a little as DI Harry Jennings passed through the door at his secretary's behest, took a deep calming breath, and made sure to keep his hands still.

'DI Jennings, a pleasure and something of a surprise,' he greeted his visitor amiably. 'Please, have a seat.' He nodded at the comfortable leather padded chair on the opposite side of his desk.

'Thank you, sir,' DI Jennings said, glancing around curiously. Clement watched him take in the book-lined walls, thick carpet and tall standing lamps, his eyes wandering with some surprise to the oil paintings that were hanging on the walls. These were Clement's own personal contribution to the décor, some rather fine English country landscapes. A fire roared away in the fireplace, since, for May, it was still a bit on the chilly side. Wordlessly, the policeman regarded the large oak and leather desk positioned impressively in front of two large sash windows, which overlooked the less-than-salubrious outer cobbled courtyard of Floyd's Row, where the morgue and coroner's offices were situated.

'Nice office you have, sir,' the Inspector commented as he took the proffered seat in front of the desk. Jennings, a man who had not long since celebrated his fortieth birthday, was slender, with thinning fair hair, a rather large nose, and hazel eyes that, at that moment, didn't look any too happy. They flitted about the room, reluctant to settle on any one spot, and Clement found his lips twitching with amusement.

'Is there something I can do for you, Inspector?' he asked, deciding to put the man out of his misery as quickly as possible.

'Er, yes, sir, there is. It's about the case you're overseeing on Monday,' Jennings said, clearing his throat.

Immediately, Clement cast his eyes to the large stack of files still sitting on his desk. 'Oh? The David … er …' For a moment he couldn't remember the last name of the deceased, and once more he silently cursed the illness that was slowly but surely nibbling away at his faculties.

'Finch,' Harry Jennings said, clearly too annoyed at having to be here at all and ask this man a favour, to realise that the old vulture had suffered a momentary lapse in memory.

'Ah yes – young lad, found hanging in a friend's barn,' Clement added crisply. 'I was reading the preliminary notes earlier this morning.' He paused, eyeing the Inspector with a gimlet glance that had the officer shifting uncomfortably in his seat. Clement had already noted that the boy's body had been found in the same village where Iris Carmody had been murdered barely a week before, and suspected a link. 'Is there something about the proceedings that I need to know about in advance?' he demanded.

Harry Jennings flushed slightly. 'The, er, deceased, is the son of Superintendent Keith Finch,' he said flatly, running a finger under his tie, which suddenly felt a little tight.

'I'm sorry,' Clement said, after a moment's thought. 'The boy's father is a friend of yours?'

Harry Jennings visibly hesitated. 'I've known the Superintendent a long time,' he finally conceded carefully. 'He's a good man. A good officer. Naturally, this business of his son has been a severe blow.'

Clement nodded, but his face was beginning to tighten. 'Inspector, if you're here to ask me to try and influence the verdict of the jury …'

'Perish the thought!' the Inspector burst in quickly. He knew, from past experience, just how withering the old vulture could be if he thought you were trying to stick your nose into his territory.

'I understand, of course, how upsetting it can be for families when suicide is suspected,' Clement said, slightly mollified but his voice still a shade cold. 'And we try and spare their feelings as much as possible, but—'

'You think it is suicide then?' Harry Jennings interjected craftily.

'Certainly not,' Clement shot back, sounding and looking shocked. 'I have yet to even hear the evidence, or listen to the witness testimony. And as you know, I never, ever, pre-judge a case.'

The Inspector hid a smile and nodded solemnly. Just as he'd known it would, the implied slur on Dr Ryder's impartiality had diverted him nicely from his intended harangue.

'No, of course not, Dr Ryder. But I am here on the family's behalf – in a way.'

Clement slowly sat forward in his chair. His watery grey gaze was now fixed firmly on the man in front of him. 'Again, if you're asking me to do anything other than conduct a proper and full inquest …'

'I'm not, Dr Ryder. I wouldn't ever be so foolish,' Harry Jennings said, and meant every word of it. Nobody but an idiot would ever try and put one over on the old vulture. Only extremely young and green constables, or the stupidly over-confident, ever tried it. 'Actually, I'm here with a request from the boy's father about what happens *after* the inquest,' he added hastily and before he got any further into the coroner's bad books.

'After?' Clement repeated, presumably slightly confused, but not by so much as a twitch of his bushy eyebrows, showing it.

'Yes, Dr Ryder,' the policeman said, deciding he might just as well leap in with both feet and get it over with. 'I'm sure you're aware of the murder of Iris Carmody in Middle Fenton nearly two weeks ago. The May Queen murder they're calling it in the press.'

'Yes, I read the papers,' Clement said with an amused twist of his lips. 'And it struck me that the killer, in posing the poor girl's body as he'd done, might have been trying to make some kind of a point. Perhaps mocking the girl, and her role as "Queen" of the May perhaps? It wasn't my case though. One of my colleagues conducted the inquest, which I believe was adjourned immediately so that the police might have time to gather more evidence?'

'That's right. We – that is, my officers and myself – have been tasked with investigating that case. But as you'll find out Monday, if you haven't already read about it in the files, young David Finch was Iris Carmody's boyfriend.'

Clement merely grunted.

'Naturally, now the boy's dead – and in such circumstances,' Harry continued grimly, 'rumours are flying around, both in the village and in the press, that the boy killed Iris and then killed himself in a fit of remorse.'

Clement sighed. 'You can't stop people speculating ahead of the evidence, Inspector,' he pointed out wearily. 'But they *will* keep on doing it!'

'Don't I know it!' the Inspector agreed bitterly. 'As it happens, so far we've found no evidence suggesting that David Finch *is* the killer. That, of course, may change,' he felt obliged to add. So far, they'd found very little evidence at all, but he was not about to say so. Apart from the fact that the medical examiner had declared that the May Queen had been manually strangled and hadn't been a virgin, they knew depressingly little more now than they did on the morning she had been found bound to the village maypole.

'Naturally, the boy's father doesn't believe his son either killed his girlfriend, or himself,' Jennings swept on. 'And he's asked me, with the Chief Constable's blessing, to ask you, once the inquest is over, to … er … further investigate David's case. Regardless of the verdict.'

For a moment, as Harry Jennings sat tensely waiting for the storm to break over his head, he mentally tossed a coin in his mind as to how the old vulture would react.

On the one hand, he couldn't be happy to be told that, no matter what his jury found in the David Finch case, the police wouldn't be satisfied with it. That would dent his pride and vanity mightily, for the former surgeon liked to think his word was law!

On the other hand, Harry knew how much the old man liked to play the investigator – and with some success, he had to admit, albeit grudgingly. And he rather thought that being *actually asked* for once to stick his nose into a ripe and juicy case would prove to be too irresistible for him to resist.

Of course, for once, it suited Inspector Jennings to have the likes of Dr Ryder poking his nose into the case. Because if the wily old so-and-so *did* uncover evidence that pointed towards David Finch being the killer, Harry's superior officers could hardly blame Inspector Harry Jennings for it! And if anyone was to take the flack for ruining Superintendent Finch's life and career, he was happy to see Clement Ryder do so.

For a second, the younger man watched, much amused, as the silent war of fury and intrigue played out in the older man's wonderful brain. It was almost as if he could hear the cogs turning.

Taking advantage of the older man's silence, he decided he might as well take the opportunity to lay down some ground rules. 'Of course, this investigation has to be, like the other times, strictly unofficial. You'll have to be careful not to let the press guess what you're up to, and on no account are you to talk to them.'

Clement smiled sourly. 'I have no love of the gutter press, Inspector, as you should know.'

Harry nodded. At least, on this point, he and the old vulture were as one. 'Bloody reporters are making my life miserable,' he unbended enough to admit. 'I daresay you saw the headlines. I think "Tragedy of murdered May Queen" was the least sensational of them. What the girl's poor parents are going through ...'

He paused, sighed, then shook his head. 'And that's another thing. You're not to start straying into *my* murder case. The death of Iris Carmody is definitely *not* in your remit, understand?' he said aggressively. 'You're only to see what you can find out about David Finch. His state of mind and so on. Anything that could help his family understand what happened. And if you discover anything that ... well, that suggests that he did commit suicide, or did have anything to do with Iris's murder, then I expect you to bring it straight to me. I hope that is clearly understood?'

Dr Ryder wore a bleak expression. 'I haven't said I'd do it yet, Inspector. And we haven't even had the inquest yet. Aren't we jumping the gun a little?'

The Inspector smiled wryly. For all his token resistance, they both knew that old vulture wouldn't be able to resist poking around.

'It might be a bit premature, yes,' Harry conceded, 'but I came to you now, as opposed to after the inquest, because I wanted to give you advance warning, so that you'd have the chance to pay especially close attention to the evidence given in court tomorrow,' Harry said. 'After all, nobody would deny that you're a very clever and experienced man, Dr Ryder, and you may hear something tomorrow that strikes you as interesting or relevant.

I'll admit, you're very … perspicacious at times, and once or twice you've seen things, well, that some of us might miss.' He shifted uncomfortably on his seat, silently cursing the higher-ups who'd put him in this untenable position. Having to actually praise the interfering coroner was giving him a headache.

Aware of the other's man's predicament, Clement Ryder bit back a rather savage grin. 'I wasn't aware that you'd noticed, Inspector,' he couldn't resist taunting him a little. But before Jennings could really take umbrage, he slipped in smoothly, 'I take it I'll be given the services of WPC Loveday again? She'll be acting as my police liaison, as before?'

The Inspector gave a huge sigh. 'Yes sir. I'll be speaking to my constable before she finishes her shift tonight. She can attend the inquest out of uniform, since I don't want the reporters finding out about her involvement until absolutely necessary.'

In a previous investigation with the coroner, WPC Trudy Loveday had got her picture in the papers accepting a reward from a grateful peer of the realm for saving the life of his son. No doubt, her appearance in the May Queen murder case would eventually cause a minor stir. Jennings only hoped she could keep under the radar for a while.

'The last thing we need is for the press to get it into their head that because David Finch was the son of a serving, high-ranking police officer, that he or his family are getting special privileges,' Harry Jennings said. *Even if they were*, he thought to himself.

'The young man's dead, Inspector, and his family in mourning,' Dr Ryder said flatly.

'That won't stop them being out in force, trying to pick up on something that they can use to tear him to shreds,' Harry Jennings predicted glumly.

Chapter 3

The Inspector's prophetic words were brought back to Clement's mind the following Monday morning as he officially opened the inquest into the death of David Peter Finch. For the press gallery was indeed lined with the avid faces of men – and two women – who watched and waited, hoping for sensationalism with the keen anticipation of their profession, notebooks open and pencils at the ready.

Amongst their number was one that he knew from of old.

Duncan Gillingham met the coroner's gaze and gave a wide, insolent grin. Clement frowned slightly, but let his gaze sweep past the handsome young man, not giving him the satisfaction of acknowledging his presence. Although he'd had the misfortune to meet this particular gentleman of the press before, he hadn't been much impressed by him.

The public gallery was also packed, as it always was whenever a case smacked of sex, scandal or intrigue. He sighed slightly, but was by now too old and resigned to mourn the more depressing aspects of human nature. Instead his eyes scanned the ranks of eager faces for one in particular, and spotted it in the middle of one of the back rows – a slender young woman with a mass of dark, curling hair, and big, appealing brown eyes.

Trudy Loveday smiled briefly back at him, acknowledging his very slight nod of greeting.

She'd been almost out the door of the station last night when DI Jennings had called her back and informed her that she would be working with Dr Clement Ryder once more on another case. She'd been absolutely delighted by the unexpected turn of events, but also very surprised. It was not often that her superior officers had actually sought them out to give them an assignment, as opposed to Dr Ryder more or less forcing their hand.

Of course, she understood that Superintendent Finch would be desperate for his son to be exonerated of implied guilt in the murder of his girlfriend, but even so, she could tell from Inspector Jennings's manner that he wasn't particularly happy about the situation.

It depressed her that, even now, he still thought that she was only useful for dealing with the female victims of crime, making the tea, filing and walking the deadest, most boring of beats. In other words, all the jobs that nobody else wanted!

Now she sat up a little straighter in her seat as the coroner called the court to order and began the proceedings. As per Inspector Jennings's instructions, she was dressed in plain clothes, consisting of a long, dark green skirt, white blouse and blue, green and white patterned cardigan. She'd deliberately left her hair long and unfettered, knowing that it helped disguise her appearance, for she knew that she looked very different with her most distinguishing feature hidden underneath a police cap. Even so, she hoped that nobody was taking much notice of her as she discreetly pulled a notebook out of her bag and prepared to use her fluent shorthand.

This was the first time in all their collaborations that she'd been given advance notice of the case she would end up investigating, and she was determined not to miss anything. Not that she expected Dr Ryder to be anything other than eagle-eyed and observant as ever, naturally.

25

She listened to him now as he went quickly through the preliminary facts, establishing that the jury were there to establish the identity of the deceased, and if possible, the cause of death. They were *not* there, he warned the jury, giving them a hard, slow stare, to speculate about anything other than the matter in hand and the evidence as presented to them.

The two women on the jury flushed a little at this, as if at a personal rebuke, and even a few of the men shuffled uneasily on their seats. No doubt they had all been reading about the brutal and flamboyant murder of the May Queen, and the press speculation surrounding those closest to her – including her now deceased boyfriend. But if they had been hoping that their being called to jury duty meant that they would be given free rein to indulge their curiosity, they had very quickly been disabused of the idea.

Trudy hid a smile as she watched her mentor whip the jury into shape, even as she felt vaguely sorry for them.

Finally, as the more routine and humdrum part of the proceedings came to an end, she could feel the excitement building up around her. As she glanced around the packed room, the sight of one man in the group of reporters caught her eye. It was his head of black hair that first alerted her to the presence of Duncan Gillingham.

Then, as if sensing that he was being watched, his green-eyed gaze flashed around, and Trudy shrank back in her seat. Luckily, she was sitting between a rather portly matron with a large hat, and an equally large gentleman in a loud houndstooth jacket.

She held her breath for a moment, but was confident that he hadn't seen her, which was just as well. The last thing she needed was to attract his attention before she'd even had a chance to get started. However, she had little doubt that, eventually, the reporter would twig to the fact that she and Dr Ryder were sniffing around, and then she could expect things to become somewhat fraught. Given their past history, Trudy was not looking forward to once again having to deal with the attractive, ambitious, treacherous reporter for one of the city's bigger newspapers.

'Right then. We'll begin with the person to find the body,' she heard Dr Ryder say in his clear, calm voice, and the usual susurration of excitement rippled through the spectators as a man made his way to the small podium to give his evidence.

From her reading of the files first thing this morning, she knew him to be in his mid-forties, although at that moment his face looked lined and weary, making him appear a little older. A few inches short of six feet, he was heavily built (his bulk the result of muscle, not fat,) with sandy-coloured hair and pale eyes – either blue or grey, Trudy guessed. From a distance, it was hard to tell.

'You are Mr Raymond Colin Dewberry?' Dr Ryder asked him mildly.

'Yes sir,' the man replied quietly but clearly.

'You are a farmer, with steadings in the village of Middle Fenton, I believe?'

'Yes sir, that's right. Worked the land all me life, like.'

Trudy gave a mental nod. No doubt that accounted for the man's build. Even with the advent of tractors and other farm machinery, she knew that being a farmer was still a labour-intensive job that required a measure of physical fitness.

'You own the land and the barn where the deceased was discovered?'

'Yes sir, happen I do.'

'Then, in your own words please, tell the jury what happened on the day in question.'

Ray Dewberry drew a deep breath, but his head hung forward, in the way that shy men not used to being the centre of attention often affected. 'Well, it were nearly six in the morning, I reckon,' he began, his voice a low, Oxonian burr that nevertheless carried well. 'I'd just helped my cowman get the ladies into the milking shed, and I had to go to the barn up the hill to check on the threshing machines in there. One of my lads told me the day

27

before he thought one of 'em needed repairs. So I went inside and saw young David, hanging from the rafters.'

There was a collectively drawn breath at this simple but ugly statement, and the man giving evidence visibly flinched, as if it was his fault that they were all having to go through this, and ducked his head even lower. 'Gave me a right turn it did, and all,' he added helplessly.

'I understand it was a shock for you, Mr Dewberry,' Clement said, his voice kind but firm. 'You recognised the deceased immediately?'

'Oh aye, known him since he were a nipper, didn't I? He was best friends with my own boy, Ronnie. As a kiddie, him and Ronnie were always running about the farm all over the place, playing, like. More often than not he'd end up having tea with us at the farmhouse. My wife was always feedin' him, like. A lovely chap he were,' he added almost defiantly. He shot a quick look at the public gallery, as if daring them to contradict him.

Clement could feel the mood in the room change to one of sympathy for the farmer, and who could blame them? It must have been awful for him to find the body of a man he'd known for nearly all of his young life. 'I understand this is upsetting, Mr Dewberry, but if you could tell us a little more about what you observed, that would be helpful.'

Ray Dewberry once more heaved a sigh, his strong shoulders slumping a little further down. 'Well … I dunno really. For a moment or two, I reckon I must have just stood there, gaping at the poor lad. Then I walked further in and saw that he was hanging from the main crossbeam, like. From a bit of old rope that had been thrown over it. And there was a stepladder lying on its side underneath his legs. The other end of the rope had been tied off around a heavy plough on the ground that had been in there for years, like. Too rusty to be of much use nowadays, but you don't like to get rid of machinery, do you?'

The man paused and gave an audible swallow.

'I looked up at him proper like, in case he was … well, still with us like … but I could see from his face … well … that he weren't. I had to go outside and was sick in some nettles. Sorry,' he added meekly.

After this embarrassing admission, Ray Dewberry gave a shrug and waited patiently for the next question.

Clement regarded him thoughtfully. He knew from the police reports that this witness was a man of considerable property, albeit mostly in the form of farmland that his family had worked for generations. But he also lived in a substantial farmhouse, and rented out several cottages to his workers. By your average man-in-the-street's standard, he was a wealthy man, but he clearly wasn't anybody's idea of a successful businessman. He'd probably worked on the farm since leaving school at fifteen, as had his father before him, and so on back through generations.

But just because he wasn't sophisticated, Clement knew, didn't mean that he was unintelligent. 'You'd known the deceased all his life, you say. What was your opinion of him?' Clement asked calmly.

'He were a right good lad,' Ray Dewberry said at once. 'Clever, I reckon, too. He was studying at university, weren't he? Had good manners too, and was always cheerful. My wife was right fond of him always – saw a lot of him growing up, like I said. He and our Ronnie were always underfoot. When he got older, he helped out on the farm in the summer holidays for pocket money, like. Trustworthy. Kind to animals. A good worker.'

The farmer seemed to run out of words and accolades, and again stood waiting patiently.

'You must know the contents of the barn where David Finch was found quite well,' the coroner changed tack. 'Was the stepladder found beneath the deceased part of its contents?'

'Ah, I reckon it were,' Ray said, after a moment's careful thought. 'Prob'ly been leaning against the wall at the back for ages. Whenever stuff got too old, but was too good to chuck out, we allus tended to leave it in the barn. Never know when summat might be needed again, do yuh?'

'Did your son and the deceased know the barn well?'

'Course they did. Young uns, looking for somewhere to play, explore everything. I reckon in its day, that there barn on the hill had been a pirate ship, or a robbers den, or a cowboys-and-Indians battleground.'

There was a warm ripple of sentiment from the listening crowd, and someone gave a muffled sob. Probably the boy's mother, Clement thought, or possibly Ray Dewberry's wife. Then he glanced down at his notes and saw that the farmer had been a widower for a few years now.

'So David would have known about the ladder,' Clement said, a comment that didn't go unnoticed by reporters or spectators alike, and a ripple of tension shivered around the room. 'Was there a lot of rope kept in the barn?'

Ray shrugged. 'Always old rope around on a farm, sir. Bits of machinery, tarps, barbed wire, you name it. I never chuck nothing out, and nor did my dad a'fore me. You never know when summat might be useful, see?'

'Yes, I understand. So what did you do after finding your son's friend in the barn that morning Mr Dewberry?'

Ray Dewberry sighed heavily. 'Well, I didn't see no easy way to get him down, so I ran back to the house and called the police. We had a telephone installed a couple of years ago, when my wife got so ill.'

'You didn't think of using the stepladder and climbing up it yourself?'

'Nah, didn't trust it would hold me. It's a rickety old thing, and I'm more solid-built than young David,' the farmer said with unthinking candour. 'And 'sides, I didn't have nothing on me to cut him down with, only my old pen knife, and I didn't know if it would saw through rope. And … well, if'n I'm gonna be honest abhat it, I needed to get out of there,' he admitted, his voice thick and his accent more pronounced than ever now. 'B'aint never been back in that barn yet, but I s'pose I'll have to go back in there sooner or later …'

Before things could begin to get maudlin, Clement briskly took him through the rest of the events of that morning – the arrival of the police and the ambulance, and that of the local doctor.

The crowd became a little impatient as this less exciting recital went on, but there was a renewed murmur of interest at the end, when the coroner rounded up his questioning.

'And when you approached the barn that morning, you noticed nobody in the vicinity?'

The farmer looked puzzled. 'No sir. Who'd be around at that time o' the morning?'

'And the previous evening – you hadn't noticed anyone hanging around, seen a stranger's car in the lane nearest to the barn, anything like that?'

'No sir, but then a'rter dark I'm in the house having my tea, and then early to bed.'

'I see. And when you found your son's friend, you didn't see anything else lying on the ground, or positioned anywhere near him – such as a piece of paper or a letter or a note?'

'No sir, I didn't then!' Ray Dewberry said, with his first sign of asperity. Clearly, he didn't like this suggestion that the young man he'd known from boyhood had left a suicide note. 'But then, I don't suppose I was noticin' much at the time,' he nevertheless felt compelled to add.

'And you have no idea why David Finch would have come to your barn?'

'Nah. Haven't seen him for a few years, not since he were a young lad and he helped out around the place for some pocket money, like,' the farmer said sadly.

'Do you know if the barn was a meeting place for, er, courting couples?' Clement asked delicately.

Again, there was the expected ripple of titillated anticipation, but Ray Dewberry seemed immune to it. He merely looked at the coroner and shook his head. 'No sir,' he said, for the first time smiling slightly. 'Reckon most lads and gals had more comfortable spots than a draughty old barn in the middle of nowhere. It's not as if it was filled with hay or anything,' he added as an afterthought.

There was a brief, nervous titter from some of the spectators at this.

'Mr Finch hadn't contacted you, or your son, arranging to meet at the barn the evening before you found him?' Clement pressed.

'No sir, that he didn't,' Ray said, sounding puzzled. 'Why would he want to meet up with me? He stopped working summers on my farm when he went up to university. And my Ronnie weren't in that night – he was at the pub with his mates. Everyone knows that,' he added, again darting a glance at the public gallery, as if daring anyone to gainsay him.

'Thank you, Mr Dewberry. That's all,' Clement said kindly. 'I think we'll have the medical evidence at this point. Calling Dr Martin Breakspeare.'

Chapter 4

The local doctor, who'd originally been called to the scene, looked nervous, as well he might. He hadn't been practising long, but long enough to know the formidable reputation of the man sitting in the judgement seat. Although he'd not studied at the same hospital where Dr Clement Ryder had been chief surgeon, he'd made a lot of friends in the medical fraternity who had – and the man's legend went ahead of him.

So, not surprisingly, as he took the podium he cast the coroner a quick, apprehensive look. There wouldn't be any wriggle room for slip-shod testimony or waffling about the facts with this man!

Dr Breakspeare took a deep breath and hoped that he didn't say anything foolish.

'You were called to the scene at … what time, Dr Breakspeare?' Clement began gently enough, but even so, the young medic consulted his notes. A tall, thin, dark-haired man with a somewhat rampant moustache, of which he was rather fond, he had a long neck and a prominent Adam's apple.

'Er, I arrived at the barn at 7.10 a.m.'

'Was it hard to get to?'

'Not really. The barn was not within sight of the farmhouse itself, but off a farm track that rose steeply, but was reasonably navigable in a trustworthy car like mine. I was directed there by the constable on duty at the house.'

'And will you tell the jury, in layman's terms, what you found, and the results of any tests or examinations of the body since then, please.'

The doctor cleared his throat and turned to the jury. 'I found the police in attendance, and the body of a young male lying on the ground. I was informed by one of the officers that the victim had been found hanging from the rafters of the barn, with the rope around his neck. This rope had been loosened, removed from the body and set aside. I observed a rope-burn mark around the sides of the deceased's neck, consistent with this testimony.'

He paused, took a sip of water then continued steadily. 'I ascertained that the victim was indeed deceased – that is, he had no heartbeat or pulse, and was in fact, cold to the touch. Using the standard measures – that is, body temperature and the passing of rigour – I gave the investigating officer a preliminary estimate that time of death had probably occurred not less than six and not more than twelve hours previously.'

Clement nodded. 'In other words, you think it most probable that the victim died somewhere from the later afternoon to the late evening of the day before?'

'That would be my opinion, er, Dr Ryder, but of course, as you know, estimating time of death is fraught with difficulties. The ambient temperature in the barn, any pre-existing medical conditions the deceased may have had, and a number of other factors can all make stating a time of death, at best, a rough estimate.'

'Carry on.'

'After declaring the victim dead, I left to continue my normal duties,' the medical man said promptly.

'Did you know the victim?'

'No sir, not personally.'

'Thank you. Call the police pathologist please.'

As the local GP stepped down with some relief, an older,

rounder, white-haired man stepped past him and took his place. There was no similar look of apprehension on his face at being called to testify, and the younger man supposed he was used to it.

'You are Dr Giles Vantham?' Clement said. He had, in fact, known Giles for years, and the two men regularly played golf together. They were also members of the same gentlemen's club in Little Clarendon Street, and each had won money from the other in poker games. But by neither a glance nor a smile did either man acknowledge their friendship.

'I am.'

'And you conducted the autopsy on Mr David Finch?'

'I did.'

'Will you please tell the jury your findings?'

'Yes. The deceased died as a result of strangulation, consistent with death by hanging.'

There was a little murmur at this in the court, which both men ignored as the irrelevance they clearly thought it was.

'I also found a not inconsiderable amount of barbiturates and alcohol in his system,' the learned man continued smoothly.

There was an even bigger sensation in the room this time, as this was the first the general public were hearing of it, although the police, of course, had long since been informed of the medical examiner's findings. And Clement Ryder had read the files thoroughly, so he also evinced no surprise.

'In your medical opinion, did these have any bearing on the cause of death?' Clement asked instead.

'No, the doses were not sufficient in themselves to cause death. The alcohol content was not so high as to incapacitate the deceased – that is, it was not high enough to say that he was seriously intoxicated – but it was significant enough to say that he would have feel the effects of it. The drug,' here the medical man named a well-known and common sleeping draught, available in almost any pharmacy in the land, 'was also present in sufficient amount to have affected the deceased. Indeed, to have made him sleep for many, many hours once it had taken effect, but it was not of significant enough dosage to constitute what you or I would call an overdose.'

'Just to make it perfectly clear then, you would say that, although the deceased would have been tipsy from the alcohol, and woozy from the drugs, they did not in any way contribute to the cause of his death?'

The medical man nodded graciously. 'That is so.'

'Did you discover any other injuries to the deceased? Bruises, marks on his hands, anything that might have indicated a struggle?'

Again Dr Ryder's question had everyone on the edge of their seats, particularly those members of the press who were hoping for something sensational.

'No,' Dr Vantham said firmly enough, but even so he hesitated slightly, and something in the way he elongated the word instantly caught Clement's attention, as his friend must have known it would.

Alerted by this, Clement thought for a moment or two, gave a mental nod, and then asked calmly, 'Was there anything *at all* that struck you as odd about that, Dr Vantham?'

Clement saw Giles shoot him a quick and appreciative look at the way that he'd just made it easier for him to convey all the facts that he wanted to – and his own interpretation of them – without having to struggle to do so.

'Yes, in my experience, people who hang themselves nearly always panic at some point in the proceedings,' he carried on smoothly and gratefully. 'The survival instinct in a human being is a very strong one, and most people, when they find they can't breathe, tend to panic and try and rectify the matter by clawing at the obstruction and trying to remove it. But there were no signs of fingernail scratching around the victim's neck, or evidence of it underneath his fingernails.'

At this graphic – and horrific – image, a general shudder

rippled around the room, and one or two women were heard to gasp audibly. An older man on the jury went a little pale.

'I see. Was the deceased, apart from the injuries caused by his death, in good physical condition and general health?' Clement swept the proceedings along briskly. In his experience, whenever a jury began to get the collywobbles it was best to give them something else to think of, and very smartly, too.

'He was.'

'And there were no signs of long-term alcohol or drug abuse visible? Nothing to suggest that the alcohol or barbiturate in his system was the norm?'

'No, he was a fit and healthy young man of just twenty years of age,' Giles Vantham confirmed grimly. Like Clement, he must have been used to seeing the young die – but it always felt wrong.

Sensing his colleague's dour mood, Clement thanked him and dismissed him, but not first without giving him a questioning look, indicating that if there was something else he wanted to say, he was willing to hear it. But his old friend left the podium without further demur.

'All right, I think it's time we heard from the police now,' Clement said briskly, but not before casting an eye at the clock. Seeing that it was still too early to call for a lunch break, he glanced around the room, catching a constable's eye. 'Who is here to speak for the constabulary?'

Trudy Loveday watched, very interested indeed, as the Sergeant at her station pushed his way to the podium.

'And you are?' Dr Ryder asked amiably, although he knew the man's name perfectly well.

'Sergeant Michael O'Grady, sir.'

Trudy's Sergeant was a slightly chubby man, around five feet ten inches tall, with a big quiff of sandy-coloured hair and pale blue eyes. Although he was of Irish descent, he'd been born in Cowley and lived there for all his life.

Trudy knew that he'd married a woman from Birmingham,

a WAAF who'd been stationed at the nearby RAF base at Upper Heyford during the war, and the couple had two children.

Although he'd always treated her reasonably well – and didn't think she was a total waste of time, as their DI did – Trudy knew that he probably didn't approve of her working with the coroner. In his view, lowly constables, especially those who had not long finished their probationary period, should be set to work at the lowest levels for at least three or four years, before being given any proper responsibility.

Thus she found herself instinctively shrinking back in her seat a little, hoping that he wouldn't notice her in the public gallery – although DI Jennings must have informed him of the situation.

Nevertheless, she was as keen to hear what the police thinking was over the death of David Finch as everyone else in the room, and she had her pencil poised eagerly over the notebook.

'Sergeant O'Grady, were you called to the scene at Mr Dewberry's farm on the morning in question?'

'Yes sir, I was.' O'Grady reached for his notebook, and like the seasoned professional that he was, proceeded to give his account without any further prompting from the old vulture.

Clement, who was well aware of the unflattering nickname he'd been given by the police, and who knew he was not the Sergeant's favourite person, chose not to take umbrage, but rather to simply let him get on with it. Besides, he knew the man to be a competent officer and he was interested to hear his opinion of things.

'Having been notified via a telephone call from the village constable of a suspicious death at Dewberry Farm in Middle Fenton, I and two police constables proceeded to the village, where I was directed to the farm by a local resident walking his dog. I found the owner of the farm, Mr Raymond Dewberry, at his residence and in a state of some distress. I took a brief statement from him, then proceeded to the barn in question, where I found the site being guarded by the constable. I then set about cutting the deceased down.'

'Just one moment,' Clement couldn't resist interrupting. 'How exactly did you set about doing this?'

Sergeant O'Grady lifted his head from his notebook and patiently looked across at the coroner. 'Before setting off, I requisitioned from the station a sharp knife and also a tall stout stepladder, which we attached to the roof of the police van, in case it should be needed. As it happened, it wasn't. To cut the deceased down, all we just had to do was saw through the rope near the end attached to the base of the plough and lower him down.'

His repressive tone of voice clearly indicated that the police were prepared for anything, as anyone of any intelligence would surely know. Several people in the room tittered nervously at this first sign of a clash of wills.

'Very perspicacious of you, Sergeant,' Clement shot back smoothly, confident that the other man would have no idea of the meaning of the long word he'd just used.

The Sergeant, magnificently choosing to suppose that he'd just been complimented, inclined his head graciously. 'I then proceeded to preserve the evidence. Shortly thereafter the local doctor arrived and confirmed death.'

Clement nodded. 'Did you find a suicide note at the scene?'

'No sir. There were no pieces of paper visible in the barn.'

'You searched the deceased's pockets, I presume?'

'Yes sir. That is standard procedure,' the Sergeant said with a bland smile.

'And made a list of the contents, no doubt?' Clement said, refusing to be drawn.

'Yes sir.' Sergeant O'Grady allowed himself an extravagant sigh, which again made those of a more nervous disposition titter nervously. 'We found a wallet, containing one pound, two shillings and sixpence, a handkerchief, a small set of keys, a roll of mints and a letter.'

The last item produced the now-anticipated buzz of interest in the rapt room.

Clement, who knew what the man giving evidence knew, played along, feeding him his lines in a now familiar dance. 'To whom was this letter addressed?'

'To the deceased.'

'And had it been opened?'

'It had been,' O'Grady confirmed.

'Presumably then, it had been read by the deceased,' Clement said, for the jury's benefit. Sometimes you had to make everything crystal clear for them. 'Did you confirm the nature of the contents of the letter, and by whom it had been written?'

'Yes sir, we did.' O'Grady took a deep breath, knowing the sensation he was about to cause. 'The letter was a love-letter, written to the deceased by Iris Carmody.'

Chapter 5

Clement waited patiently for the furore to calm down, before regarding the Sergeant steadily. 'And you are sure of the veracity of this letter?'

'Yes sir.'

Clement nodded. At this point he cast a quick glance at the section of press who were straining in their seats for more salacious information. He knew that the letter in question had been written on rose-scented stationery, had been dated less than three months ago, and had been the usual sort of missive from a pretty, young girl, mainly vowing undying love to David Finch.

But neither the police nor his office wanted these details to get into the public domain just yet. However, a few facts did need to be established here and now, as it might prove relevant to the jury's decision when it came to bringing in a verdict. 'I take it you subsequently made inquiries concerning this letter?' he asked mildly, casting the public gallery a quelling glance as they began to murmur excitedly.

Within seconds the hubbub died down, and on the witness stand, Sergeant O'Grady fought to keep the smile from his face. It took a brave soul to withstand a witheringly contemptuous glance from the old vulture, and not for the first time, he had

41

reason to be glad that Dr Ryder kept a firm control of his court-room. Although some of his colleagues hated testifying when he was presiding, the Sergeant had long since realised that, so long as you showed the man respect, there was actually very little to fear. Well …

'And what did you discover?' Clement's voice snapped the policeman back to the matter in hand.

'We discovered that, prior to his death, the deceased and the young lady in question had been stepping out together for the past four or five months.'

'I see.' Clement glanced at the jury, but decided not to lead them. No doubt they were already letting their fertile imaginations loose – with some of them deciding David Finch had murdered his girlfriend and then killed himself in a fit of remorse or fear. The more generous or romantically minded might be inclined to give the young man the benefit of the doubt, and prefer to think him innocent of murder, but that he had killed himself due to a broken heart.

Since he could already see that the writing was on the wall, and he had no doubt that the jury was likely to return a verdict of suicide there was little point, at this stage, in him trying to influence them towards a more useful Open Verdict.

'Thank you, Sergeant. I think it's time we heard from those nearest and dearest to the deceased now.'

There was a low moan of disappointment at this, but another ferocious glance from the coroner's steely grey eyes quickly had the spectators subsiding into a slightly resentful silence. His bushy white eyebrows smoothed out into an amiable line again.

He understood it, of course – the majority of them had come for answers and news, but the police liked to give away as little as possible.

'I call Superintendent Keith Finch.'

At this, any residual resentment fell away and heads turned and necks craned to get their first glimpse of the dead boy's father.

Of course, the fact that he was a high-ranking police officer, and that his dead son had to be the prime suspect in the May Queen murder case only added considerable grist to their mill.

The coroner caught Duncan Gillingham's slightly ironic glance as he watched the witness take the stand. Usually, and especially in cases of suspected suicide, the press tried to show the proper sympathies for the grieving parents, as did juries, who nearly always tried to soften the blow by bringing in the caveat 'whilst of unsound mind' whenever returning a suicide verdict.

But Clement noticed that the man taking the stand, by the ramrod rigidity of his spine and the tight-clenched line of his jaw, suspected that he couldn't expect these normal courtesies.

Clement regarded Keith Finch with plenty of sympathy, but also with a cool, analytical glance. Naturally, no father would be willing to believe that their son could strangle a young girl then hang himself afterwards. So it was no surprise that this man had insisted on a second, discreet investigation.

But the man was also an experienced police officer, used to sifting evidence and always observant and vigilant. Was his desire to see his son's reputation cleared based on more than merely wishful thinking? Well, they would soon find out. Clement cleared his throat, and said, 'You are the father of the deceased?'

'I am.' The tall, brown-haired man glanced at Clement curiously. Although he'd asked specifically for this man's unique talents to be let loose on his son's case, he'd never actually had occasion to meet or talk with him before. And as he met the old vulture's gaze, he hoped that he hadn't misjudged this man. It was taking everything he had to take a back seat in this affair when everything in him was screaming at him to take an active part in the Iris Carmody case, and thus clear his boy of suspicion.

But he knew he couldn't do it. Instead, he was going to have to rely on this former-surgeon-turned-coroner, and a still-green WPC, to pull off another miracle.

And he could only hope and pray that they could do it.

Now, looking into the sharp grey eyes of the coroner, he could see nothing in them but calm appraisal, with no hint of acknowledgement of their shared secret.

All in all, he felt assured that he'd done the right thing.

'You were called by your colleagues in order to positively identify the deceased as your son, David Finch?' Clement Ryder began briskly.

The Superintendent stiffened slightly at this sudden and painful question, then nodded curtly. 'I did. I wouldn't ask my wife to do so. She was naturally distraught.' The staccato sentences came out of him in flat, hard tones.

There was a slight shifting of bums on seats at this, and a ripple of sympathy and pity cut through the pervading atmosphere of avid curiosity somewhat. Finally, the people around him were beginning to see the witness as a grieving father, not a police officer mixed up in scandal.

'Quite so. And I'd like to extend the sympathies of the court to your wife,' Clement said calmly. 'Prior to your son's death, had you noticed any changes in his behaviour?'

The police officer slowly nodded. He'd been prepared for this, of course, and saw it as his golden opportunity to at least try to put the record straight for his dead son, who could no longer speak up for himself. And although, in the quiet desperate hours of the previous night, he'd rehearsed in his head many times what he might say in this moment, now that the time had actually come he felt terrified that he might fail. But he could only tell the truth, simple and unadorned, and hope that they believed it.

'Naturally. The girl he was stepping out with had been brutally murdered, and David was distraught.'

Excited whispering immediately broke out in the court, and Clement leapt on it at once. 'Silence!' he thundered. 'If members of the public can't conduct themselves with decency and decorum then I am going to clear the room.'

There was instant silence. Although most members of the

44

public didn't know Dr Ryder from Adam, such was his tone of voice that none of them doubted he would carry through with his threat.

In his seat, Duncan Gillingham smiled knowingly. During his career, he'd seen other coroners make the same threat, but by and large they tended to be empty, used simply as a means of making the court settle down. But he'd been present once when Clement Ryder had actually ordered the ushers to remove all but the relevant staff and witnesses, caring not a jot for the animosity it had earned him from the people being evicted. Ryder's arrogance and indifference hadn't surprised him – he'd long since come to the conclusion that the former surgeon probably believed his word was now literally law.

Not that Duncan wasn't willing to concede that, when it came to this particular man, he held something of a grudge. He was still smarting from the way he'd sabotaged his growing relationship with a certain, luscious WPC for a start.

Clement, removing his scowl from the public gallery, turned back to his witness. 'You say David was distraught. Did he ever indicate to you that he was in such despair that he might think of ending his own life?'

The court seemed to hold its collective breath as it waited for the reply – but wisely made no other sound.

Superintendent Finch flinched slightly. He took a deep breath, then shook his head; his voice, when he finally spoke, was a little rough but firm.

'No, he did not. And I believe I would have seen the signs had he been thinking of taking such a dreadful action.'

Clement made no comment, but he had to wonder – just how many other parents of suicidal children had testified to the same thing? And was it really possible to know another being so completely, that you could be so sure of anything?

Then he thought of his own children – grown up now, and gone from home. He didn't see them that often, but he thought he would know if anything was seriously wrong. Or was that just wishful thinking on his part?

'At first he was obviously upset and grieving,' Keith Finch carried on, 'but in the last few days of his life he became, if anything, more angry than despairing.' At this, he glanced across at the press gallery defiantly. Some of those who'd submitted articles hinting at other things couldn't quite meet his eyes, but the older, more seasoned professionals had no such trouble.

In her own seat, Trudy felt her heart go out to this man. It must be awful to have to stand up so straight in such a public place, knowing that almost everyone around you suspected that somebody you loved had committed that most awful and unforgivable of crimes: murder. And to have to stand there and try to defend them, with only the power of your own convictions to sustain you.

But as a police officer, Trudy was aware that it had to be simply trust and faith in his son that made him so sure that David was innocent of killing Iris Carmody. For if the Superintendent had had any solid proof, or even circumstantial evidence, he'd have handed it over to DI Jennings the moment it had come into his possession.

When news of the murder of the May Queen had first burst on the station in such spectacular fashion that early morning on the first of May, Trudy had been as fascinated and appalled by it as much as everyone else. DI Jennings had seemed both chuffed and slightly alarmed to be put in operational charge of such a high-profile case, and had quickly assembled his team around him.

Of course, she had not been let anywhere near it, and had been forced to complete the usual tasks that were her lot. Filing. Patrolling the streets where handbag snatchers were wont to try their luck. Taking witness statements from female victims.

But that didn't stop her from keeping her eyes open and her

ears on the alert for any titbits that might come her way whenever the Iris Carmody case was being discussed. So she'd overheard many conversations in the communal office that had given her at least some grasp of what was happening with the May Queen murder case.

She knew, for instance, that the medical findings had confirmed that the murdered girl had probably been dead for only a short while before she was found – making it almost certain that she had been killed around dawn. She had not been pregnant, but neither was she *virgo intacta*. And cause of death had been due to manual strangulation. Somebody – a man presumably, because of the strength it would have taken – had taken her by the neck and throat and throttled the life out of her.

She also knew that David Finch had quickly become a person of interest, as the girl's beau. He had told DI Jennings that on the evening and night before her death, he'd been at home with his parents, and at dawn the next day, had been asleep in his bed. Not that that helped much, as it would have been perfectly possible for him to sneak out at any time.

Although attending university, he was back home for a few days, no doubt so that he could share and participate in his girlfriend's big day. In the village of Middle Fenton, May Day, apparently, had always been a big day.

In normal circumstances, of course, the word of a superintendent and his respectable wife wouldn't be doubted. But these were hardly normal circumstances. And most people – particularly those responsible for writing news articles – were quick to point out that there weren't many mothers who wouldn't swear blind to the innocence of their beloved sons. Even the mothers of the most hardened criminals would swear that their darling boy was tucked up in front of the radio whenever a jeweller's was being turned over, or some poor victim was being beaten black and blue.

'You say he became angry?' Clement's voice cut into Trudy's

glum speculations and focused her mind on the here and now. Guiltily, she hastily continued to take her shorthand notes.

'Yes. After three or four days with no arrest, he became very bitter. I told him that these things could take time, but he began to … not lose faith in the police officers investigating the crime, exactly, but become impatient for a result.' Superintendent Finch shrugged a little helplessly. 'It was understandable, of course. He'd lost the girl he was growing fond of, and he wanted justice for her. He was young and impatient,' the dead boy's father added flatly.

'And what form did this impatience take?' Clement asked, genuinely curious now. Sometimes, he felt, conducting an inquest could feel a bit like conducting a symphony, with all the main players already knowing all the notes in advance, and it was merely his job to make sure things ran on a smooth, expected course. But sometimes he preferred to stray from the allotted path – like now.

Out of the corner of his eye he could see that Sergeant O'Grady, back in his seat in the front row, was looking distinctly uncomfortable, and was trying to catch his eye – no doubt with a view of trying to indicate that he wanted Clement to rein the witness in.

Clement steadfastly kept his eyes on Keith Finch.

The Superintendent considered the question for a moment, then sighed heavily. 'He said that he probably knew Iris as well as anyone, along with Iris's friends, and far better than any policeman did. And that he should be able to figure out what had happened to her if he just used his brain. I learned that he then began talking to them, and others in the village, trying to press them for information. I had to rebuke him sharply – such a thing is, of course, totally unorthodox.'

Of course, Clement thought, there were two ways of looking at the dead boy's behaviour. Either David Finch was genuinely trying to find out who had killed Iris, or else, he was trying to find out exactly what it was the police were learning, and if they were likely to stumble on any evidence that he himself had committed the crime. And playing the part of the avenging boyfriend was a good cover for such activities.

'And did he listen to you?' Clement asked.

For a moment, the man on the stand visibly hesitated, and Clement watched him closely, wondering if he was, probably for the first time, going to come out with some lie. Then Superintendent Finch's shoulders slumped slightly. 'He seemed to. But I got the feeling he was still conducting his own inquiries, only becoming much more secretive about it,' he admitted.

There was another murmur at this, abruptly cut off as Clement turned to survey the room, his expression flashing out a warning to be silent.

'I see. When you had been told the awful news of your son's death, did you search his room for a suicide note?' Clement asked next. It was a brutal question, but the police officer, apart from a quick blink, made no sign that the abrupt change of questioning had affected him.

'Yes, I did, in the company of DI Jennings, who had come to deliver the news. No such note was found. And—' here he turned to look directly at the jury '—it's my solemn belief that my son would not have committed suicide, under any circumstances whatsoever.' He paused, swallowed hard and added roughly, 'He simply wouldn't have done that to his mother.'

At this there was another murmur that swept through the room, and several members of the jury had to look away from the grieving father's flat stare. Clement decided it was a good moment to dismiss the witness.

After a few more needful but – much to the public's disgust – not particularly interesting proceedings, Clement finally gave his usual speech to the jury. He told them that they were there to establish the identity of the deceased, the cause of his death (which in this case the medical evidence made very clear was due to hanging) and, if possible, the manner by which he had come to his end.

He pointed out heavily that, in the absence of a suicide note, and with no clear forensic evidence in play, they should not rush to judgements – and that an Open Verdict was perfectly accept-able should they be unsure.

But as he dismissed them to consider their verdict he was under no illusion, and sure enough, within only ten minutes, they came back with a verdict of suicide, whilst of unsound mind.

His eyes briefly met those of Superintendent Finch before he thanked the jury and dismissed the court, and he gave an almost imperceptible nod. It was enough, he hoped, to reassure the grieving father that this was not the end of it and further investigations would duly be made.

Chapter 6

'Well, that was more or less what we expected,' Clement said to Trudy, about twenty minutes later. They were sitting in his office, sipping tea and munching on some very nice gingernut biscuits that his secretary had kindly provided, after consuming some sandwiches cobbled together by way of a late lunch.

'Yes – I felt sorry for poor Superintendent Finch though,' Trudy said.

Clement grunted. 'Well, we need to make some sort of plan of action. What do you suggest we do first?'

Trudy sighed. 'Whatever we do, it's going to be tricky. We can't step on anybody's toes by asking too openly about Iris Carmody, because that investigation is still ongoing, and the Inspector's made it clear that's *his* turf. On the other hand, it's going to be hard to find out what might have happened to David Finch without at least exploring what also happened to her. No matter which way you look at it, their deaths have to be connected, don't you agree?'

Clement nodded cautiously. 'I think it's more probable than not,' he conceded.

Trudy nodded more firmly. 'Right – either he *did* kill her, no matter what his father thinks, in which case he very likely did kill

51

himself in a fit of remorse or despair or what-have-you afterwards, and we'll just be chasing our tails trying to find evidence that points to anything else. Or he never had anything to do with her death – in which case, he still *might* have killed himself out of the grief and pain of losing her …'

'In my experience,' Clement slipped in as Trudy paused to take a much needed breath, 'young lovers killing themselves from broken hearts are more likely to be found in poetry, fiction or bad cinema films than in real life.'

Trudy couldn't help but smile wryly. 'That's a rather cynical way to look at it.'

Clement shrugged. 'I've knocked around the world a lot longer than you have,' he said, giving her a narrow smile. 'But carry on; my apologies for interrupting you.'

Trudy shook her head. 'I don't mind when you interrupt.' And indeed, she didn't. Unlike when DI Jennings or the Sarge interrupted her at work, Dr Ryder usually had something useful or encouraging to say. Which was not always the case with her superior officers! 'Anyway, er, where was I …? Yes, if David didn't kill Iris, and didn't kill himself either, then the only thing we're left with is that somebody else killed them both, obviously. And presumably they'd only kill David because he had, like his father said, been asking around and doing some private investigating of his own, and had found out something that alarmed Iris's killer.'

'Thus making it necessary to get rid of David too,' Clement nodded.

'So no matter how we look at it, Iris Carmody's death is going to prove a major factor in our considerations. But DI Jennings will have my guts for garters if I trespass onto his territory,' she wailed.

'Well – we can only do our best,' Clement said briskly. Clearly he thought nothing of crossing swords with Harry Jennings. But then, Jennings had no power over him, so he could afford to be cavalier, Trudy thought a shade resentfully.

Seemingly catching her mood, Clement suddenly grinned at

her. 'Cheer up – and don't forget – it's possible that we might find something to help Jennings solve his own murder investigation, in which case, he'll be all smiles and will forgive all.'

Trudy blinked, trying to imagine a cheerful Inspector Jennings. She shuddered slightly then sighed. 'Well, I suppose the best place to start is at the beginning,' she offered prosaically. 'And that has to be with the scene of the crime, and the barn on Mr Dewberry's farm. Have you been there yet?' she asked curiously.

'No,' Clement admitted. Before being asked to take a closer in-depth look at things, it hadn't really been necessary for him to inspect it in person. 'But from the reports I read, it's about a quarter of mile from the farmhouse itself, out of sight and up a hill, in the middle of his wheat fields. Used to house equipment and store some over-spill grain after the harvest, and some straw for winter fodder.'

'At least the weather's nice and dry,' Trudy said, glancing out of the window to make sure a sudden shower wasn't in the offing. 'So we won't need wellingtons.'

'In any other circumstances, it'd be a nice day for a walk,' Clement agreed.

Chapter 7

Because the coroner had begun giving Trudy driving lessons, he drove his 'Aunty Rover' out of the town, and then pulled over on a country lane so that they could swap seats. This meant that she could continue the seven miles or so to the village of Middle Fenton without too much difficulty or danger to other traffic whilst she was still such a novice. She was doing well, he noted with pride – very rarely now scraping the gears, and only stalling once, at a deserted country crossroads.

She carefully parked his Rover P4 in a shady part of the Dewberry farm's cobbled forecourt, which was deserted. Not even a sheepdog barked a warning, and Clement supposed that both of the Dewberrys, father and son, were out working the land.

The farmhouse was typical of the vernacular, made of local stone, a sturdy, no-nonsense square building with a vast slate roof. It had probably stood in this spot for nearly two hundred years or so.

'At some point we need to have a long talk with Ronnie Dewberry,' Trudy said as she climbed out of the car and carefully locked it, before handing the keys back to her colleague. 'They grew up together and they were best friends all through primary and the local grammar school. And David either chose to come here to die or his killer decided it was a safe spot to kill him. Not that *that's* necessarily significant – all the locals know about the barn, and anybody out taking a country walk could have stumbled on it too. But if anybody knew what was going on in David's head, it's probably his best friend.'

Clement nodded, although he didn't feel quite so confident as his companion. He knew that the boy's close friendship of childhood probably wouldn't have lasted long into adulthood even had they both survived, especially with David Finch attending university in London, and Ronnie settling into life at the farm. All too soon, they'd have lost touch, with David increasingly staying away from the village as he made his life and home elsewhere. Childhood friendships could be intense, but they rarely stayed that way into adulthood. In fact, he wouldn't have been surprised if that process hadn't already started. 'Remind me again what the dead boy was hoping to do for a career?'

'Civil engineering,' Trudy said promptly.

Yes, Clement now remembered reading that in the notes. Once, he wouldn't have had to ask Trudy for the reminder. Since he'd confirmed his self-diagnosed illness, he'd taken to doing mental exercises every day, to both stimulate his brain activity, and to monitor any rates of serious decline in his mental faculties. So far, the progression of his illness was very slow, leaving him more and more confident that he might have a few good years left, if he was lucky. And if he could keep his condition a secret for that long.

'The barn's presumably that way?' Trudy said, yanking him back from the precipice of his darkening thoughts and pointing to a grass-and-stone track that led up the hill away to the left. Years of tractor usage had sunk the track several inches into the ground, leaving ruts that made it look a bit tricky to walk on.

Clement shrugged and set off after her – but not before casually retrieving a walking stick from the boot of his car. It was a knotted length of hazel that he'd cut out of a hedgerow himself and whittled into shape a few weeks ago. It now looked suitably rustic and offhand. Not at all the sort of hospital-produced, medical affair that would suggest he had any difficulty walking.

Not that he did, as such. Well, not so that you'd notice, but he had become aware lately that he was getting into the habit of dragging his feet without realising it, and if he wasn't careful, that might one day lead him taking the odd tumble.

He glanced around at the greening barley fields with their silvery-looking feathered ears, and took a large lungful of fresh air. Above, a skylark, startled by their presence, rocketed up into the sky, singing perpetually as he rose into the clouds – a challenge that was promptly answered by a rival in the next field.

Some corn buntings, sitting at the very tops of the tallest bushes in the hedgerows – usually elders – also watched their passage with a nervous twittering. Lining the hedgerows, cow parsley frothed creamy white, a magnet for orange-tip butterflies, and Clement looked around with real pleasure. There was nothing quite like England in the springtime!

The gradient of the hill was one of those deceptive ones, so gradual it didn't pull on the knees, but so long that it gave you a surprise when you reached the top, and you looked down from quite a high panorama. Unfortunately, the hill was the wrong side of the fields to overlook the village, which meant the police had probably had zero luck by way of locating any potential witnesses. If anybody from the village had seen the lad set out on his last journey, none of them would have been able to track his progress here.

As he looked around he couldn't see a single point of habitation – only rolling arable fields, hedgerows, the shimmering line of the river in the distance, and some pigs in a field so far away they looked like tiny pink cushions.

Off to their right, however, stood the stark, black iron and wooden carcass of the barn. It sported a large set of wooden doors that had been made out of what appeared to be spare bits of timber, nailed together with more gusto than accuracy. The whole edifice had a deserted, forlorn air, as if it felt ashamed of what had happened inside its dim interior.

Of course, the police had cordoned it off once the body had been discovered, rendering it unusable anyway. Now the sight of it, looking almost accusing and lonely, made Trudy feel suddenly depressed. Although she didn't believe in the supernatural, exactly, it wouldn't be hard to imagine that the ghost of David Finch was standing right there, unseen beside them, wondering at these two disparate people who had been tasked with uncovering the mystery of his death.

Would he feel confident, Trudy wondered sadly, or would he be scornful?

She shrugged off such silly fantasies, and glanced around at the empty fields instead. 'No wonder nobody saw anything,' Trudy said glumly, unknowingly echoing her companion's previous thoughts. 'Unless somebody was walking their dog here or some-thing, who would have seen David coming up here?'

Clement nodded agreement. 'The remoteness begs an obvious question though, doesn't it? If he didn't come here specifically to kill himself, why *did* he come here?'

'To think?' Trudy proffered tentatively. 'Or to get some peace and quiet maybe? He and Ronnie would have played here as kids. Maybe he was seeking out somewhere where he'd once felt safe and happy. He must have known everyone in the village was wondering if he was a killer or not. That can't have been easy for him.'

'Possibly. Or maybe he arranged to meet someone here?' Clement said, far more prosaically.

Trudy, in spite of the May sunshine, felt herself shiver with cold. 'His killer, you mean?'

'Not necessarily,' Clement said, as always willing to play devil's advocate. 'He could have arranged to meet someone, but then they left, and someone else showed up. Somebody who was, maybe, keeping an eye on him, followed him at a distance, and then took the opportunity of the loneliness here to get rid of him.'

Trudy thought about that for a moment or two, then wrinkled her nose. 'A bit far-fetched, isn't it?'

Clement smiled. 'Yes. But you shouldn't shut off any avenue completely, no matter how far-fetched. Best to just keep it in mind, rather than get fixated on any one idea. Thinking you know what happened, when you really don't, can get you into all sorts of trouble. As of right now, for instance, it seems to me more likely than not that the boy *was* murdered. But if I become too convinced of that, I might miss clues or dismiss witness testimonies that point towards suicide simply because I've become biased without realising it.'

'OK, I'll remember that,' Trudy promised – and meant it. Working with Dr Ryder meant she was learning more than she ever had, even during her police training. 'Well, we'd better go inside then,' she added, a shade reluctantly. Although she was delighted to be working with her mentor again, and taking a break from taking burglary reports and passing lists of stolen goods around the pawn shops, she had to admit to feeling unhappy about the barn.

It was so quiet here. Even the skylarks had stopped singing now.

Clement, perhaps sensing her unease, hid a smile and brandished his raffish hazel stick. 'After you!'

Trudy set off determinedly to the barn doors, which were standing slightly ajar. She thought the officer who'd cordoned off the area probably hadn't been able to keep the doors shut. They looked warped and uncooperative. As she approached them, she glanced at the dried-mud entrance, and saw the arches cut into the ground. 'The barn was regularly in use,' she nodded at the tell-tale scrapings in the earth. 'You can see where the doors opening and shutting cut a mark into the mud.'

'It's a working farm and a working barn,' Clement agreed. 'Doesn't really help us much, does it?'

Trudy, running out of even the tiniest excuse to put off the inevitable, walked forward. Pulling one large door a little further open, she made enough room for them both to be able to slip inside, and took her first, long look at where David Finch had died.

The first thing that struck her was the musty scent and the delightful dancing motion of the dust-motes lingering in the air. Here, dried straw and the more sweet-smelling scent of dried hay competed with an even heavier musk. She knew the farm was a mixture of arable and animal, and she wondered if, at some point, potatoes had been stored here.

Right now, the back half of the barn was piled with the remnants of straw bales. A couple of threshing machines had been deposited along one long corrugated iron wall. Bags of what she presumed were fertiliser or weed killer were stacked like colourful large bricks just inside the entrance. Running along under the arched roofline were a series of rough-hewn wooden rafters. The main one, running more or less centrally, still had a length of rope left dangling from it.

'After they cut him loose, they left most of the rope in situ I see,' Clement said, going to stand under it and peering up. 'From the police report I read, there was a lot of old rope lying around, and they're pretty sure he – or someone – simply helped themselves to it. It wasn't new or bought specifically for the purpose or anything like that.'

So that was one possible lead up the spout, Trudy thought wryly. After one quick look at the ominously dangling rope, she turned around to explore further. There were odd-looking implements leaning drunkenly here and there, probably now defunct hay-rakes, or seed drills and the like. Not that she was an expert on antiquated farm implements. There was also, surprisingly, a large tin bathtub with a hole in the bottom, and some pots and pans with burnt-out bottoms. Clearly, the Dewberrys didn't believe in disposing of anything metal. Perhaps they intended to sell them to the rag-and-bone man one day?

A tallish, wooden stepladder, the only one in the barn that she could see, caught her eye, and she walked towards it, gamely ignoring the way her heartbeat started to pick up.

It still bore the telltale dark smudges of fingerprint dust, where someone had tested it at the time, but she could tell at a glance that the wood was too rough and splintered to have been of any use. No fingerprints would have been available to confirm – or otherwise – that the dead boy had handled it.

But presumably he had, for this was the ladder that David Finch had climbed, with a length of rope fashioned into a noose, just before his death. What on earth had been going through his mind when he'd found the ladder and opened it out into its triangular structure and placed it so carefully beneath the beam? Surely he must have wondered about the afterlife – if God would forgive him for what he was about to do?

She paused, wondering why she was suddenly taking it for granted that David had killed himself.

Perhaps …

Although it was dim inside the barn, with most of the sunlight filtering in through the ill-fitting gaps in the wood and from the partly open door, Trudy's keen eyesight had her quickly bending down in front of the ladder, checking the fourth rung from the bottom. Her heartbeat was now kicking into overdrive, but due to excitement now, rather than trepidation.

Yes, she was right! She'd thought she recognised the telltale signs!

'Dr Clement quickly!' she called over her shoulder excitedly. 'Come and look at this! Is that what I think it is?'

'Woodworm,' Clement said, some moments later. 'Definitely woodworm.' They were both looking at the tiny pinprick holes that peppered the wooden frame. He'd taken the ladder to the doorway, to better see what he was looking at, but he had no doubt.

'But it's especially bad just here … see, it's all along this rung.' She reached out tentatively to touch it, and gave it some gentle pressure. 'It feels spongy! Dr, do you think this would have taken David's weight?'

Clement eyed the rung thoughtfully. 'I'm not sure,' he admitted. 'Some tests will need to be made.'

'I'd better let DI Jennings know right away. He can send someone to collect it,' she said. She only hoped he'd send PC Rodney Broadstairs to do it. Rodney liked to lord it over her. Big, blond and good-looking, he thought he was the station's golden boy. And annoyingly, he probably was. Certainly the Sarge and the Inspector gave him far more interesting work than ever came her way. She wouldn't be human if she didn't resent him a bit, and it would serve him right to be used as nothing more than an errand boy for once!

'If they find out it *is* too rotten to have taken David's weight, Superintendent Finch will be pleased,' Clement agreed. 'It would make it less likely that his son killed himself.'

'Unless he used something else to climb up,' Trudy said. 'Although there doesn't seem to be anything else he could have used,' she immediately contradicted herself.

Clement, who'd seen the crime scene photographs, agreed. Although there had been bales aplenty with which the dead boy could have made a stack, none of them had been found anywhere near the hanging body. Only the overturned ladder.

'If he didn't use the ladder … if *nobody* used the ladder,' Trudy said slowly, looking from the ladder to the rope hanging from the rafters, 'then that must mean …'

'Somebody probably put the rope around his neck and hauled him up. Then tied the other end off around the base of the plough after he was dead.'

Trudy shuddered. 'So it would have to be someone strong? To take his dead weight, I mean?'

Clement frowned thoughtfully. 'Not necessarily. If someone did it that way, they could use all their own weight to haul him up. A fit and strong woman – or a heavy woman – could have done it, I think.'

Chapter 8

They left the scene of David Finch's demise in a quiet, sombre mood. Back at the farmhouse there was now some sign of movement, but only courtesy of a few red hens, who were scratching about near an outhouse and clucking desultorily.

Trudy knocked on the door, but as she suspected, the sound only echoed eerily inside, and nobody answered the summons.

She turned and shrugged at Clement, who was standing by the car, and as she watched, he slipped behind the wheel. Climbing into the passenger seat beside him, she said, 'Into the village?'

Clement nodded.

The Dewberry farm was one of three that surrounded the village, lying on the western side, and it took only a minute or so to drive into the village proper. It consisted of one main street, entitled Freehold Street, with several smaller lanes leading off it that no doubt looped and meandered about and eventually re-joined the main street at some point further on.

It boasted the usual: a square-towered Norman church, built of greyish stone, with an accurate church clock, a village primary school with a plaque stating that it had been funded by a local lord back in the mid-1880s, and a single pub.

They found the pub by following the main road to where it

diverged to form a not particularly square-shaped village square. Surrounded on three sides by a mixture of thatched and tiled cottages, on the fourth side was the pub, The Horse and Groom, and a long, low building that looked as if it might serve as a makeshift village hall. The pub was an attractive building, with a Virginia creeper growing up its ironstone walls, and a cheerfully painted pub sign depicting a grinning lad and a very large chestnut horse. The low, single-storey building next to it was built of red brick, had guttering that needed fixing, and too many uniform windows. All in all, it looked like a cheerless place to meet up and hold a village dance.

'I wonder where the village shop and post office is,' Trudy mused, looking around. 'It might be a good idea to start there.' In her experience, most villagers tended to have certain places whether they congregated to gossip – and whilst the pub was probably the chosen spot for men, she had a shrewd idea that the village shop was the domain of the housewives.

Clement glanced around, spotted the church tower and waved his hazel stick vaguely in that direction. 'Down Church Lane perhaps?' he mused, setting off.

Church Lane was a short, no-through lane that produced no sign of any shops. Back-tracking, they set off back up Freehold Street, turning off down the first lane they came to, and striking lucky within a few hundred yards or so.

The shop, which at one time had probably been a fairly large family home for someone not quite top-drawer, but fairly affluent by village standards, stood proudly in the middle of the lane. Its two large front windows displayed jars of tempting sweets and confectionery for children in one, and a more mundane selection of newspapers, packets of detergent and tinned goods for their parents in the other. No doubt the top floor had been turned into a cosy apartment for whoever was running it.

'I could do with some tobacco for my pipe,' Clement said, whilst Trudy tried to pretend she hadn't spotted the sherbet dabs.

She'd always loved sherbet, but she could hardly buy some in the presence of Dr Ryder!

They pushed open the door, and the babble of female voices that greeted them fell momentarily silent as three pairs of eyes turned in their direction, all three registering, if not hostility exactly, then certainly hard-eyed speculation.

Trudy, feeling a bit odd out of uniform – and therefore not receiving the usual deference or belligerence it evoked – felt momentarily wrong-footed. But Dr Ryder, looking every inch the learned, handsome man of 'a certain age' came in for far more speculation anyway. And as if playing to the gallery, he moved confidently forward down the middle of two aisles consisting mostly of toiletries, boxes of cereal, packets of tea and loaves of sliced bread, smiling urbanely at the three women standing at the counter as he did so.

'Ladies,' he said, wishing he'd worn his Trilby, so that he could doff it.

The oldest of the women, standing behind the counter at the till and undoubtedly the proprietor, was a large, round woman, wearing a floral apron, the kind that tied behind the back of the neck and behind the waist, and covered a multitude of sins. She had short, grey, curly hair (almost certainly permed) and wore an unexpectedly vivid shade of scarlet lipstick. She could have been anywhere from fifty to seventy.

She eyed him speculatively as he approached. In front of her and to her left, was a woman of about forty-five or so, not quite so plump, with short, blonde, curly (almost certainly permed) hair. To her right was a woman of about thirty or so, taller and thinner, with dark curly hair (probably *not* permed) and slightly bulbous brown eyes.

'Sorry, don't let me interrupt. I was wondering if you had any shag?' Clement said, fixing his eyes on the shopkeeper.

This opening gambit earned him a winning smile and she reached behind her to take down several colourful tins of shag tobacco from the shelves, all of which claimed to give the smoker the best smoking experience he could wish for.

'Certainly sir. Would any of these suit?'

Trudy hid a smile and made a show of checking out a jar of chicory coffee as she watched and observed a maestro at work.

Clement began by asking the proprietor's advice which – naturally – inclined towards the most expensive tin. Luckily, it was a brand that Clement knew and had smoked before, and within moments he had his hand in his trouser pocket, scattering half-crowns and sixpences and other assorted change onto the countertop.

The tall thin woman spoke first. 'Don't I know you?' she demanded abruptly.

Clement, surprised, turned to look at her. In his lifetime he'd probably met thousands of people – but this woman's visage rang no bells. Before he could answer, she spoke again, nodding.

'Yes, I saw you once. At the Radcliffe Infirmary. You're a doctor, right? A surgeon?' She turned to the blonde woman and said obliquely, 'You remember our Brenda's bit of trouble all those years ago?'

Clement bowed acknowledgement and made no effort, at this stage, to explain his change of career.

Trudy could see all the women look at him even more eagerly now – not only a handsome stranger, but a doctor no less! She wondered how long it would be before one or other of them managed to worm some interesting details out of him – primarily, his married status. She only hoped Dr Ryder wasn't rash enough to admit to being a widower.

'Can I get you some matches to go with that, sir? Or a refill for your lighter?' the woman behind the till wheedled, and Clement obligingly bought a box of matches.

'We're here to pay our respects to Keith,' Clement said, then added, knowing it was unnecessary, 'Superintendent Finch, that is. I'm a friend of his.' He was only stretching the truth a bit.

He was sure that the police officer would indeed regard him a friend if he could prove his son hadn't committed suicide – or had anything to do with his girlfriend's murder.

The ladies gave a collective sharply drawn breath at this, and shot each other quick, questioning glances, as if mentally debating who should go first.

'We've had lots of trouble with reporters,' the blonde woman finally spoke for the first time, not looking at Clement, but directly at Trudy, who flushed. 'We're hoping the fuss will die down now and they'll leave us in peace,' she added significantly, still eyeing Trudy with displeasure.

'Oh, Trudy isn't with the press,' Clement said. 'She's my assistant and she also knew David,' he lied blandly.

At this, all three women stared openly at her – no doubt wondering just how *well* she'd known the dead boy. So intent was their scrutiny that she could practically hear the cogs turning in their heads. *Did he dump her for Iris? Did Iris know? Was David two-timing Iris with her?*

She could understand why Clement needed to come up with some sort of story to account for their nosing around, but she wished he'd consulted her first.

'It's been a bad business all round,' Clement said mildly. 'I hope Keith's wife is coping?' This gentle probing had the desired effect, and all eyes reverted back to himself as they contemplated the current state of their stricken fellow villager.

'Betty's just about coping, I suppose,' the shopkeeper said slowly.

'Having Delia at home helps,' the blonde woman agreed.

'Oh yes, David's sister,' Clement said. 'She must be very upset about all this too.'

'She is,' the tall brunette said. 'She was always close to her little brother. And she always said that Iris was no good for him. Mind you, I don't think anybody thought that a girl like Iris would be.'

At this somewhat stark and shocking statement, Trudy felt her breath catch in surprise. Like everyone else, she'd been brought up to believe that you didn't speak ill of the dead – and certainly not of someone who had been murdered.

As if sensing the silent censure in the room, the taller woman fidgeted sharply. 'Well, we all know it's true, even if nobody has the courage to say so out loud,' she said defensively, looking around, half defiantly, half shame-faced.

The shop owner, coming to her rescue, cleared her throat. 'Well, least said, soonest mended,' she trotted out the platitude as if not really believing it.

Clement smiled at the now discomfited, red-faced brunette. 'I'm sure you're right though. From what I've been hearing about her, a lot of people thought that she and David were mismatched.'

'She was very pretty, I hear,' Trudy heard herself pipe up help-fully. She knew that if there was one thing that united middle-aged ladies it was talking about younger, prettier women.

Right on cue, the shopkeeper sniffed condescendingly. 'And she knew it, too.'

'You knew her well?' Clement slipped in.

'All her life. I've lived in the village nigh on fifty years, and the Carmodys have lived here generations, I reckon. They're all right,' she added, a shade grudgingly, Trudy thought. 'Frannie works as a daily for folks round abouts and her husband has a good solid job as a coal man. Sensible, hard-working people, both of 'em. And their three sons turned out right enough – two of 'em with wife and kiddies of their own now. Only their Bobby is still living at home. And I don't reckon he was happy about his sister's airs and graces neither,' she added, her lips thinning into a tight line.

'Oh, one of those, was she?' Trudy said with a sigh of under-standing. 'I knew a girl like that at school. Always making up stories about herself, pretending to be better than she was,' she added, sounding most indignant about this non-existent schoolmate.

'Ah, that was Iris,' the tall brunette said. 'Oh, she was pretty enough, and nobody was surprised when she was elected May Queen. But that girl had her sights set on much higher things, didn't she, Flo?'

Thus appealed to, the blonde woman nodded vigorously. 'My Jane said Iris was forever boasting that she was going to be a model, or an actress or some such. She was always swanning around in fancy clothes, wasn't she? Where did she get the money from to afford them, that's what we'd like to know.'

At this, all three women's heads nodded in unison.

'Didn't she have a job?' Trudy asked guilelessly.

'Huh! Not her – young madam wouldn't deign to chip her painted nails on anything like hard work,' Flo shot back tartly. 'Didn't stop her strutting around wearing a gold and pearl necklace though, did it?'

'Oh, you saw that too, did you?' the tall brunette said, lips pursed.

'Perhaps David gave it to her?' Clement said mildly. 'They were stepping out, weren't they?'

The three women gave him pitying looks.

'A young lad at university? Where'd he get the money from?' the blonde woman said, shaking her head. 'No, mark my words, that young lady had more strings to her bow that we knew about. Stands to reason, doesn't it? I mean … with what happened to her and all …'

She trailed off uneasily. Clement, sensing that they had begun to realise that they might have been a bit free with their tongues, and not wanting to give them time to feel angry about it, made a show of putting his new purchases away in his jacket pocket.

'Well, good day ladies, we mustn't keep you any longer.' He smiled at them in turn, and then turned away, Trudy quickly following suit.

Outside, they paused in the lane, looking around. 'Well, that was interesting,' Clement said.

'They didn't like Iris, did they?' Trudy agreed.

'No. And what's more, I don't think they're sure that David Finch killed her,' Clement mused. 'I got the distinct impression that they had pretty strong suspicions that were other men in her life, and one of them was responsible for what happened to her.'

Trudy nodded. She didn't know everything about the Carmody case, but she'd heard enough from chat at the station to know that the team working on the murder case believed that Iris was involved with other men. And she supposed anyone suspected of being intimate with the girl had already been thoroughly interviewed. But a week after the May Queen had been found so spectacularly trussed to the maypole she knew that the team was not close to an arrest. DI Jennings would be looking and sounding much more chipper if they were.

'We need to ask the Superintendent if he knows whether or not his son bought expensive jewellery for Iris,' Trudy said. 'And speaking of my superior officers, I need to use the phone box to tell Inspector Jennings about the woodworm in the ladder.'

Clement nodded amiably, and they walked down the lane, to where they'd spotted the bright red village phone box. As they approached it, two young girls playing hopscotch on the pavement paused in their game to watch them go by. No doubt, within the last week the village had been inundated with strangers – both police and press – which would have been a rare occurrence indeed. And whilst the police presence had probably dwindled now that most of the evidence had been collected, and any witnesses found and interviewed, she suspected the press would be less keen to desert a good story. Although, with the inquest into David Finch over, she supposed eventually the story would fade out of the immediate spotlight and the village could return to normal.

Well, for everyone but the Carmody and Finch families anyway.

Trudy duly fed some pennies into the slot, pressed the right button, then dialled the station number and reported in, finishing up by asking DI Jennings if he knew about the murder victim's unexplained jewellery. The Inspector ignored this, but was very definitely interested to hear about the state of the stepladder, though as usual, didn't give her any praise for her sharp eyes or quick thinking. Instead he reminded her to dodge any reporters that might still be hanging around the village and leave the Carmody case to him, before ringing off abruptly.

When she stepped out of the phone box, she saw Dr Ryder sitting on a low garden wall, the two little girls sneaking curious looks at him.

Around twelve or so, one was wearing two bright pink hair slides in her mousy brown hair, whilst the other, smaller and darker, was busy with her stick of chalk, robustly marking out further hopscotch squares and numbering them assiduously.

Clement smiled as she approached. 'All done?'

Trudy nodded. 'Where to now?'

'It's getting on for five. Time we called it a day, I think.' He called a cheerful farewell to the two girls, who waved at him in response. 'Can you come to my office about noon tomorrow? We'll have lunch here in the Horse and Groom and see what the male contingent in the village have to say for themselves. Their perspective on Iris is bound to be somewhat different, I think, from what we've heard from the women. Pretty girls can usually wrap any man around their little fingers,' he added, eyes twinkling. 'It'll be interesting to see who she bothered with, and who she slighted.'

Trudy nodded happily. However, her smile abruptly faltered as she wondered if she could get away with claiming expenses for a pub lunch. If she had to pay for it herself, she'd be short for the weekend! Then she realised that Dr Ryder, gentleman that he was, would probably insist on paying the bill anyway.

Chapter 9

The Horse and Groom looked a little busy for a weekday lunch hour, and as Trudy and Clement stepped inside and looked around, it didn't take long for them to realise why. At least three, if not more, of the men sat at the bar jawing away were reporters.

True, now that the inquest into David Finch was over, and with the Iris Carmody case generating no new information, the members of the press weren't out in as great a force as they had been when the May Queen's dead body had first been discovered. But still, Trudy and Clement prudently made their way to a table at the back and kept their heads down. Luckily, the pub was one of those low-ceilinged, small-windowed pubs that didn't let in a lot of daylight, and they were careful to stick to the darkest part of the room.

Once seated, they consulted the blackboard menu on one wall, which obliged with the usual ploughman's lunch and assorted sandwiches, and choices made, Clement made his way cautiously to the bar. He was careful to stand at the farthest end of the bar from the reporters and waited to attract the landlord's attention, before giving their choices for food. He also bought a half-pint of the local beer for himself, and a glass of lemonade for Trudy.

Even from where he was standing, he could see that most of

71

the reporters were rather the worse for drink, which might have helped him somewhat in going unrecognised.

He said as much to his companion when he returned with their drinks, but muttered, 'I don't suppose our luck will last for much longer though. Sooner or later, someone is bound to rumble us.'

Trudy sighed. 'I know. Let's just hope it's later.' She took a sip of her lemonade and glanced around. There was no way they could chat to the locals until the reporters left, and she had a feeling they were not likely to be going anywhere fast, which made the pub a bit of a lost cause right now. She made a mental note to come back another time.

When their sandwiches came, they ate slowly, ears on the alert for any stray titbits of information that might come their way. On the next table over to their right, two men dressed in well-worn trousers, knitted jumpers and solid work boots, played dominoes. They looked like farm labourers taking a rest from their tractors, but they played with a silent intensity that spoke of a long-time rivalry.

Seated behind them, however, was a rather florid-faced, middle-aged man dressed rather more respectably, and an older man who was busy chomping his way through some cheese and pickle. They seemed to be rather more vocal, and luckily for Trudy and Clement, weren't bothering to keep their voices down.

'I'll be glad when we get the village back to ourselves,' the red-faced man said, casting the gaggle of noisy reporters a jaundiced glance as he did so. 'Muck-rakers the lot of 'em,' he added under his breath.

The older man swallowed a morsel of Red Leicester and nodded. 'It'll die down once the coppers pull their fingers out and close the case, you'll see,' he remarked.

'Do you think that's likely to be soon?' his companion wondered aloud.

Trudy and Clement, both ear-wigging without a qualm, kept very quiet as they listened to the talk behind them.

The older man sighed. 'Hope so. I think they'll decide that that boy Finch did it, and close the case. Stands to reason, don't it? Who else would have killed Iris?'

His friend was silent for a moment, then said slowly, 'Not sure that I agree with you there, Charles.'

'When pretty girls end up strangled, mark my words, it's usually the man in their lives that did it,' came back the response. His voice was somewhat world-weary, and he gave a heavy sigh. 'Least ways, that's how it often pans out.'

'Ah, yes,' his younger companion said, 'but that's just what I'm not sure about, see? Iris was a lovely young girl, wasn't she? And everybody knows that that boy she was gadding about wasn't the only fish she had on her hook.'

By now, Trudy hardly dared swallow any of her drink for fear of missing a stray word.

'Oh, she was a flirt, I'll give you that,' came the response. 'Especially when it came to men old enough to be her father! Little minx, I think she liked to tease them and get them all aflutter. But that doesn't necessarily mean anything, no matter what the women in this place want to believe. And why shouldn't a young beauty like Iris flirt, hmm?' the older man said, his voice now having more of a smile in it. 'Nothing wrong with a pretty girl flirting. It's only natural. Besides, it peps everyone up, and no harm done.'

'That's all very well if that's all it was,' the red-faced man muttered, his voice lowering. Although she couldn't see him (since, no matter what the Sarge said, she couldn't develop eyes in the back of her head!) Trudy could imagine him casting a quick, anxious look at the reporters at the bar. 'I keep hearing it was more than that.'

'Who from?' the older man snorted, making Clement wonder if the dead May Queen hadn't done a bit of flirting with the man now doing the talking. 'The women around here were all jealous of her, you know that. She was young and pretty and going places, and they were all eaten up with jealousy, the old biddies. Just because she had her sights set on getting out of the village and getting on in life.'

Clement smiled into his beer. Oh yes, definitely, the old boy had to have been one of Iris's conquests.

'Oh, I know all that,' the red-faced man said, maybe a shade impatiently. 'But you can't deny she was always causing trouble. I have it on good authority that the Finch boy had a big falling out with his best friend over her not long before they found her at the maypole.'

'Best friend? Oh you mean Ronnie Dewbury?

'Ssshhhh,' the younger of the men hissed. 'Don't want big ears overhearing us.'

Trudy had a nasty moment at that, thinking that she and Dr Ryder had been caught out. Then she wilted in relief as the villager carried on smoothly, 'Those bloody reporters will twist whatever you say, and before you know it, you'll be seeing your name appearing in tomorrow's papers as some sort of "source". Bloody vultures, the lot of 'em.'

At this Dr Ryder grinned openly. He knew – of course – that most members of Trudy's profession referred to himself as 'the old vulture' so it was nice to know he had company! Although, come to think of it, being grouped with members of the press was probably a worse insult.

'Oh, they're all too busy drinking and boasting of past sexual conquests to hear us,' the older man said disgustedly, but not before lowering his tone a little – luckily, not so low that Trudy and Clement still couldn't hear him.

'I suppose so,' his friend conceded grudgingly. 'But still, it pays to be careful. Anyway, let's talk about something more cheerful.' And then, maddeningly, he started to talk about his companion's success with the fly rod, and Trudy had to listen to a boring treatise on the merits of a ledger over a float when it came to catching chub.

74

By tacit consent, she and Clement finished their lunch without more ado, and left about twenty minutes later, again sticking to the shadows and keeping their faces averted from the men at the bar.

'Do you think it's true?' Trudy asked, once they were outside. 'About David Finch having a fallout with his friend Ronnie? Over Iris?'

'It's possible,' Clement said. 'I don't suppose you've heard anything about it at the station?'

'Not really, the DI and the Sarge are careful to keep things under wraps. There's a lot of interest in the May Queen murder, and they don't want anything leaking out to the newspapers,' she said regretfully.

They were both too intent on talking to notice the man in the car park. He'd just pulled into the pub grounds and had been about to climb out of his car when he spotted the familiar figures of WPC Trudy Loveday and the city coroner emerging from under the hanging baskets.

Hastily he hunkered back down a little behind the steering wheel, his handsome face slowly creasing into a smile.

So, Trudy and that bloody interfering coroner were sniffing around were they? Now that was interesting, Duncan Gillingham thought, his smile turning into a wolfish grin. Very interesting indeed – for where this particular duo showed their faces, news had a habit of following.

He watched them walk off down the village street, wondering where they were going and, for a moment, wondered wistfully if he could follow them without being spotted. He rather thought that he couldn't though, which was a pity.

He waited until they had disappeared around a bend in the lane and then climbed out of his car. He'd always wanted to have another chance at seducing the lovely Trudy Loveday, once the dust had had time to settle after their last encounter – and if he could pick up any scoops on the May Queen murder, all the better.

Perhaps now was a good time to test the waters …

Chapter 10

The Finch family lived in a large, square house on the junction of two lanes. Set in a large garden, it looked solid and respectable – just the sort of place you might expect a solid and respectable police officer and his family to live.

'Did your DI ask Superintendent Finch about any expensive jewellery his son might have bought Iris?' Clement asked as they paused at the garden gate to admire the house.

'If he did, he hasn't told me,' Trudy said morosely. 'But then, I spent most of this morning doing really important things like filing and making tea for the Sergeant and the likes of PC Rodney Broadbent,' she added with a flash of spirit. 'It's not as if any of them think of me as someone who should be kept in the loop.'

Clement grunted. 'More fool them, then, hmmm?' he said absently, but the compliment cheered her.

'Anyway,' Trudy said, 'it's far more likely that his mother would know about things like that,' she said. 'Mothers are more aware of what their children get up to than fathers, in my opinion,' she added with a smile, thinking of her own mother, who, at certain times during her childhood, seemed to be positively clairvoyant, not to mention omnipresent.

'So, let's go and talk to her then,' Clement said soberly. 'If anybody can give us an insight into David Finch's state of mind shortly before he died, it's probably her.'

Trudy felt herself tensing up. Talking to the bereaved was always an ordeal, even if a necessary one. She only hoped that one day, even if she never got used to it, she would at least feel less incompetent at it.

She took a deep breath and pushed open the garden gate. It creaked loudly as it did so, and made her smile, helping to lighten her mood a little. A proper copper's trick, that creaking gate – it meant that nobody in the house would ever be taken by surprise by a visitor coming in through the front way. And she would have bet her last shilling that any side or rear entrances to the property were firmly locked or barred.

Betty Finch was a short, slightly plump woman, with dark curling hair and large hazel eyes which had, at the moment, blue smudges beneath them. She was pale but composed when she answered the door, and somewhat to Trudy's surprise, seemed to recognise them immediately.

'Oh, Dr Ryder, hello. And you must be WPC Loveday? Thank you for dropping in. Won't you come in?' As they passed her into a small, neat hallway, she added, 'My husband told me about you and what you're doing for us. I can't tell you how grateful we are.'

So they had been expected to call in at some point, Trudy thought, silently agreeing as they followed Mrs Finch into the front room. It made sense that her husband had kept her informed about all that was happening in their son's case.

The room was obviously seldom used, but had recently been dusted and the scent of furniture polish hung in the air. A vase of daffodils, probably picked that morning from the garden, rested on a sideboard, catching the sun's rays. The room had a stuffy feel, however, and as if reading her mind, their hostess went quickly to a window and opened it to let in the warm but fresh spring air.

'Would you like tea?' she asked. She was dressed in a simple black dress and wore ballet-like black pumps. Although neither of them wanted tea after their drink at the pub, they both nodded, knowing that it would give her something to do and help settle her for the interview that lay ahead. She couldn't have been married to a police officer for all these years without having some inkling of why they had come and what they needed from her.

As they waited, Clement glanced around the small but pleasant room, decorated in shades of apple-green and cream, and shifted slightly in his chair. He'd popped a breath mint into his mouth as they'd walked up the path, careful not to let Trudy see it. One of the symptoms of his illness could include bad breath, and now he was careful to always have a supply of strong mints on hand any time he expected to talk to people.

'Here we are – I hope you like shortbread. I baked some this morning. They're my daughter Delia's favourite. I like to keep busy.' Mrs Finch said the words in a rush, running the sentences together and then she sat down the tray abruptly onto the table, rattling the cups and saucers a little. She sat down equally abruptly in the chair facing the sofa, where Clement and Trudy had elected to sit. She looked, to Trudy's eye, as if she'd suddenly run out of energy.

'I'll pour, shall I?' Trudy said kindly, and set about adding sugar lumps and pouring milk. She noticed Mrs Finch, after accepting her cup, immediately set it down again, without taking so much as a sip.

'So, you've come to talk about David,' Betty Finch said firmly, straightening her shoulders a little and looking determined to do her best, even though she was almost coming apart at the seams. It made Trudy's heart ache for her.

'I know that he didn't kill Iris, and I know that he didn't kill himself either,' Betty said, but her eyes were staring at a point somewhere between the two of them. 'And yes, I know that all mothers probably say the same things, in situations like these.' She shrugged and looked down at her hands, which were now twisting together in her lap. 'And I know there's no way I can convince you that I'm right. I mean, how can I? You never knew David. But I did. And I *know* I'm right.'

She smiled bitterly at this and then, with an effort, forced herself to look directly at them – firstly at Clement, and then at Trudy. 'My husband told me that I wasn't to be fooled by your youth, my dear,' she said, making Trudy's eyes widen in surprise. 'He says that you and Dr Ryder have an uncanny way of getting at the truth, and that's why he insisted you investigate everything discreetly. And I trust my husband's judgement,' she added. 'Besides, I think DI Jennings and his team are under pressure to close Iris's case as quickly as possible, which given the media attention is understandable. And the temptation for them to simply blame David and close the case must be enormous. So I'll do anything I can to help you. What do you want to know?'

Trudy swallowed hard and felt a momentary sense of panic. Until now, the problem had felt, not academic exactly, but not altogether quite 'real' either. But now, facing this grieving mother who was placing so much trust in her, brought it home to her just how much responsibility there was resting on her shoulders. Especially when she wasn't sure herself whether or not David Finch had first committed murder and then suicide.

'Well, there are one or two things we'd like to ask you about,' she said, knowing that she had to start somewhere, or she might start to feel paralysed by her own sudden lack of confidence. 'Before she died, Iris was seen wearing an expensive necklace. Do you know if David bought it for her?'

'Oh no, I'm sure he didn't,' Betty said at once. 'He was a student, with a part-time job during the holidays. He had no spare money. And his father and I only gave him a small allowance – enough to cover the basic necessities. He didn't have the wherewithal to buy Iris all the things that she was always wanting and angling for.'

The last sentence was said bitterly, and Trudy followed up on it quickly. 'Yes, we're picking up things about Iris. I take it she was the sort who liked the good things in life?' she said mildly.

'Oh my, yes, that was Iris,' Betty Finch said coldly, but then her face suddenly crumpled. 'Oh no, I shouldn't have said that. I keep forgetting that the poor girl's dead. And the way they did it! How *could* anyone do that to her? Make a mockery of her like that, tying her to the maypole with those ribbons? It was like someone really hated her. Her poor parents.'

Clement reached forward and put a hand over her own. 'Easy, Mrs Finch. We won't keep you much longer,' he said quietly.

Betty nodded, gulped, took a deep breath and straightened her shoulders again. 'Sorry. I'm all right now, really I am. What else can I tell you?'

'Do you know anything about an argument that David might have had with Ronnie Dewberry, Mrs Finch? We've been hearing rumours that they had a falling out?' Trudy tried next.

'Really? Well, I know that David hadn't been very happy with Ronnie for some time, but I don't know that it meant much – nothing serious, anyway. They'd been friends for so long, and they always made up any differences they might have had. David never said anything to me about it.'

'Why hadn't he been happy with Ronnie?' Clement slipped in his first question, and Betty waved a hand vaguely in the air.

'Oh, I think that was because Ronnie was always warning him against Iris. For some reason, Ronnie never thought much of Iris, and wasn't afraid of saying as much to David. Of course, they've been best friends for simply ages, ever since they were knee-high to grasshoppers, and so I suppose Ronnie expected David to listen to him and follow his advice to jilt her. But of course …' Here, the dead boy's mother shrugged. 'When a boy's smitten, properly smitten I mean, especially for the first time … well, even long-time friendship doesn't count for much, does it?'

Betty smiled sadly again and looked from one to the other questioningly.

'So David carried on seeing her. Hmmm, I'm surprised Ronnie was set against Iris,' Clement mused. 'She really was a stunningly lovely girl, wasn't she?'

'Oh yes, you had to give her that,' Betty said promptly. 'But I'm afraid it went to her head a bit. She had all sorts of fancy ideas – becoming a model, or a film star, or something, so they say. Silly really. She was so desperate to get out of the village and make this grand life for herself …'

She abruptly clamped her lips together as she evidently realised she was in danger of speaking ill of the dead yet again. Instead, she sighed and shrugged. 'It was all so pointless! I knew David was just a passing fancy for her, you see. It was obvious. Oh, he was a good-looking lad, my David, and our family is well respected in the village. So …' She trailed off, clearly struggling to find a way of saying that they were a step above the girl's working-class roots without sounding snobbish.

'The Carmodys would have thought of your son as a good catch,' Trudy helped her out with a gentle smile.

'Exactly,' Betty said gratefully. 'Not that Iris saw things the same way. To her, I think David was, well, just a bit of a plaything, really. Or worse – camouflage.'

'Could you expand a bit on that for us, Mrs Finch?' Trudy asked gently. 'I know it's hard, not wanting to say anything against someone who can't defend themselves, but I promise you, anything you tell us won't be repeated.'

Betty sighed heavily. 'It's just that … Well, although David thought the world of her, I could tell that Iris didn't feel the same way. Not that he brought her home to tea, or anything, but I'd still see them out and about, and I could just tell. A mother can, can't she? He wasn't what she was after, you see – which, to be frank, was somebody who could do her some proper good. Someone with money, say, or power to help her achieve her silly dreams. I wondered, to be honest, why she was wasting her time on him at all. He was still a lad at university after all, with hardly two pennies to rub together. Oh, he would have got a good job once he'd got his degree – been able to afford a nice home and all that. But Iris was a girl in a hurry – she wanted nice things now. I just had the feeling she had other fish to fry, do you know what I mean? And going out with our David was just a way to keep her parents happy and thinking that she wasn't up to anything they wouldn't approve of and … well … make it all look respectable.'

'You think she was going out with other boys behind his back?' Trudy said, and when the other woman nodded, said, 'Do you think that's what Ronnie tried to warn David about? Is that why they argued?'

'I suppose it could have been,' Betty said slowly. 'I know David said that Ronnie had it in for Iris for some reason, and it was making him mad. Naturally, he didn't like it when anyone said that they didn't think she was wonderful too,' she added wryly. 'Boys who think they're in love have some strange ideas. They think *everyone* must agree with them about how wonderful their beloved is, and be equally smitten.'

'But Ronnie clearly saw through Iris's beauty and charm,' Clement said dryly. 'Odd that. I would have thought the lad would be as smitten as everyone else. Do you think it could have been the case that Ronnie was secretly hankering after her too?'

Betty Finch thought for a moment, then smiled. 'Well, I always thought he had his eye on someone else … but it could be. I remember when I was at school, this boy, Derek Parks was infatuated with my friend Doris. Everyday he'd pull her pigtails and pretend he couldn't stand her.'

Trudy nodded. 'It was the same when I was at school. Everyone knew that if a boy put you down it meant he was really interested in you. So you think that Ronnie was rather smitten with Iris too, and his pretending not to like her was just a front? That all the time he was really jealous of David and wanted to split them up so he could have a chance with Iris himself?'

Betty shrugged helplessly. 'Who can say? I only know David

complained that Ronnie bad-mouthed Iris all the time, and he was fed up with it.'

'But you don't know if they ever actually fought?' Clement asked.

Betty blinked and straightened in her chair. 'If you think Ronnie had something to do with David's death, I can tell you now, you're barking up the wrong tree. Those kids were always as thick as thieves. And I know their friendship would have survived Iris, once she'd dumped David and moved on. Because I know, as sure as eggs are eggs, that's that what would have happened if …'

She broke off and shook her head. 'But what does any of that matter now? They're both dead, aren't they?' she added hopelessly.

'Do you have any idea who killed Iris?' Trudy asked gently.

'I wish I did,' Betty Finch said bitterly. 'I only know it wasn't my son.'

'But her death must have affected him,' Trudy said again, even more gently.

'Of course it did. He was wild with grief,' Betty said angrily. 'But he was determined to find out who had killed her. That's why I know he didn't kill himself.' She paused and took a long breath, clearly nerving herself up for something, then said flatly, 'I think he found out who killed her, and whoever it was, murdered him to keep him quiet.'

She looked almost satisfied for a moment. And then, once again, her face crumpled. 'Please, you have to find out the truth.'

At this appeal, Trudy shot Clement a helpless look. For the first time, she felt truly frightened; because what if they *couldn't* find out the truth? What if this case became one of those unsatisfactory ones that remained technically open, but really shelved, with everyone assuming David Finch's guilt, but having no evidence to actually prove it? How could this poor woman and her husband – a superintendent of police – live the rest of their lives with that sort of nebulous black cloud following them everywhere?

'We'll do our best,' she said, realising just how inadequate that sounded. 'Did David ever tell you who he suspected might have killed Iris?' she swept on, hoping that Betty hadn't picked up on her doubts.

'No,' Betty admitted, her shoulders finally slumping in defeat. 'He was always quite a secretive child, but what happened to Iris … It made him even more careful. I think he knew in his heart of hearts that she had been running around with other men, and that only made him even more tight-lipped than ever. You know – as if even mentioning the possibility out loud would be unforgivable and disloyal. So he never told me anything about what he was thinking or doing. His father either,' she added, the tears finally rolling down her pale face at last. 'I only wish he had.'

Trudy wanted to ask more – about the last time she'd seen her son alive for instance – but she could see that the poor woman was in no fit state to answer any more questions. She was looking utterly wrung out. So it would have to wait for another time.

Beside her, Clement, too, was making motions to rise.

Trudy thanked Mrs Finch, told her to stay where she was and that they could see themselves out, and quietly followed Clement as he made his way back to the front door.

Outside, a ginger cat sitting in the sun on the path saw them, got up and came sauntering up to be petted.

'Well, that was awful,' Trudy said, bending to oblige the cat with a quick ear-scratch.

'It always is,' Clement said sombrely. As a coroner, he'd had to deal with more than his fair share of grieving relatives. 'But it was also very interesting,' he added, almost under his breath.

Chapter 11

When Trudy got home that evening, she heard the sound of the radio coming from the kitchen. As she recognised the Shadow's number one hit, 'Wonderful Land' she smiled and walked on through. For all her mother claimed not to think much of 'this modern pop music' she was often to be caught out listening to it! A quick glance around the small but cheerful room showed her that her father had yet to get in from his bus driving job, as the small table pressed up against one wall was empty. Usually Frank Loveday liked to bring back with him an evening paper, which he spread out on the table and studied whilst waiting for his tea.

Intriguingly, she noticed a lovely bunch of flowers standing in a jug of water on the worktop near the back door.

Her mother, Barbara, was at the sink busy peeling potatoes and she glanced around as she sensed movement behind her. 'Oh, hello love. You're a bit early,' she said, glancing at the clock.

Trudy nodded. 'Dr Ryder said we might as well call it a day. Nobody wants to talk to you when it's getting towards the end of the day. What's for tea?'

'Spam fritters, chips and peas.'

'Lovely.'

'You still working with Dr Ryder then?' Barbara said rather too nonchalantly. Trudy, trying to think of a tactful way of avoiding having to satisfy her mother's inquisitiveness, was relieved when a knock came on the door, saving her the need to respond.

'Oh, it's the meter man,' Barbara said, peering through the window. 'Let him in will you love?'

Trudy opened the door to the man who came to read the electric meter every three months or so, glancing again at the delivery of flowers that must have come to the house some time that day. The same man had been reading their meters ever since she could remember, and he knew he could rely on the Loveday household to sit and have a chat if he had time. Trudy let him in with a smile and watched him go through to the hallway without breaking stride.

'Hello Tom, time for a cup of tea?' Barbara called over her shoulder right on cue, as he crouched down to open the door under the stairs and peer in to read the dials on the machinery there.

'Would love to, but I've still got most of the main street to do before I can clock off. Maybe next time, hmmm?'

Trudy showed him back out with a cheerful wave, and again admired the large and exquisitely colourful bouquet of mixed flowers sitting in a pail of water by the kitchen door.

'Mum, who sent the flowers?' Trudy asked curiously. The bouquet looked expensive. As she turned to look at her mother at the sink, she was surprised to see her mother was beaming at her.

'You tell me, our Trudy,' she said with a knowing twinkle in her eye. 'They're for you.'

Trudy almost felt her jaw drop, but she managed to stop herself from gaping just in time. 'For me? Are you sure?' Feeling a sense of excitement, she crouched down to check. Sure enough, attached to a slender black stick, a small envelope had been thrust down amongst the stems, with her name prominently displayed.

Wonderingly, she pulled it free and stood up, staring at it. The only person she could think of who could afford to send her such a marvellous gift was Dr Clement Ryder. But why should he? It was not her birthday …

'Well, don't just stand there gawping at it, our Trudy, open it,' her mother encouraged impatiently, wiping her hands dry on her apron front and coming to stand beside her. No doubt, Trudy mused, she'd been on tenterhooks ever since it came, since Barbara Loveday's curiosity was legendary in the family.

'You kept quiet about it, I must say,' her mother teased. And on seeing her daughter shoot her a baffled look, added, 'having an admirer, I mean.'

'But I don't have an admirer,' Trudy assured her, working her finger with some difficulty under the sealed tight and tiny flap of the envelope before managing to pry the card within free. Quickly, she pulled it out and read the message.

For Trudy
I hope you haven't forgotten me?
Duncan G.

'Who's Duncan G. when he's at home then?' Barbara asked, her voice a mixture of caution and warmth as she peered unrepentantly over her daughter's shoulder.

'He's no one, Mum, honest,' Trudy said shortly. 'He's just some reporter I used to know.'

'Really? Young, is he?'

'Well, a few years older than me,' Trudy said reluctantly.

'How many years?' Barbara asked suspiciously.

'I don't know Mum! Maybe five or six,' Trudy said exasperatedly.

'Good-looking lad, is he?'

'Very,' Trudy said, before she could stop herself, then added, 'and engaged to someone else.'

'Oh,' her mother said, somewhat deflated, and then sniffed disapprovingly. 'Then he has no business sending you flowers, does he, the cheeky young pup!'

'No, he doesn't,' Trudy agreed. But she couldn't help but give the bouquet a lingering look. She'd never had flowers sent to her before. You couldn't really count some daffodils picked from the family garden, that had been her one and only boyfriend's previous gifts. But these sumptuous blooms had clearly come straight from a high-end flower shop, she could tell. And carnations were one of her favourites – they smelt so nice. Roses too … 'But they'll make a nice display anyway. Mum, why don't you arrange them in Auntie Jane's big green vase, whilst I go and have a wash?'

Before her mother could launch in with yet more questions, Trudy beat a hasty retreat and ran up the stairs to her small bedroom. Once there, she sat on the edge of her bed, took off her shoes with a sense of relief and pushed her feet into some slippers. But all the time she was thinking of Duncan Gillingham.

She'd first met him during her last case with Dr Ryder. At first, she'd thought he was rather interested in her, and had been a little flattered, but she'd quickly learned that he was not a man that could be trusted. Not only was he ferociously ambitious, and would do anything to get a good story, he was also engaged to the daughter of the man who owned the newspaper he worked for.

A fact that he'd been very careful not to mention to her.

Luckily, Dr Ryder had saved her from making a bit of a fool of herself, and now she gave a small sigh.

She hadn't thought of him for months … well, not really. Not often, anyway. And now he was back, sending her beautiful flowers. Of course, it didn't take half a second for her to realise why.

Somehow he'd found out that she and the coroner were digging into the Carmody/Finch case. And he thought he could get some sort of inside scoop by buttering her up again!

Hah! Trudy gave a mental snort. If he thought he could sweet-talk and fool her again he was in for a shock!

Chapter 12

The next morning they arrived bright and early at the Dewberry farm, but even so Clement suspected that father and son had probably been up for hours and had already seen to all the first chores of the day. Luckily, they had returned to the farmhouse for what was probably their second breakfast of the day – for when Ray Dewberry answered the door to their knock, Clement could smell porridge bubbling on the stove.

The main entrance to the old farmhouse opened directly into the kitchen, and an old black cat sat in the middle of the stone-flagged floor, lackadaisically washing its face. It paused briefly to study them, then resumed its ablutions. Seated at the large, well-scrubbed wooden table, nursing an empty mug in his hands, Ronnie Dewberry peered at them suspiciously.

'Who's that, Dad?' he asked. 'Not more police!' He snorted. 'I thought they'd done poking around the village asking about Iris.'

'T'ain't the police, boy. This is the coroner. I 'ad to tell him all about finding young David in court, and such.' The farmer's eyes moved shyly to Trudy then rapidly away again.

'I'm Dr Ryder's assistant,' Trudy introduced herself, not quite truthfully, but not actually lying either. She was finding it hard to have to explain herself, for usually her uniform did it for her.

Being in plain clothes was still a treat, but sometimes it had its drawbacks.

'May we come in for a few minutes, Mr Dewberry? I just have some follow-up questions,' Clement put in smoothly. 'Inquests can be long-winded things, and we have to cross all the T's and dot all the I's. Everyone thinks a case is over when the court rules on a verdict, but alas, that's not quite so.'

'Oh, I daresay,' the farmer said, clearly having no idea about such matters – and probably caring even less. 'Paperwork be the bane of my life sometimes too,' he muttered as he led them towards the table. 'What the taxman wants to know …' He shook his head sadly and moved to the old wood-burning range to give the porridge a stir and prevent it burning on the bottom of the saucepan.

'We just wanted a quick word with both of you, really, about David and what happened to him,' Clement said, glancing inquiringly at one of the chairs tucked under the table and then at the younger Dewberry male. Ronnie scowled slightly, but then shrugged, nodding his head in unspoken permission.

Clement, ever the gentleman, first pulled out a chair for Trudy, and as she sat, she contemplated Ronnie thoughtfully. She knew from the files that he was the same age as the dead boy, which would make him just twenty. A few inches short of six feet, she judged, though it was hard to tell with him sitting down. He was a handsome enough lad, she supposed, with straw-coloured hair and nice blue eyes. A slight smattering of freckles had probably caused him to be teased at school, but when he bothered to smile, she imagined he would make a few female heads turn in interest.

'As I understand it,' Clement said, glancing at the younger farmer, 'the evening David died, you were at the village pub?'

Over by the range, the boy's father gave a brief snort, but said nothing.

Ronnie shot him a glowering glance. 'Just to have a pint of cider and play a game of darts with the lads,' he muttered. 'No harm in that.'

'And you stayed till closing time?'

'I left just before,' he said, a shade defensively, Trudy thought.

Clement nodded. So the boy had an alibi for only part of the time period when David had probably died, which meant his best friend was by no means in the clear, if they were indeed looking at a case of murder.

'Did you see David that day?' Clement asked curiously.

'No, not that day,' Ronnie said heavily. 'I wish I had. If I'd'a seen him, I might've got an inkling about what a bad way he was in, and done summat about it. Jollied him up a bit, like.' He shrugged his shoulders wearily. 'Or at least … I dunno. Done something,' he added morosely, staring into his empty mug. 'I just don't get it. How he could'a done it, I mean.'

'Perhaps he didn't,' Clement said softly.

Over by the stove, Trudy noticed Ray Dewberry stop stirring the contents of the saucepan. It wasn't hard to understand why. Her friend's comment had had the same effect as that of a grenade tossed into the room.

'But I thought the jury said it was suicide,' Ronnie said, sounding puzzled.

'Juries have been known to be wrong,' Clement said mildly. 'So you don't think he was the type to kill himself?'

'Nah, I don't then,' Ronnie said somewhat belligerently. 'And nor I don't believe he would ever hurt Iris neither. Now then!' He shot Clement a challenging look, his chin jutting out slightly, but the coroner only smiled amiably and nodded.

'I hear that you and David had a falling out over Iris not long before he died. Is that true?'

The boy's father, not liking the way the conversation was going, stirred restively by the range, but his son shot him another scowl, this time his sharp blue eyes clearly carrying a warning. Whatever else his parent might think, he didn't like his father fighting his battles for him.

At this display of grit, Trudy felt herself warming a little more to the unhappy lad. After all, he was clearly missing his best friend, and genuinely seemed to be mourning him, as well as sticking up for him and his reputation – unless, of course, it was all just an act?

'Not to say a proper falling out,' Ronnie answered the coroner, holding Clement's mild gaze with his own, his jaw clenching slightly. 'Me and David never really fell out about anything. Not bad like. He was the brother I never had, see.'

'Me and the missus had three girls, straight off, before our Ronnie came along,' Ray felt compelled to put in gruffly. 'All of 'em married with kids of their own now of course. Wish the wife had seen 'em all … She'd'a loved the grand-kiddies … Ah well.'

Pointedly ignoring his father, Ronnie smiled grimly. 'I grew up the youngest boy surrounded by girls who all delighted in telling me what to do. David was my ally, see. He helped me find frogs to put in their beds, and helped me dig up worms to put in their shoes …'

Clement grinned. 'So you were still close, even after he'd gone off to university?'

'He came back for the holidays,' Ronnie said petulantly.

'But wasn't that more Iris's doing?' Clement asked, and the boy, after a quick scowl, grunted in acquiescence.

'Yeah, I suppose it was,' he agreed sadly. 'Mad about her, he was.'

'A lot of people in the village have remarked how lovely she was,' Trudy put in, deciding it was time she added something to the mix. She watched Ronnie closely and sure enough, at this praise of the dead May Queen, angry colour swept up into his face.

'Oh yeah, she was something to look at right enough,' Ronnie said. 'Pretty as a picture and rotten through and through.'

Once again his father moved a little agitatedly forward, as if to try and silence him, and then thought better of it.

'You didn't like her then,' Clement said dryly.

'That I didn't, mister,' Ronnie said flatly. 'Everyone knew she was doing the dirty on him, seeing other men and what-not.

She had half the silly old sods in the village wrapped around her little finger, and not just people our age neither, but married men who should'a known better. Old enough to be her dad, some of 'em! It was sickening. She even had some arty type promising to take her picture and make her famous and promising all sorts. And she lapped it up – all the attention. Made her feel like Gina Lollobridgida or something, I dare say.' He shot his father's stiff and disapproving back another scowl. 'I don't care if you're not supposed to speak ill of the dead! Everyone saw her, going around in fancy clothes that she couldn't afford to buy for herself, sprayed in French perfume and wearing gold. Where'd she get all those little gee-gaws, ey? From some silly old duffer who should have been old enough to know better, that's who. Flirting, and playing up to them! The only one who couldn't see it was David.' He finally ran out of bile, his voice dropping to a more despairing tone now. 'He would never hear a word said against her. Poor fool! And look where it got him!'

He slammed his hand down sharply on the table, making both his father and Trudy jump. Only Clement continued to watch him, unruffled.

'I'm sorry you lost your friend,' the coroner said gently. And for a moment, Ronnie Dewberry's blue eyes swam with unshed tears. Then he shook his head and cleared his throat. 'Yeah. Well …'

'So you never fell for her charms yourself?' Trudy ventured to break the small sad silence that followed.

'No. Unlike some, I had more sense!' Ronnie shot back.

'She must have had *some* redeeming features though. Nobody's all bad,' Trudy tried again, but Ronnie was having none of it.

'If she did, I can't think of one. She was a nasty bit of goods through and through. She even treated her best friend like dirt. Now what does that say about her, hey?'

'Her best friend?' Trudy echoed.

'Yeah, Janet Baines. Now there's a decent enough girl,' he added quietly. 'She dresses proper, like, and doesn't think she's the queen bee. Mind you, she has a bit of a bad time with her mother, I reckon. She's the over-protective sort,' he added, as Trudy's eyebrows rose in query. 'Smothers her a bit, you know the kind. Janet's her only child, and tries to keep her tied to her apron strings. I think that's why Iris was able to get her claws into her – Janet, I mean. You know, she helped Janet get away from her mum for a bit and have some fun. If you can call it fun. Not that Janet … Well, it's none of my business is it,' he said with a final shake of his head. 'Anyway, if you've finished, I got work to do.'

'Have some porridge,' his father said half-heartedly, but the younger Dewberry simply shook his head and stumped out of the house.

'You ain't gotta take anythin' the boy says to heart,' his father said heavily. 'Things ain't been the same around here since I found young David … well, since I found him.'

'We're sorry to intrude, Mr Dewberry,' Trudy said quietly. 'Thank you for speaking to us. We'd appreciate it if you didn't spread it around the village that we're here tying up some lose ends,' she added, thinking of Duncan Gillingham. 'There are still reporters lurking about …'

But Ray Dewberry snorted disdainfully. 'Don't have no truck with the likes of them!' he promised. And for that, Trudy could only feel very grateful.

Chapter 13

Once outside, Trudy and Clement walked thoughtfully towards the Rover. 'So what do you think?' Trudy mused. 'Is it a case of "methinks the young man doth protest too much" or do you think he genuinely didn't like her?'

Clement smiled. 'Hard to say. But I think we can be sure, for some reason or other, that he definitely wasn't indifferent to Iris. But whether or not he disliked her as much as he claimed, or whether he was secretly pining after her …' He shrugged. 'We'll probably never know.'

'But if he *was* smitten with her, and was even seeing Iris behind his best friend's back,' Trudy persisted, 'does that give him motive to kill either Iris or David? I mean, let's just say for argument's sake that he had a great passion for Iris – he might have killed her if she turned him down. Or if she didn't turn him down, and they'd been seeing each other, what if he found out that she was two-timing both himself *and* David? We keep hearing how Iris was popular with practically all the male population of the village, after all.' Trudy paused and took a much-needed breath, then frowned. 'But why then would he turn around after killing Iris and kill David? That doesn't make sense, does it?'

She slipped into the passenger seat and waited for Clement

to settle behind the wheel before she was off and running again. 'And if he didn't kill Iris, but secretly loved her, could it be that he believed David murdered her, and killed David in revenge?'

Clement grunted, amused by all the eager speculation, and reached into his pocket to pull out the car keys. As he did so, he felt his hand begin to tremble and twitch. He knew he couldn't fit the keys into the ignition right then without drawing attention to his most recent fit of 'the shakes' so he sat back instead, waiting for it to pass. At least, with his young friend in such a talkative mood, he wouldn't be pressed for something to keep her distracted!

'That's a lot of speculation,' he said slowly. 'Let's take it a step at a time and see if we can't sort it out.' He glanced out of the window as a black and white sheepdog darted across the farmyard and slipped into one of the outhouses. 'If – and that's a big "if" by the way – we say that Ronnie *is* the killer, are we saying that Ronnie lured David to the barn and killed him in cold blood?'

Trudy stared thoughtfully out of the window. 'Well, it's a starting point, isn't it? I mean, why did David die in the barn at all? If he committed suicide he could have done it anywhere. He could have slit his wrists in the bath at his home, or taken pills with alcohol on the village green, where Iris died. Or …'

Clement couldn't help but grin. 'All right, I get the picture. But don't forget that if he did kill himself, and his preferred method was hanging, then the barn would make perfect sense to him. He knew it well, remember, because he played there as a kid. He would have known about the handy rafters, and the rope lying around.'

'Yes, but all of that goes equally well for Ronnie too, if he was the killer,' Trudy pointed out reasonably. 'He could have asked David to meet him at the barn – I don't know, telling him he'd found something out about Iris or what-have-you. And once he was there, he offered him a drink laced with the sleeping pills. And then, when he was feeling woozy, put the rope around his neck and hauled him up.' She stopped abruptly at that, suddenly appalled by the image that swept into her head. 'That's awful. To be betrayed and killed by your best friend.'

'*If* it happened at all,' Clement reminded her steadily, glancing down unobtrusively to check his hand. It was fluttering gently now, down between the door panel and the side of his leg, but it wasn't trembling quite as much as it had been. 'We still don't know if suicide can be ruled out. Has your DI Jennings done anything about checking out the condition of the stepladder that he supposedly used?'

Trudy nodded. 'Yes, he's got some expert on woodwork looking at it. He expects to have a report soon.'

Clement sighed. 'Well, until we have something evidentiary to go on, it seems to me we have far too much to contend with. Did David kill Iris, or didn't he? Did David commit suicide, or didn't he? If he did neither, did the same person who killed Iris kill David? It's possible – but not likely, I admit – that one person could have killed Iris, and someone else killed David! If we're not careful, we'll start running around like headless chickens.'

Trudy sighed, but she knew the coroner was right.

'We need to keep our focus on one thing – and that's David,' Clement reminded her firmly. 'His state of mind before he died. What he was doing, who he was seeing, what he was saying about Iris. Because if his father is right, and David was actively trying to find out who killed Iris …'

'Then by following his tracks, we might find out who killed her too?' Trudy put in eagerly.

'Well yes, there's that,' Clement agreed, turning the car keys thoughtfully in his hand, relieved to find he could manipulate them quite well now. 'But we're not actually supposed to be investigating Iris's death, are we? Didn't your inspector make that very clear?'

Trudy bit her lip. 'Yes. I mean …' Her eyes shifted to him slyly. 'But if we *do* happen to find out who killed Iris …'

Clement laughed outright. 'You want to show your sergeant and Jennings what you can do?' Well, that was understandable, he thought with a smile.

Trudy sighed again, but said nothing. He was right, of course. She was desperate to prove to her superiors that they shouldn't leave her out of the big cases in future.

'Well, we won't accomplish anything sitting in the car,' Clement said, leaning forward and so blocking her view of what he was doing. He got the key into the ignition on the second try, then leaned back in his seat again.

'I think we should talk to this girl Janet Baines, don't you?' he murmured. 'If David was trying to find Iris's killer, he must have talked to her best friend. Even *I* know that girls tell things to other girls that they'd never confide in a month of Sundays to the chap they're actually stepping out with.'

'Good idea,' Trudy agreed.

But after asking a young lad playing with a whip-and-top in the street the way to the Baines' house, they found they were out of luck. Janet Baines wasn't home.

But her mother was.

Chapter 14

The Baines' house turned out to be a fairly large, detached house a little way down the lane leading from the village green. It had a colourful front garden, and an old man was busy working in it, tying up lupin plants. Clement suspected that Mrs Baines probably employed retired villagers to maintain both her house and gardens, which meant that she couldn't be short of a bob or two.

Unlike Iris's working-class background, her best friend came from a family a step or two up from her on the social ladder, and he suspected that had probably rankled.

'Do we know anything about the family?' Trudy asked him, as they opened the gate and walked up to the front door, watched curiously by the old man with green fingers.

'I don't. None of the Baines family were called as witnesses,' he pointed out. 'So they wouldn't have been included in my files.'

Trudy didn't like going in without prior information, but since they were severely hampered by the fact that their investigation was being conducted without official sanction, she had no choice. So she knocked on the door and hoped for the best.

The woman who answered the summons a few moments later was tall and thin, with shoulder-length brown hair and large brown eyes. She was not quite beautiful, and dressed in a twin-set

99

the colour of peaches. She looked to be in her early forties. 'Yes?' she asked sharply, looking instantly at Clement.

'Dr Ryder, city coroner. Mrs Baines, is it?'

'Yes, I'm Angela Baines. I'm afraid I don't understand …' She trailed off politely, and Clement smiled his best, most soothing smile.

'I resided over the David Finch inquest, and I'm just in the village doing some final tidying up of the case. I was hoping that I might speak to your daughter Janet.'

'Janet? Why? She hardly knew David,' Angela Finch said sharply, and Trudy gave a mental nod. Ronnie Dewberry was right – this was definitely a protective mother all right. She already looked ready to go into battle on her daughter's behalf, and Trudy only hoped that Dr Ryder would be able to charm her around a bit, otherwise they'd quickly have the door slammed in their faces. She had already come to the conclusion that Mrs Finch regarded Trudy as beneath her notice. She probably regarded all young women around her daughter's age as insignificant.

'Oh, I'm sure that must be the case, Mrs Baines,' Clement said smoothly. 'I just wanted to ask her a few questions about Iris Carmody and whether or not David had asked her any questions about what had happened to Iris. It goes to state of mind, you know,' he added as if confiding in her. In fact, what he'd just said was all but meaningless, but Trudy admired the psychology behind it. People were always flattered to think that they were being allowed access to confidential information of which their friends or neighbours were unaware.

At the mention of the dead May Queen, Angela's face instantly tightened however. 'Oh *her*. I see.' She sniffed, then cast a quick, anxious glance up and down the street. 'You'd better come in then, but Janet's not here right now. Still, no point in giving the neighbours something else to wag their tongues over.'

And so saying, she stepped a shade reluctantly aside to let them pass. 'Please, go on through to the end.' She indicated a short, rather ill-lit corridor that led off the hall.

'Is your husband home, Mrs Baines?' Clement asked. No doubt he was hoping that if he was, he might be in a more talkative mood than his wife.

'I'm a widow. Have been for some years now,' Angela said briskly, following them down the corridor and then indicating a door off to the left. Clement, in the lead, obligingly opened the door, revealing an extremely tidy and clean room, done out in shades of magnolia and beige. There was a fairly new-looking three-piece suite done out in some knobbly material the colour of oatmeal, and a deep-pile carpet in a similar colour.

'I'm sorry to hear that. If you'd rather have someone else here with you whilst we talk … a sister perhaps?' Clement asked casually, making Trudy cast him a swift, slightly surprised look. She was pretty sure that Angela Baines was the sort of woman who believed she could cope with anyone or anything on her own, and sure enough, the woman's already stiff shoulders stiffened even further.

'That won't be necessary, I'm sure,' she sniffed. 'Brian left us very well provided-for, as you can see,' she gave a quick, casual wave that was meant to take in the entire house, not just the well-appointed room, 'and I've been managing our affairs quite well on my own ever since he passed. Now, what's all this about Iris? Oh, please sit down. Tea?' she made the last offer abruptly, an obvious afterthought and one which she believed they'd forgo, because she was already sitting down herself.

'No thank you, Mrs Baines, we're fine for the present,' Clement said, taking his cue from her without batting an eyelash. Here, he understood, was a woman with a one-track mind who would not be distracted by social niceties.

Consequently, he got right down to business. 'We understand that Iris and Janet were friends? Best friends, in fact?'

Angela drew in a sharp breath. 'Supposedly,' she said. 'At least, I know that's how *Janet* saw things,' she amended.

'You saw them differently?' Clement asked.

'Of course. I'm older and wiser than my daughter, Dr …'

'Ryder.'

'Yes. Well. Janet was far too trusting in my opinion. She thought Iris was her friend, when it was clear the girl had no real feelings of friendship towards her at all.'

'That sounds rather harsh,' Clement mused mildly.

Angela's thin lips tightened mutinously. 'It may be so, but it's true nonetheless. Oh, I could see right through *that* little Miss, right from the time they met in primary school. Even then, as a five-year-old, Iris was as jealous as jealous could be of Janet. It was as plain as a pikestaff,' she added, nodding firmly.

'Oh? In what way?' Clement continued to keep his voice light and vaguely disinterested. This, he knew, would goad her on more than anything.

'In every way,' Angela said sharply. 'She was green with envy because I gave Janet things that her own family couldn't afford. Clothes, toys, books, you name it. If I gave Janet a new doll, Iris would somehow have to ruin it. Drop it, break it, get the clothes muddy. She just couldn't bear for Janet to have nice things that she didn't.'

'Children can be very fierce sometimes,' Clement said.

'Oh, that was just the beginning. When they were little, I could make excuses for Iris, because she was, as you said, just a little child. But as they grew older, she became even worse – more sly and cunning. She began to deliberately get my Janet into no end of trouble at school. She'd do things and then run off, leaving my daughter to the take the blame. I think her teachers soon cottoned on to that though,' she added with satisfaction. 'They soon realised what was what. Iris was a good-looking girl, but then so is my Janet – in a less obvious way. They could see that Iris was always trying to undermine her.'

'And this … rivalry … continued as they grew into adulthood, I take it?' Clement asked.

Angela looked as though she might have snorted at this, if she hadn't been so ladylike. As it was, she contented herself with a magnificent sniff. 'I should say so! If ever a boy showed any interest in Janet at all, Iris had to snatch him away. If ever Janet had her hair cut in the latest fashion, Iris had to go one better. The same with clothes. If I took Janet shopping for a new outfit, Iris wouldn't rest until she had something even more showy. It was pathetic really.'

'And Janet never realised any of this?' Trudy ventured timidly.

Angela Baines spared her a quick, pitying look. 'Oh no. She always thought I was being hard on Iris if I said anything against her. Iris had a way of making herself look liked the sinned-against, rather than the sinner. But she didn't fool me!'

'It sounds as if she was a very manipulative young lady,' Clement said.

'I'll say she was.'

'We've been hearing that she might have been seeing other men, other than David Finch I mean,' Trudy put in.

'Of course she was!' Angela said scathingly, as if it could be in any doubt. 'That dreadful man, Mortimer Crowley for one – art dealer my eye! The man's an obvious crook. Riding around in his fancy car, with all his arty friends and so-called "celebrity" pals coming up from London to spend weekends at his country place.' Angela shook her head. 'In my younger day, he would have been given the cold shoulder by the whole village. Everyone was respectable in those days. Nowadays though …' She sighed as if in regret. 'People are so influenced by money and a flashy reputation, aren't they? Oh, Iris thought she was being so clever, getting her fingers hooked into him. No doubt she thought he could do her some good – help her become an artist's model or something, I have no doubt. It wouldn't surprise me one bit if she didn't take off her clothes …' She stopped abruptly and shook her head. 'But then, I have no proof of that. I only know I didn't like my Janet hanging around with her. Who knows what might …' Realising she was in danger of revealing more than she might have liked, she broke off abruptly and scowled.

'I don't see what any of this has to do with that poor boy David taking his own life,' she said, glancing suspiciously at Clement.

'We were wondering if perhaps David had spoken to Janet before he died about Iris,' Clement repeated. 'Do you know if David called on her after Iris was found on the village green, Mrs Baines?'

'Not to my knowledge,' she said flatly. 'And I wouldn't have encouraged him if he had. No, I really don't think that Janet can possibly be of help to you,' she added with unmistakable finality, and stood up.

The interview was terminated.

Chapter 15

Trudy meekly followed Angela back to the front door, and only when they were clear of the house did she let her breath out in a whoosh.

'Poor Janet!' she muttered.

But Clement was frowning thoughtfully. 'Yes, no wonder she was friends with someone like Iris.'

'A free spirit, you mean?' Trudy said with a grin. 'Those two must have been like chalk and cheese. Did you believe her – Mrs Baines I mean – about what Iris was like?'

'Putting aside her antipathy, I think I probably do. Look at it from Iris's point of view. Janet was almost as pretty as her, which must have rankled, plus she was an only child and the apple of her mother's eye. Iris had brothers, didn't she?'

'I think so – at least three.'

'Right. And I don't suppose there was much money to spare, whereas Janet clearly had a lot of money to spend on nice things. Why wouldn't Iris resent her?'

'How do you know Janet Baines is pretty? Her mother is bound to be biased,' Trudy suddenly asked, distracted.

'I saw the photographs of her on the sideboard,' Clement said simply. 'Didn't you notice them?'

Trudy felt her face flush in shame. 'No. I was too busy concentrating on what Mrs Baines was saying,' she admitted, feeling cross with herself. 'Did you get the impression that there was something a little … well … fanatical about her? When she was talking about Iris, I mean?'

'Oh yes. But I think that was because she was afraid of her,' Clement said, making Trudy, walking alongside him, stop for a moment in surprise.

'Afraid of her? Why would she be afraid of Iris?'

Clement also stopped walking and shrugged. 'I think she was afraid of Iris's influence over Janet. More specifically, that she might lure Janet into getting into *serious* trouble.'

Trudy instantly caught on. 'Oh! You mean with men … oh! She thought Iris might make her become … promiscuous, like herself?'

Clement smiled at the way his young friend had lowered her voice and looked rather embarrassed.

'Yes. I think that's very much what she was afraid of,' Clement agreed. 'Which would have given her a good motive for getting rid of Iris, wouldn't it?'

Chapter 16

Trudy pondered this comment for a while and then said judiciously, 'Yes. But she'd have no motive for getting rid of David, would she?'

Clement smiled. 'Not unless David suspected her of killing Iris and challenged her about it.'

Trudy sighed and clutched her head. 'Oh don't! This is all giving me a headache, and I doubt she'd have the strength to … Oh no!' she broke off, groaning out loud. 'This is just what I need right now.'

'What?' Clement asked, glancing at her then quickly following her gaze to where a good-looking young constable was striding purposefully towards them, grinning hugely. Fair-haired, square-jawed and with bright blue eyes, he was probably used to setting feminine hearts fluttering. But Clement's young friend looked merely exasperated.

'Friend of yours?' he couldn't help but tease.

Trudy rolled her eyes. 'No, he isn't. PC Rodney Broadbent – I knew he was working the Carmody case with Sergeant O'Grady but I'd hoped I wouldn't run into him. The silly idiot is going to ruin my cover! I don't want anybody knowing I'm with the police just yet.'

So saying, she began to walk forward to intercept him, a grim look on her face. Before he could speak, and no doubt ask her something inane in his loud and carrying voice, she said, 'Hello Constable. You're still making inquiries about Miss Carmody, I see?' and thrust her hand out to be shaken.

For a moment Trudy wondered if the big clot was going to ask her what on earth she was going on about, and she noticed two middle-aged women, standing on the pavement on the opposite side of the road, watching them with interest.

Then, with a sigh of relief, she saw comprehension dawn in Rodney's blue eyes just in time and his grin faltered a bit. No doubt, the Inspector had had to tell his team about the confidential nature of Trudy's own assignment, and the golden boy couldn't have been pleased to see her, a mere 'girl', be given yet another plum job working with the coroner.

Reminded of this, he nodded curtly at Dr Ryder, but at least lowered his voice somewhat as he said, 'Hello Miss, yes we're still asking people if they can tell us anything relevant about Miss Carmody's death.' He turned to look pointedly at the two women who had the grace to look uncomfortable and carry on walking. Albeit rather slowly.

'I thought most of the door-to-door interviews were over now,' Trudy said quietly, when she was sure that they couldn't be overheard.

Rodney shrugged indolently. 'They are. But the Sarge wanted to keep a police presence in the village. You know, reassure people their daughters were safe, and make myself available in case someone saw me and thought of something new they wanted to say.'

By that, Trudy translated, Rodney was hanging out at the pub and seeing if he could pick up any gossip.

'And have they?' she asked curiously.

'Not yet but … Hey! I thought you were supposed to keep your nose out of our case? Isn't David Finch your main priority?' he challenged her territorially, his impressive chin jutting out.

Trudy sighed. 'Yes, it is,' she was forced to admit. 'We've just been talking to Mrs Baines. Oh, by the way, you don't know where her daughter might be found when she's not at home, do you?'

If she knew Rodney Broadbent (and, alas, she did, only too well) he would have found a way of ferreting out all the pretty girls the village had to offer and 'interviewing' them personally. She wondered, cynically, how many of them had been foolish enough to go out on a date with him.

'Ah, the lovely Janet. Yeah, she's probably at work. Well, I say work,' he added with a smile, 'it's not what you or I would think of as work. She helps out at some charity thing in Oxford. You know, one of those places selling jumble and bric-a-brac to feed some starving kids somewhere.'

Clement felt his lips twitch as Trudy sighed heavily. 'Yes, I do know what a charity shop is Rodney. Where in Oxford, do you know?'

'Some shop off St Ebbe's I think,' he answered vaguely.

Trudy nodded. They'd be able to find it, she was sure. 'Well, thanks. I don't suppose you've heard anything that could help us? About David Finch, I mean? Anyone see him on the day he died, maybe going towards the Dewberry Farm?'

'Nah, nothing like that,' Rodney said, obviously happy to be of no use whatsoever.

'What are the villagers saying about him?' Trudy persisted, but again he just shrugged, not in the least interested in doing her any favours.

'Half of 'em think he did it then did away with himself, the other half seem to think some arty bloke might have done it.'

This was not the first time that people had mentioned the artistic man who had been rather closely associated with the dead girl, and therefore might have had a possible reason to kill David. Trudy and Clement already had him firmly on their 'to be interviewed' list.

'OK. Well, thanks Rodney, you've been very helpful,' she said ironically.

The big idiot just beamed at her and strolled on – no doubt to find a shady spot to sit and lounge the day away.

'A lovely specimen,' Clement remarked drolly, watching the golden-haired youth saunter off.

At this, Trudy had to smile.

Chapter 17

As Trudy had expected, it wasn't that hard to find the charity shop where Janet Baines sometimes volunteered to work. Tucked away in one of Oxford's many little medieval (or older) alleyways, it did indeed offer the jumble, bric-a-brac and other assorted and unwanted items that Rodney had predicted.

When they went in, a smartly dressed woman with white hair and sharp, pale grey eyes glanced up from behind the counter. Such was the force of her personality that Trudy instantly felt compelled to check on the bookshelves of second-hand books so that she might find something to purchase, for there was no way she would feel comfortable without spending some of her hard-earned pennies in here.

Luckily, she spotted an Agatha Christie that she hadn't read yet, and as Clement approached the counter, she hastily snatched it and scuttled after him to pay for it.

'I was wondering if you could help us,' Clement said with a charming smile that unfortunately had no effect whatsoever on the guardian of the counter. 'We're looking for a Miss Janet Baines?'

The older woman's eyelids flickered in some surprise as she eyed first Clement with such an openly speculative glance that

Trudy almost blushed for him, and then, with more puzzlement, Trudy.

'We don't encourage our gels to have male visitors when they're in the shop,' the woman said, her cut-glass accent so acute Trudy almost had trouble understanding what she was saying.

Clement, who could do a good range in haughty looks himself when he wanted, gave one now. 'I'm Dr Clement Ryder, city coroner. I need to speak to Miss Baines on a professional manner. This is my assistant,' he added vaguely, gesturing at Trudy.

She didn't mind being relegated and ignored, as she understood at once what he was doing, and why. People like this always reacted to authority. And, right on cue, the dragon lady relaxed slightly. But only slightly.

'She's in the office sorting through some crockery that was dropped off. We don't sell chipped or cracked cups and saucers here,' she added severely. 'I'll just inform her that she's needed.' And so saying, she opened a door and called briskly upwards, 'Janet, would you come down for a moment please?'

Clearly, she was not about to leave the shop unattended, and Trudy couldn't help but wonder if she and Clement looked like her idea of shoplifters. But perhaps they did? Trudy knew from her own patrols and bitter experience, that shoplifters came in all shapes and disguises. Once, a woman dressed as a nun—

Her trip down memory lane abruptly ended as she heard light footfalls coming down a set of uncarpeted wooden stairs, and a moment later, Janet appeared in the doorway. 'Yes, Miss Boisier?' she asked meekly.

She was a tall girl, with a figure that a fashion editor would no doubt have described as 'willowy'. She was dressed elegantly but simply in a pale blue summer frock, and had long, very thick and slightly wavy dark brown hair. Her eyes were large and velvet-brown, and set in a perfectly oval and very pale face. Her features looked serene and interesting rather than pretty, and it took you a moment or two to realise just how beautiful it was – in total contrast to Iris Carmody's more conventional beauty of fair hair, heart-shaped face and blue eyes, Trudy could nevertheless understand how Janet's more subtle beauty would give her dead friend cause for jealousy.

'This is Dr Ryder. He says he has business with you,' the inimitable Miss Boisier said, her voice totally neutral but somehow endeavouring to make it clear that she didn't believe a word of it.

'Oh?' Janet turned her large brown, deer-like eyes onto Clement.

'I'd like to talk to you about your friends, Iris and David,' Clement said, determined not to satisfy the older woman's curiosity any more than he could help, and which he could sense was bubbling away beneath her tightly contained surface.

Janet blinked slightly at this, then nodded. 'I see. Perhaps we should talk outside? We wouldn't want to inconvenience any customers,' Janet said, with just the smallest hint of a smile in her voice that told them that she, too, was determined to deny her co-worker the satisfaction of overhearing their conversation.

Once outside, she led them a little way down the narrow alleyway to a bus stop on a wider road that had the benefit of a wooden bench. Luckily, the seat was currently empty. She sat down in the sun with a sigh, and pushed back a long lock of hair behind her ear.

'Are you really the coroner?' Janet asked listlessly, looking up at him.

'Yes. I resided over David's inquest, but not Iris's,' Clement answered truthfully.

The girl nodded, but without any apparent curiosity. She looked even more pale than before, but still composed.

Trudy sat beside her and decided this time it was up to her to take the lead. They were the same age and she had a feeling that this witness would respond more readily to herself than to a middle-aged authority figure. 'I'm really sorry about Iris. I can't image what it's like, to lose your best friend,' she began gently.

Janet nodded, managing to give a small smile so lacking in any

113

feeling at all that it was utterly meaningless. 'I still can't believe it. Not really. I keep expecting Iris to call around and ask me to go out with her somewhere.'

'To a nightclub, you mean?' Trudy asked, then smiled as Janet shot her a quick, assessing look. 'It's all right – I hear they're very exciting. I've never been to one myself though.' She hoped she'd managed to inject some envy into her tone. 'My dad would kill me if he found out.'

'My mum would kill me too, if she knew we'd been to one,' Janet admitted.

'But Iris was brave.' Trudy nodded, making it a statement, and Janet nodded back.

'Yes she was. That's what Mum doesn't really understand. Life was exciting with her. Do you know what I mean?'

'Yes, I can imagine,' Trudy said quietly.

'I really miss her. I just can't believe somebody *did* that to her,' Janet said, for the first time showing some real emotion. 'Just … strangling her then tying her to the maypole on the village green like that, where everyone would see her. As if he was mocking her. It was so … *horrible*!'

'Yes it was awful,' Trudy agreed grimly. 'Do you think David Finch was capable of doing something like that? From what we've been hearing about him, he seemed a nice enough boy.' Trudy spoke bluntly, encouraged by having broken through the other girl's previous calm dullness.

Janet cogitated this for a while, obviously giving it some serious thought and in no hurry to rush to speech. It puzzled Trudy a little, for surely this girl must have already thought long and hard this past week or so about who it was that might have murdered her friend. And David was the village's favourite chief suspect.

Finally she stirred. 'I'm not sure. I don't *think* so. But I don't know. How can I?' She shrugged helplessly. 'I always liked David well enough, and like you said, he seemed a nice boy,' she said wearily. 'But on the other hand, he really had it bad over Iris.

Maybe, if he found out about Mort … some bad things that she was doing, he might have … I don't know …' She shrugged again. 'Gone mad for a moment or two and killed her before he got himself back under control? Men do *do* that, don't they?' She looked at Trudy earnestly. 'You read about it sometimes in the papers, men going berserk.'

'It's been known to happen,' Trudy agreed. As if losing your temper gave a man a right to hurt their loved ones. And yet how many times had she heard wife-beaters say self-pityingly that it was all the woman's fault for rousing his ire? 'Did David have a bad temper?' she asked curiously.

'Not that I saw,' Janet was compelled to admit. 'But when Iris was with David, I didn't hang around much. I mean, you don't like to, do you? Feel like you're playing gooseberry?'

Trudy smiled understandingly. 'You said before that Iris was into some bad things. What did you mean by that?'

But this was obviously a question too far, for Janet shifted uncomfortably on the bench and her mouth set in a stubborn line. Oddly, it only enhanced her beauty. 'Oh, I don't know specifically,' she said, clearly lying.

Wisely, Trudy remained silent, and let Janet stare down at her hands, giving her time to feel more and more guilty for holding back. At last, the other girl shrugged listlessly again. 'I know that Iris was up to something, because she was boasting about going to London to become a model. I mean for real, this time,' she added, biting her lip. 'Before, when we were still at school, she was always threatening to run away from school and get away from this silly little village and go to London and become famous. But that was, you know, just a dream. We all knew that, because of course, you don't really intend to do it, do you? How can you? Even if you had the money – and Iris's family didn't have much spare money – how would you go about finding somewhere to live, in a big city, all on your own? But lately, she was *really* excited. I could just tell that something had happened to make

115

her believe that it was suddenly all actually possible. She was all … gleeful and bubbling over.'

Trudy caught Clement's gaze and frowned thoughtfully. If Janet was right, and the murdered girl *had* found some way to make her dreams come true, had Iris gone so far as to break things off with David? She'd hardly want to take her boyfriend to the capital with her and have him underfoot whilst she enjoyed her big adventure, would she? And if she *had* jilted him, maybe she hadn't been particularly kind about it? She could just see someone like Iris, all caught up in her own world, being callous and unthinking about the feelings of others. And if she'd been particularly brutal about it – maybe even laughed at him – it might have led to him strangling her in a fit of rage.

'Did she actually say what her plans were?' Trudy asked cautiously.

'Oh no. But then, Iris liked to be mysterious,' Janet said, half admiringly and half bitterly. 'You know, cultivate an air of … oh, I don't know … glamour, I suppose. She would tease and taunt you with some outrageous claim, until you thought she was talking so much pie-in-the-sky, but then the moment you called her on it, she'd pull it off. Like saying she was going to wear a pearl necklace at the next village hall dance, but not showing up in it. And then, when you teased her about it, she'd turn up in the village shop wearing it when she bought a loaf of bread. She liked to keep people guessing about her. I think it made her feel important.'

Trudy smiled. 'She sounds as if she could be a bit of a handful.'

'She was,' Janet said flatly.

'She sounds like she might be hard work though – to have as a best friend,' Trudy tried again.

But again it became clear that no criticism of the dead May Queen would be tolerated as Janet's pretty lips firmed ominously again. 'I liked her, no matter what people said,' she insisted firmly.

Trudy knew she'd never get anywhere whilst the dead girl's

memory remained sacrosanct, so she tried to find a lever that she might use to prise open Janet's lips again. 'Someone told us that she had the habit of stealing other girls' boyfriends,' she mused. 'Was David going out with someone else before Iris? Maybe someone who was jealous of Iris for stealing him away?'

Janet thought about this intriguing possibility for a moment, but then sighed. 'I suppose it's possible that he met someone at that college he was going to, and jilted her when he and Iris got together,' Janet said indifferently. 'But he'd not been going with any girl from the village.'

Janet nodded, again catching Clement's knowing eye. Unless Janet was a very good actress, *she* hadn't been going out with David Finch herself then. Unless she *had* been secretly interested in him, but knowing of Iris's poaching ways, had been careful to hide her true feelings?

Then, remembering the warm way Ronnie Dewberry had talked about her, she tried another angle. 'Did you and Iris ever double-date? With his best friend, maybe?'

'Ronnie?' Janet said very casually. 'No, I've never stepped out with Ronnie,' she said, her eyes never wavering from a dead stare straight ahead.

Trudy gave a mental nod. Unless she was much mistaken, Janet might not have ever dated the handsome young farmer, but she had probably wanted to. Unless, again, she was being manipulated by a very clever young woman who was as intelligent as she was lovely.

Just supposing Janet *had* been in love with David? Passionately and deeply in love. Iris, who probably had superlatively accurate radar when it came to her best friend's emotional state, would almost certainly have picked up on it. And if Janet's mother was to be believed, Iris would then have made it her mission in life to steal David away – and then probably have grown bored with him once she had.

And how would Janet feel about all that? Perhaps her so-called best friend's latest betrayal had been a step too far? It wasn't impossible for a woman to strangle another woman, was it? Janet was taller than Iris, and although willowy, was probably strong enough. And then what? With Iris dead, and displayed so contemptuously on the village green, had her thoughts turned to punishing David? Regardless of whether or not he'd even known of any feelings Janet might have had for him, someone emotionally fraught and unbalanced enough to kill once, surely wouldn't hesitate to kill again.

But killing a fit young man was a vastly different proposition from killing a smaller woman. Hence the need to drug him with the tainted alcohol first. And then, once he was too woozy to put up a real struggle ... But would Janet have the strength, once she'd placed the rope around his neck, to haul his body into the air and tie off the rope? Trudy just couldn't see it somehow.

She gave a small sigh, but all that speculation meant that she had hesitated too long to ask the next question, and Janet was quick to take advantage of it.

'Look, I'd better get back to the shop. Miss Boisier doesn't like being on her own in case we get a lot of customers in all at once.' And so saying, she slipped lithely to her feet and turned to head back towards the narrow alleyway.

'Thank you for your time, Miss Baines,' Clement said gallantly. It earned him nothing more than a brief, distracted smile, and then she was gone.

She even walked elegantly, Trudy thought dispassionately, watching Janet's willowy form in the sky-blue dress disappear into the shadows.

'So, what did you make of her?' Trudy asked her mentor curiously. 'She really is quite beautiful, isn't she?'

'Yes,' Clement admitted, sounding mildly amused. 'She and Iris must have made quite a dazzling pair. No wonder half the male population of the village seemed smitten with them.'

'Do you think Janet might be in danger as well?' Trudy asked, suddenly alarmed. It had never occurred to her that Iris's death wasn't a one-off thing, but Clement's sudden grouping of them together made her feel afraid now for Janet. What if there was a maniac in the village intent on going around killing beautiful girls? Iris might only be the first!

To her dismay, Clement took his time in answering, and when he did, she didn't find his response particularly comforting.

'How can we know? Until we know who killed Iris, and why, nothing's certain, is it? Do you get the feeling that the relationship between those two girls was rather an odd one?'

'What – oh you mean because you can't really tell whether they were friends or rivals? Best buddies, or secret enemies?' Trudy said. 'Not really. Girls can be like that sometimes,' she said thoughtfully. 'You can really like someone, and really hate them at the same time.'

Now it was Clement's turn to look vaguely worried. 'Really?' And he wondered if his own daughter's school friendships had been so convoluted.

Trudy smiled, deciding it would only confuse – and alarm – him more if she tried to explain a teenage girl's mentality to him. 'We're not really seeing things any more clearly, are we? With the case, I mean.'

Clement sighed. 'No. But I think there's someone who might be able to lift the fog for us a bit, don't you? Someone who might have known Iris rather well if the gossips have it right?'

Trudy only had to think for a moment. Then she nodded. 'You mean this arty-type chap who's either a crook, or a celebrity, or something very disreputable, depending on who's doing the describing?'

'That's the chap,' Clement said amiably.

119

Chapter 18

'So what do we actually know about Mortimer Crowley?' Clement asked as they sat in his car, watching a female blackbird industriously investigating the bottom of a nearby garden hedge for caterpillars and beetles.

He'd driven back from Oxford and parked near the village green. It seemed appropriate somehow, although all signs that the pretty spot had once been the sign of a particular nasty murder were now gone. Even the flattened grass, where many constabulary boots had once trudged, had now sprung up bright and green again and was rife with daisies, courtesy of the spring rain and sunshine. The permanent maypole, though, was still rooted in place, and he wondered, idly, if tradition would win out and it would be allowed to stay there, or if some future village committee would elect to have it removed.

Trudy sighed. 'I heard he was a person of interest in the Iris Carmody case quite early on, but nothing much seemed to come of it,' she admitted with a rueful smile. 'I overheard the Sarge talking about him to one of the other constables on the team,' she further confessed.

'Were you curious enough to do a little digging around about the murder case?' Clement asked mildly, careful to keep his eyes on the village scenery. The last thing he wanted was to make her feel he was putting her on the spot, or questioning what she did – or didn't do – at work. Although they worked well together, he was always aware that her job meant a lot to her, and he never intended to trespass on her priorities if he could avoid it.

Trudy smiled, even more ruefully than before, and made no sign that she regarded his question as intrusive. 'That's the thing about being given all the paperwork and filing to do,' she said super-casually. 'Often you drop papers on the floor and have to pick them up.'

'And naturally your eyes can't help but pick up the odd word or two as you replace them in their correct order,' Clement mused idly.

'You can hardly avoid it,' Trudy agreed. 'As far as I can tell, the Iris Carmody case is suffering from a real lack of physical evidence and or witnesses.'

Clement sighed. 'And now that David Finch has died – probably by suicide – perhaps the investigating officer is thinking that the case is all but closed anyway?'

Trudy thought about it for a moment, and wondered. Was DI Jennings assuming David had killed his girlfriend then himself, and thus, the case could be wound down? Was allowing herself and Dr Ryder to 'investigate' the circumstances surrounding David's death nothing more than sop to a grieving father and a superior officer? Or did Jennings still have an open mind?

'Well, if he is, Inspector Jennings isn't likely to discuss it with me,' Trudy said wryly.

Clement nodded at this, but refused to be defeatist. 'So, how bad is our local Lothario?' he asked briskly. 'Does he deserve the scorn of the housewives of Middle Fenton? Or was he more sinned against than sinning?'

Trudy sighed. 'Well, for a start, Mr Crowley is very well off. He owns a lot of real estate around here – some land he leases to farmers, but mostly he buys up local cottages when they come up on the market and then he leases them back out again. A few of the more upmarket ones he does up and rents out as country or second homes to incomers from London and Birmingham. That's how he comes to have a place in the village – he often uses one of them he did up for himself. His main residence is in London, though, I think. So that alone doesn't really endear him to the locals.'

'Hmmm. Does he spend much time here?'

'A fair bit, yes, from what I can tell.'

This made Clement frown thoughtfully. 'Which makes me wonder just what the attraction can be?' he muttered, glancing around the quiet, pretty-but-unspectacular village. 'You'd have thought, if he was into a bohemian kind of lifestyle that he'd rather stick to clubs in Soho, the world of cinema, nightclubs and avant-garde art parties. But there's nothing like that around here, and he doesn't sound like the kind of man to indulge in bucolic pleasures.'

Trudy shrugged. She was not quite sure what 'bucolic' meant and she didn't want to show her ignorance. 'All I can tell you is that he owns art galleries in Chelsea and Solihull, and one in Brighton. But from what I could gather, they're all run by managers. He has some stocks and shares, but he has a broker for that.'

'So he's hardly a workaholic,' Clement mused. 'Again, it makes me wonder just what he does with all his spare time? Especially around here.'

Trudy shrugged. 'He has no criminal record, I know that. It was one of the first things the Sergeant asked to be checked out. He's not married either – well, not now, anyway. He *was* married, to a woman called Alison Browne-Gore, but she died about five years ago. She was rich too – an heiress of some kind to a gin, or wine dynasty or something like that. Her family made a lot of money out of booze. I think he still owns a lot of breweries he inherited from her. They had no children though.'

'Is he old?'

'Pretty old – forty-one.'

Clement hid a wince at that, and supposed that, to a girl of twenty, forty-one might seem fairly aged. She probably thought of himself as positively ancient. And as if thinking about his advancing years had triggered it, he felt his left leg begin to tremble slightly.

He ignored it.

'Where did he go to school?' he asked curiously.

'Eton, then Oxford,' Trudy said at once.

'You must have dropped a lot of files,' Clement said, highly entertained.

Trudy flushed a little, but didn't deny it.

'Did you find out just how well he knew our dead May Queen?' Clement asked, turning the key in the ignition to start the motor. 'If he came to the serious attention of your sergeant, I would imagine there had to be more against him than mere idle village gossip.'

But here Trudy had to admit to her dearth of knowledge. 'I don't know. The actual case files are kept locked in the DI's desk.'

'And you don't have a key?' Clement couldn't help but tease.

Trudy shot him a reproachful look and said nothing. Taking the hint, Clement let his smile fade. 'Whereabouts in the village does he live?' he asked instead.

'Near the manor house, off Church Lane,' Trudy said promptly.

Clement looked at his watch and frowned. 'Might be a job for tomorrow morning,' he said, and Trudy nodded. With a grunt, Clement put the car in gear and set off to drive his young friend back to Oxford.

Chapter 19

Mortimer Crowley's house was a handsome Georgian building, typically square and with elegant proportions, built out of the local Cotswold stone which glowed in the morning light. An ancient wisteria had colonised nearly all of the south-facing façade. It had a large, well-tended garden, and a small stable block had been converted into garages.

Trudy couldn't imagine living in a place like this.

'Let's hope he's home,' Clement, less impressed, said mildly as they walked up the thickly gravelled driveway. On the front step, he reached for a black, wrought-iron bell-pull and yanked on it. In the distance, behind the solid oak door, they could just hear a faint tinkling sound.

The man who opened the door nearly a minute later looked distinctly hungover, and was barely out of his twenties. Rumpled clothes matched his rumpled brown hair and unshaven chin, and his bloodshot eyes blinked blearily. He regarded them without interest for a moment and absently scratched himself on the chin.

'Huh? Yeah? Wannah-you-wan'?' he slurred.

'We're hoping to have a word with Mr Mortimer Crowley,' Clement said clearly and slowly.

For a second the young man continued to look at them blankly, but then slowly nodded. 'Oh, Morty? Yeah … he mus' be around somewhere …' So saying, he stepped back and beckoned them in, revealing a rather lovely hall.

It had the usual black-and-white tiled floor, and housed a fine example of a late-eighteenth-century grandfather clock, that was standing flush to one wall. Although it was ticking ponderously, it was running late. A small but charming wooden staircase swept in an elegant curve off to the left, inviting the visitor upstairs, but the young man gestured vaguely past it and into the darker far corner. 'In there somewhere, pro'bly,' he said, and then left them somewhat abruptly.

Trudy and Clement just had time to see that he'd plunged into a downstairs lavatory before the door swung back behind him. A moment or two later came a vague sound of retching.

'Well, so far our party-loving friend seems to be living up to his reputation,' Clement said with a slight smile of distaste.

'You think he often has friends over who get too drunk and have to stay the night?' Trudy asked, part-scandalised, part-intrigued. 'Do you think they all come from London?' She had never been to London in her life and regarded it as almost a foreign country – slightly dangerous and unknowable.

Clement shrugged. 'I'd imagine so. Well, shall we see if we can find the man himself?'

Trudy nodded, and set off towards the far side of the hall that had been indicated by their not-very helpful friend. As she moved, her head swivelled from side to side, taking it all in. As befitted an art dealer, there were indeed a lot of paintings hung on the various walls, but somewhat to her disappointment, none of them were of nude women – or men, for that matter. For the most part, they were landscapes, or dark portraits of various men and women in period costume, but she had no idea if they were great works of art or cheap reproductions. Her secondary school had been hot on teaching 'the three R's' but it had been rather more reticent when it came to art appreciation.

She glanced at Clement, who was also looking at the paintings, but didn't want to appear ignorant by asking what he thought of them. She had no doubt that he would know if they were authentic though; a man of refinement like Dr Ryder was bound to know. Instead she chose to think things through for herself, and came to the conclusion that a man who owned art galleries was unlikely to hang anything on his own walls that wasn't a credit to him.

Unless he was the sort who liked to play jokes, and had the kind of humour that would allow him to find it funny to hang worthless daubs in his private residence?

The door indicated by the drunken young man opened to reveal a large and rather fine library. Two tall windows, probably as much as ten feet high, allowed the sunshine to fall on a colourful Persian rug that lay on well-polished floorboards. Row after row of bookshelves lined all four walls, full of books of all descriptions, their mostly leather bindings glowing richly in the light. The room had the slightly dusty, musty but infinitely pleasant smell of old books. It also contained a large, round and highly polished mahogany table that was littered with upmarket magazines and a selection of daily newspapers. Four green leather button-back armchairs (that reminded Clement of so many gentlemen's clubs in London) were scattered around, offering a comfortable seat in which to sit and read.

It was also, alas, empty of human life. Consequently, they shut the door and tried the next one down. This opened onto a long sunroom, flooded with light from yet more enormous windows. And standing looking out across the gardens through a set of French doors was a man who barely acknowledged the sound of the opening door.

'Want some hair of the dog, Froggo?' he drawled over his shoulder, without bothering to look around.

'Depends on the hair and species of dog,' Clement drawled back.

The man's shoulders stiffened slightly and he spun around.

Trudy's first impression of Mortimer Crowley was one of lazy, effortless elegance. He was slim, and maybe a shade under six feet tall. His dark hair was just going silver at the temples, reminding her of the pictures of the romantic heroes on the front of the romance books her mother liked to read so much. He was dressed in well-fitting bottle-green slacks and a paler green jacket of some kind that seemed to be made of velvet. Trudy had never seen anything like it before.

'Who the hell are you pair?' the man said, his eyes narrowing slightly. With the light behind him, Trudy couldn't tell what colour they were, but she guessed they'd be pale – blue, or grey maybe. 'And how the hell did you get in?' he added as an afterthought.

'A young man opened the door to us, but became rather indisposed shortly afterwards,' Clement said with a man-of-the-world smile. 'He indicated you could be found down here somewhere. You are Mortimer Crowley, I take it?'

'I am. Care to share the knowledge around?'

Clement swept forward, hand out. 'Dr Clement Ryder, coroner of the city of Oxford. This is my assistant, Miss Loveday.'

Mortimer's stiffened form relaxed visibly – too visibly for it to be real, Clement thought. And right on cue, his square, good-looking face creased into an affable smile.

'That sounds rather ominous,' he said mildly. 'I didn't think coroners made house calls. I know my dissolute lifestyle isn't likely to let me see old bones, but I hadn't realised you fellows actually came touting for business.' He flashed them a smile to show that it was all in good fun, giving them a view of some very impressive white teeth.

Clement obliging exposed his own molars in a similar flash of manufactured humour. 'Oh, it's frowned upon, no doubt about it,' he shot back. If he wanted to go down the hail-fellow-well-met route, he could be as insincere as the best of them. 'Which is why we're not here on your behalf, but on that of another unfortunate resident of the village.'

Mortimer sighed heavily. 'Oh hell, not more about that poor wretched girl Iris?' He moved from the window with a heavy sigh, and indicated a long, traditional sofa, done out in chintz, wordlessly inviting them to sit. 'I've been so thoroughly grilled by the local police about her, I'm beginning to sympathise with lamb chops. Well, sit down, we might as well all be comfortable.'

It was interesting – but perhaps understandable – that their host had assumed they were here to talk about Iris rather than David Finch, and neither Clement nor Trudy, for the moment at least, were in any hurry to disabuse him.

Instead they sat down, watching as Mortimer selected a smaller two-seater sofa opposite them, and spread his legs out in front of him, neatly crossing his legs at the ankles. Under the velvet jacket, Trudy now saw that he was wearing a silk cravat so white it almost made her want to squint.

'Poor Iris. I really do hope you find out who killed her, you know,' Mortimer said, having clearly decided to tackle them head on. 'I rather liked her. She had spirit, you know, and ambition.' He smiled and shrugged. 'You don't really see much of either of that around here,' he added, glancing out of the window, where, in truth, little of the village could actually been seen. Just a few roofs from the cottages facing the house across the lane. 'And, of course, she was lovely to look at. And as an art-lover, you can forgive anyone or anything so long as it's beautiful.'

'Yes, we're getting the impression she was quite something in that department,' Clement said blandly. 'No surprise she was elected May Queen then?'

At this, their host snorted disparagingly. 'Oh, this village and their bloody May Queen! Just because the village elders made such a song and dance about the celebration of it in days of yore! No doubt it gave them an excuse to leer at all the village maidens. You'd think this bloody village invented May Day, the fuss they made about it! Still, she thought it was a great feather in her cap to be chosen and she was pleased to bits about it. Iris would have made a great May Queen, the poor cow, no doubt about it.'

Although the words sounded shockingly derogatory, Trudy thought she detected a genuine note of pity under all the man's posturing. He might be trying hard to come across as the uncaring sophisticate, but she also sensed a wariness and nervousness that was distinctly making her policewoman's nose twitch.

Clement sighed gently. 'It must have come as a shock for the whole village – what happened to her.'

'Oh, you bet. Hit it like an earthquake,' he said flatly. 'Nothing of the kind could have happened here since the first peasant built his first hovel back in the time of the great plague! The excitement! Such high drama!' His lips twisted grimly. 'Mind you, it gave all the self-righteous old biddies the chance to nod their heads sagely and say I told you so. Makes me sick! Just because a beautiful young girl had a bit of vim and get-up-and-go about her … oh hell, what's the point?' He raised his arms and then let them fall. 'It's always been the same – the old and ugly always despise the young and beautiful.'

At this he glanced at Trudy appreciatively. 'You have lovely hair,' he said abruptly.

At the unexpected compliment, Trudy felt herself instantly blush, and wished she could get out of this schoolgirl habit. She knew her long, dark, wavy hair was one of her best features, but she was used to it being hidden beneath her policewoman's cap.

'Thank you,' she said somewhat primly. She wasn't sure that she liked a man like this paying her that sort of attention. It made her feel gauche and out of her depth.

Mortimer Crowley blinked at her decidedly cool tone, then grinned. 'Sorry, don't mind me. I have a habit of looking at people with an artist's eye.'

'Do you paint yourself?' Clement came to her rescue, forcing the man's attention back to himself.

The other man's lips twisted wryly. 'Only as a hobby, and purely for my own pleasure. I sell art and appreciate art, but alas,

I haven't any real talent for it myself. My own particular skills lay more in being a facilitator. Matching buyers with artists, finding and encouraging new talent, that sort of thing.'

'A regular patron of the arts then?' Clement said.

Mortimer gave him an assessing, slightly unhappy look. 'If you like,' he admitted.

Clement nodded. Like Trudy, he was picking up on the fact that underneath the act, this man was not all happy to be answering their questions.

Which, of course, only made him want to ask a lot more.

'Was Iris one of the talented ones?'

Mortimer snorted in laughter. 'Good grief, no! I doubt she could draw a daffodil. At least, she never had any daubs that she wanted to show me, which is a relief, I can tell you. The amount of people who seem to think I'm interested in their etchings and insist on showing them to me … ugh!' He gave a shudder. 'I wouldn't mind, but they're never even remotely interesting.'

'But you seem to have known Iris well?' Clement put in, letting the insinuation drift along at its own pace.

Mortimer gave a long-suffering sigh. 'This bloody village! What's the gossip been saying about us? No, don't bother, I can imagine. I was debauching her, or maybe she was debauching me? It has to be one or the other. The way people's minds work around here. Bourgeoisie doesn't begin to cover it! But I can assure you we weren't lovers. I like my women a little older and far more sophisticated. Not that Iris wasn't … well. And she *was* eager to become …' Again he paused and then smiled ruefully. 'I'm trying to find a nice way of saying this, a way that doesn't make it sound worse than it is, but …'

'I think I get the picture,' Clement said, with another man-of-the-world smile. 'Would it be fair to say that Iris was a girl who meant to make something of herself, and was eager to learn how?'

'Yes, that's fair to say.'

'And in you, she had found an obvious target for a mentor

and ... shall we say, a facilitator? An older, sophisticated, well-to-do man from the big bad city who could show her the ropes?'

The art dealer shifted a little uneasily on his chair at this. 'Well, if you want to be blunt, then yes, that was no doubt what she had in mind. But really, there was in truth little that I could do for her. I wasn't in the market for a mistress myself, so as a potential source of pretty baubles and fashionable clothes I was a bit of a washout.' He grinned a little at that. 'In fact, I rather think I was a disappointment to her all round. I even refused to invite her to my parties. But really, as keen as she was to grow up and spread her wings, I would have felt a right bast ... er ... rotter, throwing her to the tender mercies of some of my circle. They'd have gobbled the poor girl up and spit her out.'

He said this casually, as if it was taken for granted, and Trudy could feel herself growing ever more disapproving, and wondered if she was being silly and prudish. But the truth was, she simply didn't like this man. She didn't like his attitude to life, or the careless way in which he talked about a girl who had been so brutally murdered. Not only as if she didn't matter, but as if his indifference to it didn't matter either.

'But she was often seen in your company,' Clement repeated, and Trudy felt a flush of pride and pleasure that her friend wasn't letting him get away with anything.

Mortimer flushed slightly, his first real sign of anger, and then shrugged. 'Yes, all right, she was a bit of a pest and hung around, and I didn't like to give her the total brush off. She was so desperate to get to London and get a high-profile job, something to make her parents go grey overnight and give the old village biddies something to really get their tongues wagging. It was like having a puppy following you around, looking at you with big pleading eyes. In the end, I sort of introduced her to a few artists I trusted not to treat her too shabbily, and who were in the market for a pretty model. I knew if nothing else they'd at least pay her well. And if they promised her that they could get her a break into real modelling, or introduce her to someone from a proper modelling agency …' He shrugged fatalistically. 'Well, who was I to rain on her parade? Anyway, that seemed to satisfy her.'

'That was big of you,' Clement said with another flash of his teeth, and again Trudy felt pleased to see their handsome host look discomfited. 'Do you think you could give us the names of these artists you … introduced her to, out of the goodness of your heart?'

Mortimer sighed ostentatiously and rapidly shot off a few names. Trudy wished she had her notebook with her and could jot them down, but she was sure she could remember them.

'But I don't know if any of them ever did get her to model for them, you understand,' Mortimer warned.

'So who do you suppose *did* supply her with her baubles?' Clement asked out of nowhere. 'You said *you* weren't in the market for a mistress, but we know that Iris had been given a rather fine pearl and gold necklace, amongst other things.'

'Oh, right. How on earth should I know?' he asked indifferently, beginning to sound bored.

Clement nodded. 'Of course, the death of Iris wasn't the only tragedy the village has had to cope with, is it?'

'What?' For a moment, the art-lover looked genuinely bewildered, but then his face cleared. 'Oh, you mean the boyfriend – the one who hanged himself? No, that was rough. Poor little sod. Fancy dying when you're not even twenty-one yet. Or had he got that far?' he asked nonchalantly.

'Did you know David Finch?' Clement asked shortly.

'What, a policeman's son?' Mortimer said, mock-scandalised. 'No, not well,' he added more gruffly, when neither of them responded to his wide grin. 'I mean we'd spoken once or twice, but since he'd mostly got the wrong end of the stick about me and Iris, we didn't exactly get the chance to become best buddies.'

'Oh?' Clement almost felt Trudy begin to quiver alertly, and only hoped his own interest wasn't so obvious. Like his young friend, Clement didn't like this man much, and wasn't in any rush to make life easier for him. 'How did he get the wrong end of the stick exactly?'

But if he'd hoped to penetrate their host's determined bonhomie, or even disconcert him a little, he was to be disappointed, for Mortimer merely shrugged.

'Oh, he'd been listening to the gossip I suppose,' he yawned widely and settled himself more comfortably on the sofa. 'Seemed to have some sort of a bee in his bonnet that I'd been giving her fancy ideas, promising her a new life in London, or some such rubbish. Turning her head, and generally interfering with his precious courtship of her.' Mortimer laughed. 'Naturally, I soon put him right. Told him flat out she'd been too young and silly for me.'

'And did he believe you?' Clement asked sceptically.

Mortimer's pale eyes (pale blue, Trudy noted, now that she could see them properly) narrowed slightly. He obviously didn't appreciate the older man's patent disbelief, but then he was once again flashing his big white teeth.

'Not at first, you're right,' he admitted affably enough. 'But eventually I was able to convince him that girls like Iris are far more trouble to me than they're worth, and he got the idea. In the end he went off quite happily, I think. Mind you, not before jotting down something in that ridiculous little journal of his though.'

Chapter 20

Seemingly totally unaware of the bombshell that he'd just dropped, Mortimer yawned again. 'I think I was meant to consider myself "warned". That my words were being *noted*!' He gave the last word a dramatic twist. 'Naturally, I couldn't care less how I came across in his grubby little diary or whatever it was.'

He stretched luxuriously. 'Why is it that people seem to think you care a tinker's cuss about their lives?'

'What journal?' Clement said.

'Hmmm? Sorry, what was that? I didn't get much sleep last night.'

Clement held onto his temper and repeated cordially, 'You said he wrote something down in his journal or diary or something?'

'Yes, he did. He didn't think I'd seen him, but after he walked away I watched him for a bit, just curious I suppose, and he stopped and pulled what looked like a small notebook or pocket diary – you know the kind, one of those black or brown leather things? – out of his pocket and jotted something down.'

'Did it make you feel uneasy? It sounds as if he thought you were a person of interest, or had said something important. Did that worry you?' Trudy couldn't help but ask, earning herself a patronising smile in return.

'Hardly! What do I care what people think of me?' came the somewhat predictable response.

It was also, Trudy supposed, a rhetorical question.

'And is that the only time you saw David Finch?' Clement asked.

'As far as I know,' the other man responded, making no effort to hide his boredom now.

'You never saw him on the day he died for instance?' Clement probed.

'Don't think so,' Mortimer said.

'Not out of the window, perhaps. Going by? Maybe on his way out of the village, towards the farm track that leads to the place he died?'

'I doubt I was paying that much attention. The comings and goings of the village don't really interest me that much.'

'Yet you own some real estate here. You have this place.' Clement swept a hand around the room, indicating the house and environs beyond.

'Oh well, sometimes I like a bit of peace and quiet,' Mortimer smiled widely.

Clement hid another rush of temper with a smile. More likely, he thought sourly, this man liked to indulge himself in a quiet village where he didn't have the eyes and the ears of the city watching him. It made Clement wonder just what sort of parties he liked to throw out here, in Middle Fenton. And whether or not a pretty girl like Iris Carmody had been drawn to them and welcomed with open arms, despite his denials that she'd ever been invited?

'What sort of things do you think he might have wanted to note down?' Clement, determined to keep his mind focused on the job in hand, went back on the attack. 'David Finch, I mean? I doubt that he was interested in simply jotting down your denials about having designs on his girlfriend. That, after all, was to be expected. And from what I've been hearing about him, he was a bright lad.'

Mortimer's brow furrowed slightly, perhaps suspecting some sort of a dig, but after a moment's thought, he merely nodded. 'No, you're quite right,' he agreed. 'He was, I think, after specific information about Iris. When I'd last seen her, what she'd said, did I know of anybody who she might have been planning on meeting – you know, artists or photographers or such. More especially, if she'd asked me if I could ask my contacts in London if they could do her any favours or help her find work. Or if I'd seen her talking with anyone in the village, maybe arguing with them, in the last few weeks or so. That sort of thing.' He shrugged and smiled. 'He seemed intent on becoming a rural version of Sherlock Holmes, in fact.'

So he *had* been serious about trying to find Iris's killer, Trudy thought.

'And were you able to enlighten him?' she heard Clement enquire drolly.

'Not really,' Mortimer said languidly. 'Like I said, the girl was something of a pest, even though I could sympathise with her desperation to get out of this place and make a life for herself. Just not to the extent that I was interested in her comings and goings.'

Clement nodded and glanced at Trudy to see if she had anything else to ask. Seeing by her quick glance that she didn't, he made to rise. 'Well, thank you for your help, Mr Crowley,' he said dryly.

The other man airily waved a hand in the air. 'Oh, think nothing of it,' he said, equally dryly. 'Shall I show you out?'

'Oh, I think we can find our own way,' Clement demurred.

The moment they left the room, however, Mortimer Crowley's smile faded and he got to his feet and cautiously approached the window. He watched as, a short while later, their figures emerged from the house and walked down the path towards the front gate.

He swore softly – and with some originality – under his breath. So far, he'd only had to deal with the local flatfoots and that

136

by-the-book ninny, Jennings. Which had left him feeling relatively sanguine and inclined to relax. But Dr Clement Ryder was a far different proposition. He was no know-nothing country bumpkin but a sophisticated man with a sharp mind and sharp eyes. The sort who wasn't so easily fooled.

As he turned away from the window, he contemplated a quick return to London. Or would that look like he was running away? The last thing he needed now was to throw suspicion on himself.

He collapsed moodily into a chair, resentful about the sense of unease that now bothered him. Damn that girl, he thought savagely. Trust a beautiful, grasping bloody woman to ruin everyone's fun.

He brooded, contemplating exactly what he should do next. He would have to be careful, obviously, and do nothing too rash or silly. As far as he knew, the police hadn't found out anything damaging about him, and he wanted to keep it that way.

If only he knew what that damned coroner was thinking!

'So what are you thinking?' Trudy asked as they walked back to the Rover.

'I think we need to find out more about this journal or note-book or whatever it is that he claims David had on him. This is the first we've heard of it, and I trust that … that … *insect*, about as far as I could throw him! I wouldn't put it past him to make up a lie about it to put us off track, just to amuse himself. On the other hand, he strikes me as someone too intent on taking care of his own skin to do anything that might bring himself to our attention needlessly. I take it no diary was found on the body?'

'No, I'm sure it wasn't,' Trudy said. If David had kept a journal, it would have been meat and drink to her DI.

Clement nodded. 'I agree it can't have been. It would have been listed amongst his personal possessions for a start, and noted in my files. Do you know if any of the other witnesses questioned about Iris mentioned David keeping a diary?'

'I don't think so. But I can't be sure,' Trudy was forced to admit. 'DI Jennings, like I said, would hardly be likely to confide in me.'

Clement grunted. 'Well, we'll just have to ask around for ourselves then, won't we? We need to call on his parents again at some point anyway – and if anyone would know, they probably would. And Ronnie, the best friend too, should be able to clear it up one way or another. Even if they weren't too close right at the end, if David was the kind to keep a diary Ronnie would still have known about it.'

'Maybe Janet Baines would know too,' Trudy offered. 'If David *did* keep a regular diary, you can be sure that Iris would have known all about it. Girlfriends ferret out all sorts of information about the men that they're seeing, and she'd almost certainly have mentioned it to her best friend. But what if it's a more recent thing?' she pointed out. 'You know, something he took up only after Iris was killed?'

Clement glanced at his watch. 'Time's marching on. I've got to get back to my office. What say we pick this up again tomorrow, first thing?'

'Suits me,' Trudy said happily. 'Is it wishful thinking, or do you think we might be getting somewhere at last?'

Clement smiled. 'Let's hope so.' But she was right. He too, felt as if the case was finally beginning to take some sort of a shape. And it was starting to look more and more as if they had a double-murder on their hands.

Chapter 21

Duncan Gillingham had planned his move carefully. He knew it was no use trying to catch Trudy on her own in the village of Middle Fenton, since from what he had seen so far, she and the city coroner were always together. And there was no way he was going to risk Dr Clement Ryder's cynical gaze as he tried to cajole her to let him take her out somewhere.

Likewise, he could hardly call around at her home – even though he'd gone to the trouble of finding out where she lived. Again, he didn't fancy running the risk of being introduced to the parents or have her daddy's gimlet eye fall upon him! And he didn't think she would be happy if he showed his face at the police station, asking for her. No doubt the news would quickly reach her superior officers and she'd be hauled over the coals, wondering if she'd been leaking information to the press. Which was hardly going to help endear him to her after their last, disastrous dealings.

So his only option was to catch her before she got *into* the station. So it was that he found himself in position, lounging beside a pillar box late in the afternoon, when he recognised Clement's Rover P4 pull to a halt in a parking space about fifty yards from the entrance to the police station. Perfect!

He'd guessed she would have to return to the station sometime, and although he'd been prepared to wait for hours if need be, as luck would have it, he'd only had to lounge around for twenty minutes or so.

He saw her climb out of the passenger door, bend down to say something to the driver, then close the door after herself. He sprinted across the road, hoping the coroner hadn't spotted him, and sidled along the edge of the pavement closest to the buildings lining the street. He was moving fast, since he needed to catch up with Trudy before she got to the entrance to the station, but that didn't stop him from keeping a careful eye on the Rover as it pulled out into traffic and swept past him.

Once he was sure the eagle-eyed Ryder was safely out of sight, he sprinted openly up the street.

Behind her, Trudy heard the sound of someone running, and stopped automatically, turning around, feeling slightly tense. Since walking a beat, she'd become wary of hearing footsteps behind her – especially running ones! Because she wasn't in uniform she didn't even have her truncheon with her, and so didn't know whether to feel relieved or annoyed to see Duncan Gillingham bearing down on her.

At least he wasn't someone she'd once arrested, taking the chance to verbally abuse or annoy her, she supposed.

She made sure she kept her face calm and neutral as he panted to a stop beside her. He was dressed in a smart navy-blue suit and his red tie was rakishly askew. His dark, somewhat floppy near-black hair needed cutting, she noticed, and his green eyes were crinkled attractively at the corners as he smiled at her.

It was really annoying that he was so good-looking.

'I thought it was you!' Duncan said with a grin. 'I've been wanting to talk to you for ages.'

Trudy smiled cynically. 'Oh? And the fact that you're after a story about Iris Carmody has nothing to do with your sudden interest in me again?' she asked caustically.

'Actually it doesn't,' Duncan lied, sounding a little hurt. 'Did you get my flowers?' He changed the subject quickly.

'My mum loved them,' Trudy said flatly.

He spluttered with sudden laughter. 'Well, that wasn't five bob spent in total vain then.'

Trudy felt her lips twitch in the beginnings of a spontaneous smile, and ruthlessly stopped the movement.

'What do you want, Duncan?' she said, sighing exaggeratedly.

When they'd first met, this man had been determined to make a name for himself by using his newspaper position to all but accuse the police of condoning a cover-up in a murder case. And he hadn't been above feigning an interest in her in the hopes of gleaning information about the on-going investigation. So she was about as likely to trust him now as she would trust a cat to keep watch over a goldfish bowl.

'I can't help you, if that's what you might be thinking,' she warned him, before he had a chance to answer. 'I'm not on the Iris Carmody case, I'm just a lowly WPC remember?' she taunted.

Duncan nodded. In which case, he wondered cynically, why was she in civvies, snooping around the village of Middle Fenton with the likes of Dr Clement Ryder. 'Yes, I thought that must be the case,' he said smoothly. 'So that proves it, doesn't it? I'm not here in my official capacity. Pax?' he asked, crossing both sets of his forefingers and holding them up in front of her.

'So if you're not here as a reporter, why are you here?'

Duncan smiled winsomely. 'I feel bad about the way we left things,' he said, realising as he spoke that he actually meant it. Well, mostly. 'I didn't want you to think that … well, I mean, I just wanted to say that I really liked you. I still *do* like you,' he added. 'I admire you too. The job you do. You've got spunk. I just didn't want you to think it was all a con. You know, that it wasn't real.'

'Real?' she repeated tensely. 'What was real?'

Duncan shifted a little on his feet. 'You know … that spark between us.'

'Spark?' she repeated again, not giving an inch.

Duncan gave a rueful smile, genuinely not knowing whether to curse her for making this so hard, or admire her for not giving in to his bullshit. She was unlike any other young woman he'd ever met, and he was damned if he knew, really, how to handle her, or what she might say next. She certainly had the ability to keep him on his toes, which was, in many ways, rather exciting.

But he wasn't about to let her get the better of him. Apart from anything else, he really wanted to get to know her better.

'Did I really get it so wrong then?' he asked, letting his eyes flicker uncertainly, in a way he'd learned before hitting his sixteenth birthday. It was remarkable, he'd realised, what a show of vulnerability could do to the feminine heart. 'I thought we … well, connected in some way. Was I wrong?'

Trudy looked him steadily in the eye. 'Are you still engaged?' she asked simply.

Duncan sighed. 'That situation really is complicated, I told you before.'

Trudy nodded. 'Oh yes, I remember. You're engaged to the boss's daughter, poor you.'

Duncan stiffened, feeling a flush of genuine anger creep over his face. 'Actually, it's not that funny. I don't want to hurt her feelings, because she's a great girl, and how can I break it off without feeling like a right heel? On the other hand, I'm just not sure we're suited.'

'So why don't you just tell her that?' Trudy asked, intrigued to see what lie he would come up with.

But Duncan was too canny to spin out any of the usual trite excuses. Instead, he just shook his head. 'It's not that easy. As I told you before, apart from anything else, she *is* the boss's daughter. Do you think I'd still have a job tomorrow if I just up and ditched her? Come on, I grew up in the same circumstances as you did. I can't afford to lose my job.'

Which was actually true. And because it was true, he suspected this had far more of a chance of making its way through her defences than anything. Of course, he didn't intend to work for an Oxford paper forever. He had his eyes set on Fleet Street. But for now, he needed to get a few good years in and break some big stories if he was going to catch the eye of one of the big editors in the capital.

Trudy shifted a little uneasily on the pavement. She supposed, in all fairness, he was in a bit of a cleft stick. She knew how much working-class people such as themselves needed to keep a good job. 'Well, I'm sorry, I hope you manage to sort it all out. But speaking of work …' She indicated the police station entrance a few yards away. 'I have to go.'

'At least have a cup of coffee with me some time,' Duncan asked. 'Just to show there are no hard feelings. I really didn't make a fool of you last time, you know, but I have a horrible feeling that you might think I did. Or that I pretended to feel … Oh look, we can't discuss it here on the pavement.' He made a show of glancing around at the curious shoppers moving past them. 'Can't we just have a cup of coffee somewhere and talk about it rationally? We are two adults, after all! Being childish is just silly.'

Trudy's lips twisted slightly. Who was the one being childish? 'Oh, all right,' she sighed. It would probably just be easier to let him talk and have the chance to soothe his ego – and then she could be rid of him once and for all.

'Great. I'll call you,' he promised. 'Soon.'

Can't wait, Trudy thought cynically. But as she walked away from him, she couldn't help but feel a little bit pleased. After all, it always made a girl feel good to have a good-looking young man acting so anxious to please her.

Her heart beating a little bit faster than before, she stepped inside and girded her loins to report back that day's findings to her inspector. Not that she expected him to be that impressed.

Chapter 22

The next morning started with a rain shower that had, luckily, all but played itself out by the time Trudy and Clement returned to the village of Middle Fenton. This time, they swept down the main street to the end, and then followed the smaller lane that led off to the Dewberrys' Farm.

The sun came out, quickly warming the rain-dampened air, and lifted the scent of spring flowers and blossom so that it was a delight just to breathe in. Through the open window of the car, Trudy smiled gratefully.

When they pulled up in the now slightly steaming farmyard, Ray Dewberry was already climbing into the seat of an old tractor but he paused at the sound of the engine and turned to look at them warily.

Trudy climbed out and called over to him. 'Is your son at home, Mr Dewberry?'

The farmer indicated the house and as they walked to the kitchen door, the sound of the rumbling engine filled the courtyard, echoing slightly off the cobbled yard.

Ronnie was at the sink washing the breakfast dishes when they passed the window, and they saw him startle slightly as their shadows cut across the windowsill, then indicate that he would meet them at the door.

'Hello again,' he said a moment or two later, looking from one to the other. He looked unhappy to see them again, and Trudy supposed that was only natural. Like a lot of people in the village he was probably hoping that things would blow over sooner rather than later, and that they could all be allowed to get back on with their lives in peace. Life in farming villages changed little from one year to the next, and the vast majority of people who chose to live here must prefer it that way.

But until her DI arrested someone for Iris Carmody's murder, and she and Dr Ryder had found out what had really happened to David Finch, she was afraid Ronnie Dewberry and the rest of the village were just going to have put up with the upheaval.

'Did you want to come in? I can put the kettle on,' he offered diffidently.

'Tea would be nice,' Clement said, noting the way the young man's shoulders first slumped slightly, then braced, at his cheerful acceptance of a beverage.

'Don't mind Bess,' he said, indicating a black and white sheepdog that was both barking at them and also backing away from them as they stepped across the threshold. The dog waited its moment, then slipped quickly past them and dashed out into the courtyard.

Ronnie set about filling the kettle, watching as his father, on the tractor, drove through an open gate and into the field beyond. He looked, Clement thought, as if he wished he was with him.

'We just have a few follow-up questions about David,' Clement said when, tea steaming away in mugs in front of them, they were all seated around the scrubbed kitchen table.

'Huh-huh,' Ronnie said, bobbing his head and taking a sip of the hot tea. He winced slightly as it burned his tongue.

'We understand he kept a diary,' Trudy put in abruptly, presenting it as a fact rather than a question and watching him closely for his reaction.

He tensed visibly then frowned. 'A diary? David?' Ronnie said slowly. 'That's news to me.'

'Are you saying he didn't keep a journal?' Clement asked, something just a little sharp and formal in his voice causing the younger man to look anxious. He opened his mouth, thought better of giving a spontaneous reply, and chose instead to take another sip of too-hot tea.

He made a show of wincing again, then blew on the top of the mug's surface. Finally, he shrugged. 'I'm not saying he didn't have a diary. Just that I never knew about it. It's not the sort of thing you share, really, is it? Not with a mate. Anyway, David was always more at home with books and learning and all that stuff than I was. I liked to read adventure stories and what-not, but I wouldn't have ever thought about writing stuff down.'

He made a show of shrugging and looking around at the not-particularly-clean farmhouse kitchen. 'I mean, what would I write? Six a.m., milked the cows. Seven a.m. mended some barbed wire fencing …' He laughed. 'But I suppose David might have had more interesting stuff to write about – leaving the village, going to university …' He hesitated visibly, then said, 'And about Iris, and stuff like that. But if he did write it down, I never saw him do it.'

'And he never mentioned keeping a journal?' Clement pressed.

'Not to me,' Ronnie said adamantly.

Clement nodded. 'Well, thanks. You've been very helpful.' He started to rise, then stopped. 'Oh … just supposing he did keep a journal, you wouldn't have any idea where he might have kept it, would you?'

Ronnie, who'd just begun to think the ordeal was over, blinked, then looked puzzled. 'What do you mean?'

'We didn't find it amongst his personal effects,' Clement explained patiently. As yet, they hadn't asked the Finch family if they'd come across any such item at the family home, but it seemed unlikely they had. Had the boy's father found it, he would have produced it at the inquest, especially if, as they suspected,

146

David had been using it to jot down information about his investigations.

'Did David have a favourite hiding place when you were boys?' Trudy put in helpfully. 'You know, in a hole in a tree, or under a large stone, or hidden somewhere here, on the farm?'

'Oh, I see what you mean,' Ronnie said, already shaking his head. 'To be honest, I never did like that hiding game as a kid. We made the usual "dens" in the woods, and there's an old abandoned pigsty that we used to pretend was a Roman fort – but it would be too open to the elements to hide something made out of paper.'

After they made their farewells, Ronnie watched the car drive away, biting his lower lip nervously.

Was it possible David had kept a journal?

He felt the sweat begin to prickle on his forehead and on his palms and he began to feel physically sick.

If he had been keeping a record of what had been happening in his life in the past few months … what the hell might he have he written down in it?

Chapter 23

Janet Baines felt both surprised and worried when Trudy and Clement pushed open the gate to her front garden and started up the path. Luckily, she'd been sitting in the window seat overlooking the small garden that fronted the house, and was thus able to bolt out into the hallway and open the door before they had a chance to ring the bell.

She had hoped that they'd been satisfied with what she'd had to say the last time, and that she wouldn't have to go through it all over again, and she felt a flash of anger shoot through her, that she quickly suppressed.

As she stepped outside, she was careful to close the door behind her, preventing them from entering the house and surprising Trudy by the hostility implied in the action.

Then she smiled uncertainly and said, 'Mum's in the kitchen preparing our lunch. Hope you don't mind, but I'd rather we didn't disturb her. She can get … well, *rather emotional* about things sometimes. I don't want to get her upset if we can avoid it.'

Trudy nodded, at once seeing Janet's point of view. It was hardly surprising that she was anxious to keep her mother out of her business; who could blame her? After only having met the woman once, she had had no doubts that she was the kind of

148

woman who liked to know where her daughter was, and what she was doing, every minute of the day. And that must surely be very wearing on a person's nerves. 'That sounds like a good idea. Is there somewhere private we could talk?' she asked with a conspiratorial smile.

Janet nodded, casting a quick glance nervously over her shoulder. 'We can go around the side of the house and sit under the apple tree.'

She led them through the large and well-maintained garden, blooming with columbines and forget-me-nots, wine-red peonies and a rather magnificent double lilac in full and fragrant bloom, to a spot under a blossoming fruit tree. Clement fastidiously brushed aside a few stray twigs and leaves before sitting down on the garden bench that was placed there, with Trudy next to him in the middle, and Janet on the far end.

'We've just been talking to Ronnie Dewberry,' Trudy began, not missing the quick glance Janet threw at them. As Janet flushed slightly and refused to meet her eyes, Trudy wondered, not for the first time, if there might not be something going on between this pretty young girl and the farmer's son.

'Oh? Is he all right?' Janet asked casually.

'Well, he misses his best friend,' Trudy said lightly, 'but yes, he's fine. We wanted to ask him something about David.'

Since she was sitting so close to her on the bench, Trudy was able to feel the way Janet stiffened slightly. Perhaps aware of that, she raised a hand to her face and tucked a stray lock of hair back behind her ear and tried to shift a little further along the bench. Unfortunately, it was a snug fit, and she didn't quite manage it. 'Oh?' she finally managed.

'Did Iris ever mention David keeping a diary?' Trudy asked mildly. As the other girl had tried to shift away, *she* had moved very slightly closer, so that the tops of their arms were pressed tightly together, and there was no mistaking the shock the question had given her. Trudy felt it like a quick electrical quiver run through her that came and went in a flash. When she turned to look sharply at Janet's profile, however, her expression gave nothing away.

But Trudy knew what she'd felt.

'Iris didn't really talk about David much,' Janet heard herself lie, and was almost impressed with the casual honesty of her tone. She hadn't realised, until now, just how well she could act a part. It had always been her best friend who had been so skilled at subterfuge.

Aware that they were still waiting for an answer, she shrugged lightly. 'Iris liked to talk about herself and her plans for the future, and what she was doing, and what she wanted, and things like that. Other people didn't really interest her – unless they could be useful to her, I suppose.'

Which was all true enough, Janet mused, with an inner smile.

'She sounds like she was a bit full of herself,' Trudy commented.

Janet sighed. 'I suppose she was, in a way. But you didn't really mind. It's hard to explain, but she made you feel so *alive*. You could never be bored with Iris. She was so cheerful and … I don't know … like a force of nature. You could believe somehow that she really *could* take on the world and win, somehow. Being with her was exciting … I suppose that's why all the boys wanted to date her,' she finished with a wry smile.

'David was beating them off with a stick, was he?' Trudy teased lightly.

'I suppose he was, yes. And Iris loved it when he got jealous.'

'And she gave him a lot of reasons to be jealous, or so we keep hearing. And it wasn't just the young, single, unattached men either, was it?' Trudy carried on, again careful to keep her tone light.

'Oh you mean the older men … that wasn't anything serious, it was just silly flirting. The men in this village …' Janet sighed and gave a brief bark of laughter. 'Well, men can be so silly about girls who like to josh them along a bit, can't they? Some of them

150

might have taken it a bit too seriously, but Iris would always put them in their place if they did.'

'I don't suppose their wives liked it much though,' Trudy said with another light laugh.

'No, but Iris didn't care about them,' Janet said off-handedly. 'She called them boring old housewives. She always said she'd never get married or have a brood of children … and now she won't, will she?'

Trudy glanced at her profile, a little surprised by the lack of sympathy in her tone, but again Janet's face was bland and unhelpful.

'So you don't know anything about a diary or a journal that David might have kept?' Trudy returned to the attack, aware that she had allowed the conversation to get slightly off track.

'First I've heard of it,' Janet lied blithely. Inside, she felt proud of herself. There really was nothing to this acting lark, she thought, almost scornfully. Anybody could do it, if they tried. You just had to pretend that things were different, that was all. And to think of all the fuss Iris made about how hard it was to be a great actress!

'And you've no idea where he might have kept it, if he had been keeping a record of his life?'

'Sorry?' Janet said, only having caught the tail end of the question, so caught up had she been in her own personal reverie.

'It's just that David might not have wanted to keep a private journal at home, say, where his mother might find it. We were wondering if you knew where he might have hidden it where it would be safe?' Trudy elaborated.

Janet's heart gave another little leap, but her shoulders gave a nonchalant shrug. 'Sorry, but I'd have no idea. Although we all went to school together, I wasn't close to David,' she murmured, turning her face away to glance at a robin, peering down at the lawn for anything six-legged that might be moving through the stems of grass. Although she was gaining in confidence, she thought it wise not to look either of her two visitors in the face.

The girl seemed rather nice and blissfully clueless, but the quiet, thoughtful Dr Ryder had alarmingly penetrating eyes.

'All right. Well thanks for your time,' Trudy said, sounding a little disappointed.

'That's all right,' Janet said, with rather more obvious relief than she would have liked. She got up with them and walked them around the side of the house and back to the front garden. At the gate to the lane she gave them a brief smile then turned and made her way back towards the house. All the while her knees had felt a little stiff, and she was sure she must be walking awkwardly. She was almost convinced that she could feel both sets of their eyes boring into her back, right between her shoulder blades; but knew that was probably just her guilty conscience playing her up. And sure enough, when she dared to glance back she saw that they were nowhere in sight.

But just in case they might be watching her through a gap in the hedge or something, she opened the front door and went inside, shutting the door gratefully behind her. Her heart pounding, she leaned on it for a few moments, taking deep, calming breaths.

Although lying to them the way she'd just done had felt surprisingly wonderful, the strain of it had also taken a toll. Grimly, she wondered if Iris had been right when she used to mock her and call her a goody-two-shoes who'd never be able to have any fun in life.

'Hello love, did I hear the front door?' her mother's voice came through from the kitchen, making her almost jump out of her skin.

'No, it's just me. I thought I heard the postman, but it was nothing. I'm going upstairs to read, Mum.'

'All right, love. Lunch will be at twelve.'

Janet ignored this, and went upstairs, her legs still feeling curiously rubbery beneath her.

She clutched her secret close, savouring it like a miser gleefully savours the feel of gold. Because, of course, Iris had long since told her all about not only David's diary, but also about his habit of using other little notebooks too, that he used to keep on him to write down ideas or thoughts as and when they occurred to him. It was probably the budding engineer in him, Janet had supposed, but Iris often laughed about it. 'Really, Jan-Jan, I wonder what on earth he ever finds to write about! He's so boring, and his life is so boring, and everything here is so *boring* …'

As she threw herself on her bed and lay staring up at the ceiling, Janet could almost hear her dead friend's voice in the actual room, so clear did it sound.

Trust Iris to make a joke about something so private, Janet mused now. She'd asked Iris once if she'd ever read David's personal diary, but her friend had denied it. She'd said she was hardly interested – she knew all there was to know about him anyway.

Which was probably true, Janet concluded, her lips twisting into a grim smile. If there was one thing you could say about Iris, it was that she had a way of learning everybody's little secrets … especially those of the opposite sex.

She turned onto her side, wondering if Ronnie had any secrets … But the thought displeased her, so she pushed it away and concentrated instead on the here and now.

For a long time she lay on the bed, forcing herself to relax, to try and calm down, and to think rationally. But it wasn't easy. She felt so excited! For it was slowly dawning on her that for once in her boring life she knew something that nobody else did. And with it, came a feeling of power.

Which was a unique feeling indeed for Janet.

Normally her mother always knew best, or Iris had the upper hand, or the old dragon at the shop was lording it over her, or, well, anybody else in her life, if it came to that. All her life, she'd done as she was told, and been a good girl, and played everything safe.

And now it felt just so deliciously heady and wonderful to feel as if she might have the upper hand at last.

Possibly.

Slowly Janet sat up and hugged her knees under her chin. She needed to think. Really *think*. She had to be very careful about what she did next. Very careful indeed.

Chapter 24

'Was it me, or do you think Janet is getting over Iris's death pretty quickly?' Trudy asked. They were walking away from the Baines' cottage and further into the village, where the Finch family lived.

'No, I got the feeling her mind was on other things too,' Clement said.

'She nearly jumped out of her skin when I mentioned David's diary,' Trudy said. 'I'm sure she—'

'Sssshhh,' Clement hissed a warning, but he had a feeling he was too late. Three children, two girls and a boy, aged between eight and ten or so, suddenly shot out of the bushes where they'd been hiding, and ran off giggling.

'Oh damn!' Trudy said in frustration. 'Do you think they heard me?'

Clement sighed. 'I'm afraid so.'

Trudy could have kicked herself. She knew how villages worked. Before tea-time, the entire inhabitants of Middle Fenton would be talking about the dead boy's diary.

'It probably won't matter,' Clement tried to console her. 'So far, we only have Mortimer Crowley's word that it ever existed.' Inside, though, he couldn't help but feel a little uneasy. *If* the journal or some sort of notebook *did* exist, then there was a good chance that its contents might just pose a threat to whoever had strangled the May Queen; and more and more he was inclined to believe that that somebody was *not* David Finch.

So once the killer got to hear the rumours about the possibility of the journal's existence, they'd surely become desperate to get their hands on it, and that thought wasn't a pretty one. Especially since Clement was inclined to believe that the person who *had* murdered Iris Carmody in such a dramatic way must have been in a very emotional state to begin with. To give vent to his (or her?) feelings in such a way that he needed to leave the poor girl's body trussed to the maypole in full public view, spoke of a very disturbed mentality indeed. The act screamed of someone crazed with love, rage or despair – or maybe a combination of all three.

And he doubted that such high emotions could easily be repressed. Now that they would soon have to add fear to the mix, the combination could turn the killer even more volatile. Because when a killer feared for their safety …

'I wish we had our hands on that damned diary,' Clement muttered.

Trudy nodded. *She* wished she hadn't been so careless as to talk about the case out in the open in the village. She'd certainly never do so again – that particular lesson was well and truly learned. She should have realised that their presence was bound to attract the curiosity of the village children, and learning what they were doing would be high on any kiddie's list. The bragging rights it would give them with their friends would be phenomenal.

She felt distinctly deflated as they made their way to the Finch residence in taut silence, and tried to snap out of her gloomy mood as Clement knocked briskly on the door. Castigating herself wasn't going to help anyone or anything, and she couldn't let herself get distracted. As Dr Ryder had just pointed out, they needed to find that diary of David's and his parents were likely to be their best chance of doing so.

She was expecting Mrs Finch to answer the door again, and was therefore very disconcerted, when the door swung open, to find herself in the presence of Superintendent Finch himself. Not that she'd ever met him in person, but she recognised him from when he'd given his evidence at the coroner's court.

She felt herself instinctively straighten to attention. 'Sir,' she said smartly. She was half-expecting him to barely acknowledge her, so used was she to men in authority always seeking out other men in authority to engage with first. So she felt utterly stunned when her superior officer's face creased into a welcoming smile, and he reached out his hand to her.

'WPC Loveday, I'm very glad to see you. Congratulations! I can't tell you how pleased I am by your progress. Come on in and tell me all about it. I knew I was right to ask you two to investigate David's case!'

Trudy blinked and shot Clement a baffled look. Congratulations? On what, exactly – and what progress had they made?

Clement shot her back an equally blank stare and gave an almost imperceptible shrug of his shoulders.

Feeling full of trepidation, Trudy stepped into the Superintendent's hallway and followed him through to the small front room. There was no sign of his wife, and he indicated a pair of armchairs impatiently as he took a seat on a small sofa.

'I can't tell you how glad I was to get DI Jennings's call last night,' he swept on. 'That was a very clever piece of deductive reasoning, Constable,' he added, running a hand over his face. In spite of his ebullient mood, he looked tired and pale, and Trudy felt her heart go out to him, even as her mind scrabbled to understand what this was all about.

'Er, thank you, sir,' she said, a shade helplessly. Although she reported to the station every morning, that morning DI Jennings hadn't been in his office, so she was literally in the dark.

'Although in itself the evidence isn't conclusive, it's certainly suggestive. Oh yes, I think we can say that. Certainly it's cast the verdict of suicide into doubt.'

Trudy gulped, realising that she could put it off no longer – there was nothing else for it. She was just going to have to admit, humiliatingly, that she had no idea what the Superintendent was talking about, and feel like a perfect fool. Just when she was already still kicking herself for her earlier mistake with the village children, too.

Luckily he burst into speech before she could do so.

'Yes, getting that ladder tested was a stroke of genius!' Keith Finch said, giving her another grateful look.

The ladder!

Trudy, who hadn't realised how tense she'd actually been, felt her shoulders all but slump in relief as comprehension finally came. So the test results must have come back in on the woodworm and the state of the rungs. And it didn't take a genius to work out that the experts' verdict had been that the wood had been in no fit state to take a man's weight.

'Of course, Jennings pointed out that David knew the barn well, and might have known the ladder was a bit rickety from playing there as a kid. But I told him – in no uncertain terms, you can be sure – that was all but irrelevant. Nobody who was in the act of killing themselves, especially when befuddled already by a sleeping drug, was going to have the presence of mind to avoid stepping on ladder rungs that they might have guessed were unable to take their weight, would they?' Superintendent Finch looked from one to the other. 'I mean, it's just not feasible, is it?'

'I wouldn't have said so, no,' Clement said, sensing that Trudy's nerves were probably a little fraught right then. 'I take it that DI Jennings …' He broke off diplomatically.

'Is now having to rethink the whole thing?' the Superintendent finished happily. 'Yes he is. Well, I suppose it would be more accurate to say that he's not quite so sure that the case is as cut-and-dried as it first appeared. Which as far as I'm concerned, is a major step forward. So …' He leaned forward eagerly in the chair. 'Now that things are moving at last, what's your next move?'

He looked at Trudy expectantly.

Chapter 25

Under her superior officer's unwavering gaze, Trudy gulped. Their next move? For a hideous second her mind went a total blank and she groped for the first thing she could think of.

'Well, we've spoken to someone called Mortimer Crowley. I don't know if DI Jennings mentioned him?' she heard herself say. Luckily (and astonishingly,) she heard herself say it in a calm and even confident manner.

Beside her, Clement leaned forward slightly in his chair, and as if sensing she might need for a moment or two to pull herself together, took over smoothly, 'I take it he's been living in the village a few years. Have you met him, Superintendent?'

Keith Finch's lips twisted grimly. 'Yes, to both questions. DI Jennings mentioned that he was a person of interest in Iris's murder not long ago. Apparently, he holds a lot of wild parties with friends of his that come down from London. The Inspector is not sure if the rumours of drugs and debauchery that surround his set are accurate or not, but the village on the whole tends to regard him as a bad lot. And Iris was known to be friendly with him.'

'Something he denies,' Clement grunted.

'Yes, well, that's hardly surprising is it?' Keith Finch responded laconically. 'And yes, naturally, I've seen him out and about in the village and we exchange the odd pleasantry, but I can't say that I know the man. Or want to. But since I learned he was on the radar for Iris's killing I've put out a few feelers amongst my friends both here and further afield and from what I can tell he's – legally at least – above board. He inherited a lot of money from his late wife, and has invested most of it in real estate and art galleries.' The Superintendent paused and put the tips of his fingers together in what was obviously a subconscious habit, before smiling wryly. 'Now as I'm sure you're aware, there can be a lot of hanky-panky going on in the art world – I had a word with a chap who specialises in art forgery and whatnot, and the things he told me made my hair stand on end! I can tell you, I'll never go into another museum and look at the pictures in the same light again. But having said that, our friend Crowley's name hasn't been mentioned in connection with anything remotely shady. He tends to steer clear of fake Corot's and what-have-you, and specialises instead, in a quiet sort of way, with promoting and selling new painters. There's a growing market for them apparently.'

He shrugged. 'Not that a clean sheet in his business-practices means anything. If Iris *did* fall foul of him in some way, it won't have had anything to do with his work, but with his social life.'

'Yes I tend to agree,' Clement mused. 'Correct me if I'm wrong, but the thinking is that she met someone a bit wild at one of the parties and things got out of hand, yes?'

The other man nodded but frowned. 'Yes, but I'm not sure how seriously DI Jennings is pursuing that line of inquiry. It presupposes that Iris met some man who really lost his head over her and strangled her in a fit of … well, who can say?' He shot a quick look at Trudy, who was looking rather young and innocent, and had to remind himself that she was a very able police officer. He cleared his throat and carried on gamely. 'But if Iris did meet someone who was off his head on drugs or mentally unstable, or a bit of a sexual sadist, it seems odd that they've been able to find no trace of him. This is a small village, after all, not a big city. Anyone out of place would have been clocked and observed almost at once.'

Clement nodded glumly.

But Superintendent Finch wasn't quite finished. 'However, I'm not inclined to let Crowley off the hook quite yet. When I was asking around about him, a friend of mine from the golf club told me in confidence that he knows a chap called Rhys Owen, who apparently is well in with Mortimer Crowley and his arty friends. He told me this Rhys fellah is often as drunk as a skunk and in a bragging mood, and liked to hint about his daring peccadilloes with the opposite sex. And had boasted that he'd attended one or two parties locally that had proved very interesting indeed. I wanted to talk to him and narrow that down a bit, but unfortunately he's a slippery bastard, and I couldn't manage to get hold of him. I don't know whether he was so anxious to avoid me because I'm with the police, or because I'm David's father. But you might have more luck?'

He turned to Trudy as he finished speaking.

'Yes sir,' Trudy said, taking that as an order. 'We'll make that a priority.' Then she took a deep breath and glanced at Clement. 'There is one more thing we've come up with that might prove very helpful. Do you know if David kept a journal or a diary, sir?'

The Superintendent looked at her quickly, his eyes flickering rapidly in thought. 'I'm not sure,' he finally said. 'What makes you think that he might have done?'

'Somebody mentioned him writing something down in a note-book or pocket diary-type thing,' Trudy said vaguely, aware that she was being evasive, but not wanting to give the grieving father false hope. 'Of course, it may have been something he had taken up recently – after Iris died.'

Keith nodded. 'That sounds like something David might do. He was very methodical, you know. Painstaking. I suppose it had to do with his love of engineering …' He broke off and cleared his throat again. 'My son didn't kill that girl, Constable, I'm sure of it.' He stiffened his shoulders briskly. 'But you're right. If he did keep some sort of a record, it's vital that we find it.'

'You haven't come across it in his things then, sir?' she prompted gently. 'Here in the house, I mean?'

'No. But his mother might have some idea …' He clicked his fingers angrily as something obviously occurred to him. 'I'll go and search his student digs myself. We haven't got around to collecting his things from there yet. What with one thing and another, neither of us have felt like facing it. I could kick myself for not doing it sooner. I'm sure DI Jennings would have sent someone already, but they might have missed it. David was a dab hand at finding hiding places.'

Trudy opened her mouth to protest – sure that DI Jennings would not be very happy about this – then abruptly closed her mouth again, her objections unspoken. The last thing she wanted to do was get in the middle of a power-struggle between her superior officers.

'Yes sir,' she said meekly instead.

'Well, we'd best let you get on with things,' Clement said, rising to his feet. It was only when she too rose and looked across at him that Trudy realised that he was looking rather grim-faced.

It was so unexpected it made her heart skip a beat. What had made him look so displeased? She tried to cast her mind back through the interview they'd just conducted and couldn't think of anything that might have caused the coroner's jaw to set in quite so firm a line. But their host was also rising and walking with them to the door, and she had to concentrate on saying her farewells.

Once they were outside and walking to the car however, she cast Clement another quick look, but his expression hadn't changed.

'Is something wrong?' she asked, her nervousness making her sound more defiant than she really felt.

They were standing in the street, face to face, talking quietly. Trudy, not about to make the mistake she'd made before, had already checked that their surroundings were deserted and free of eavesdroppers.

Clement grunted and shook his head. He wasn't looking forward to the next few minutes but he knew what had to be done. Once he was sure they were out of sight of the house, he turned and looked her square in the face. 'I don't like the idea of the Superintendent searching for David's diary,' he said flatly. 'And much as I hate to say it – and this is something I never thought I'd ever find myself saying – you should find a phone box and report back to DI Jennings immediately and tell him *everything* we've found out. Not only about the possibility of the diary's existence, but tell him that he needs to send someone to David's university again to thoroughly search his lodgings.'

'But why? I doubt it would be there anyway,' Trudy said, surprised by the hard tone of her friend's voice. 'If he was keeping a record of Iris's movements or trying to find out who killed her, wouldn't he have it with him?'

'Very likely,' Clement conceded. 'Then again, there might just be two books – a regular journal that he could have been keeping and left behind at his university lodgings, and a more recent note-book that he had on him in the village,' Clement said doggedly. 'Don't forget, originally he would have thought he'd be leaving college only for the May Day celebrations, and would have been expecting to go back the next day. He might not have brought his journal with him for such a short trip.'

'In that case, there's not likely to be anything relevant in it then, surely?' Trudy said stubbornly, still feeling unsettled because she still couldn't see what her mentor was driving at, nor why he was so unhappy with her – because he clearly was.

'Only his thoughts on Iris!' Clement all but barked. 'And who knows what he might have written down in it? His suspicions of other men that she might have been friendly with, casual remarks about dates when he'd been stood up – and she could have been meeting someone else – and who knows what other clues. It's vital that the team investigating Iris's murder get their hands on it,' Clement said, before adding significantly, 'and that Superintendent Finch doesn't.'

He was looking at her almost coldly now, standing rigidly, aware of the tension creeping over him. He knew what he had to say next wasn't going to go down well, and he hated the thought of them having their first proper argument, but he could sense it was coming.

Trudy blinked. 'What do you mean? Why would you want to stop the Superintendent finding his son's journal?' she demanded. 'It might have something in it that proves his innocence. You said that yourself.'

'Yes,' Clement gritted. 'But use your head, girl,' he admonished, beginning to feel angry himself now, because it was falling on him to teach her some hard facts of life, and he didn't particularly feel like doing it. 'For all we know, *the boy's journal might prove the exact opposite!*'

For a second Trudy floundered – and then, with a rush of indignation, she understood.

'You think David did kill Iris after all – and wrote about it in his journal?' she accused, feeling, for some strange reason, oddly betrayed.

Clement bit back a swear word. 'I don't know, and nor do you,' he pointed out coolly. 'And that's precisely the point. In fact, I think it very unlikely that *if* David *did* kill her that he would then be so stupid as to admit as much in writing! But he might have killed her nevertheless, and *not* admitted it in his diary. In which case, his previous entries might well provide clues as to how he was feeling – his growing disenchantment with Iris for example. He might have written down entries when he was angry, giving away his true emotional state. All of which would add to the case against him. And if his father

165

finds it ...' Clement took a deep breath. 'What's to stop him from destroying it?'

Trudy was so stunned by the accusation, that she actually took a step back. She stared at Clement's stern, challenging face for a moment, and then took a second step back.

'You can't ... you can't just say something like that about someone like *Superintendent Finch*,' she said weakly. 'He wouldn't do something like that!'

'No? Why not? He's a grieving father after all, and desperate to save his son's reputation. And maybe his own career as well. It's not likely he can advance any further if it's an unacknowledged fact that his own son is believed to be a murderer, is it?'

Trudy's eyes flared. 'You can't say that!' she repeated. But even as she felt the indignation and anger building inside her, now that the shock of the accusation was receding a little, in her head she was beginning to concede that her friend might have a point. What was to stop him destroying the diary if he thought it implicated his son? The man was only human after all. But ... still she found it unthinkable. She knew that the Superintendent's reputation as a police officer was totally unsullied. And having met the man, she just couldn't see him betraying everything he'd worked for, and stood for ... and yet ...

Clement watched her go pale, then red, then pale again. He waited patiently for her to sort it all out in her mind, but he knew that she must be in turmoil. Everything loyal in her, and everything she'd been taught, would be telling her that superior officers were honourable and trustworthy and incorruptible.

But she wasn't the totally green and innocent young girl he'd first met any longer. In the past two years she'd seen five murderers caught, and had to deal with the tragic aftermath of their crimes. She was learning, and learning fast, that the world didn't operate in monochrome shades of pure black and bright white, but in an almost infinite number of shades of grey.

And now she was faced with a choice. Did she 'do the right

thing', inform DI Jennings, as he'd told her she must, and 'betray' Superintendent Finch? Or did she keep a diplomatic silence?

Clement felt his left leg begin to tremble and cursed inwardly. No doubt the stress of the moment was bringing on an episode. Surreptitiously he leaned back against the garden fence behind him and carefully shifted more weight onto his right leg. At least Trudy was too distracted by her own woes to notice his, he thought gratefully.

He took slow, deep breaths and watched her struggle with her dilemma – and grimly acknowledged that there was nothing at all he could do to help her.

Chapter 26

Angela Baines was beginning to get worried. It wasn't like Janet to be so late in getting home. Already she'd had to put their dinners to keep in the oven on a low heat. It simply wasn't possible for her to eat on her own, not knowing why Janet wasn't home. She'd always been a considerate girl and she knew when the evening meal was served.

She paced nervously up and down the front window, pausing every now and then to stare at the garden gate, hoping to see her daughter's form push it open and walk through. But only a lone chaffinch, searching for mayflies to feed its growing brood, darted around the garden, providing movement.

She glanced at the wooden sunburst clock on the wall again. It was a recently purchased and rather fashionable item that would normally give her pleasure to look at, but today she barely noticed this symbol of her determined modernity. It simply kept telling her the same thing – time was ticking away and her daughter was not home.

Angela tried to stem her growing sense of panic. Janet was a sensible girl, after all, and a thoughtful one. She was sure to be home soon with a very good excuse. Maybe she'd been into town, and the bus had broken down? It was sure to be something like that and nothing serious at all. Unlike some girls, who could cause their parents no end of trouble, Janet had always been a good girl.

Not like that little madam Iris.

Angela was glad that Iris was gone and felt no guilt whatsoever for feeling this way. The little so-and-so had been nothing but trouble ever since she could start to walk and talk, but more recently she and her radical ideas about running away to London had become downright dangerous.

How many nights had Angela lain awake, worrying that the atrocious girl might succeed in luring Janet to go away with her? And who knows what might have happened to Janet then if she had? You heard such awful stories about young girls going to London and simply vanishing.

At least that particular nightmare no longer bothered her, she thought with intense satisfaction. A mother had a sacred duty to protect her children, didn't she?

She paused at the window again, and glared at the still stubbornly shut garden gate, and felt her stomach once more start to churn with anxiety.

What on earth could be keeping her? Angela took another look at the placidly ticking clock and felt like dragging it from the wall and breaking off the silly wooden sunbeams that radiated out. She wanted to smash it to pieces and then throw the whole thing in the dustbin.

What on earth had made her buy the wretched thing?

She forced her trembling hands down to her side and took deep calming breaths. It was no use getting into 'one of her awful tizzies' as her mother had always called them.

Of course, they had only been childish tantrums, and she hadn't had a spell like that for some time. Not since her husband died, in fact. Not that she could remember anyway. But there were times, in the middle of a particular dark or long night, when she could lie awake for hours, worrying. Whenever she'd had a particularly stressful day, she'd wonder if she might have had 'one of her tizzies' and then gone off into a daydream and forgotten about it.

How would she know if she had?

Angrily, Angela Baines shook her head. What on earth did it matter, when Janet wasn't at home, like she should be?

She commenced pacing again, wringing her hands. She couldn't bear it if anything happened to Janet. She just knew she couldn't. She was all she had.

But her daughter would be home soon. She had to be.

Of course, Janet had never been the same since Iris died, Angela mused. Not that it worried her much – she knew that for all her daughter's insistence that the wretched girl had been her best friend, Janet hadn't *really* been fond of Iris, not *deep down*, of that Angela was positive. So her loss would cause her beloved daughter no serious harm.

But then David Finch had been found hanging in the Dewberry farm, and somehow, something had changed. But she wasn't sure exactly *what* had changed, and that worried her. Angela was used to knowing everything about her daughter – what she was thinking, what she was feeling, what she might be planning, where she was and what she was doing. Angela had always prided herself on being a good mother. Having no husband to help her, she'd always made sure that Janet came first. Unlike some modern mothers, who seemed to think their children could raise themselves!

But there was no denying it. Ever since David Finch had died, something subtle, but something persistent, had been occupying her daughter's waking moments, and she felt a chill begin to creep up her spine at the thought of what that might be.

Angela's fists clenched in a mixture of fear and fury as she gave a muffled cry of apprehension and frustration.

Where is she?

Whilst Angela Baines paced her home, watching the sun begin to slowly set and becoming more and more frantic, Mortimer

Crowley sat in his comfortable study, lounging back in his favourite chair with a black Bakelite telephone receiver pressed to his ear.

He was trying to keep his patience, but it was costing him. 'No, Reggie, I'm telling you, I'm not holding any more parties until things settle down a bit here,' he repeated. 'And it's no use whinging about it …'

He sighed, letting the upper-class accent moan on in his ear. The Right Hon. Reggie Arbington-Smythe, he suspected, spent his every waking moment half-cut, and today was obviously no exception. His words were so slurred he could almost swear that he could smell the booze on his breath over the telephone wire!

Which meant you simply just had to wait until he ran down a bit and then forcefully yell whatever information you wanted to impart into his ear, over and over again until you were sure it stuck.

Of all his 'special' friends, he was really only worried about Reggie, and maybe that old reprobate Welshman. Reggie, because he was capable of almost any indiscretion when he was really blotto, and Rhys because he had no damned sense of self-preservation at all. To him, the world was one big joke and he couldn't care tuppence about anything except his own pleasures.

Unfortunately he hadn't yet been able to reach Rhys, but Reggie had been easy enough to track down to one of his favoured Soho haunts.

'Listen Reggie, you need to keep your mouth shut, all right?' Mortimer said loudly, once he'd got the chance to get a word in edgeways.

'Shut, ol' boy? Can't do that – can't drink port with a shut mouth …' The gratingly upper-class accent made Mortimer wince as the other man began to snigger.

'I mean about the parties,' Mortimer persisted grimly. 'And about that girl, Iris, in particular.'

'Iris? Iris – oh pretty little Iris the country milkmaid …'

'Yes, her,' Mortimer hissed, pushing back his mounting sense of fury. 'If anyone comes asking about her, anyone at all, you know nothing about … our party games. All right?'

'Ssshhhh,' the Right Hon. hissed down the line like a demented snake, and Mortimer could almost picture his silly face, a finger pressed up against his lips. 'Got you, ol' boy. No mention of pretty Iris.'

'Promise me Reggie?' Mortimer pressed.

'Scout's honour, ol' boy,' the furry voice came back, and then, without so much as a goodbye, the phone was hung up. Probably the bartender at the club had offered to refill his glass, Mortimer thought sourly, and Reggie had promptly forgotten all about him.

He sighed and hung up. Well, he'd done his best. Not that he seriously expected the coppers to get onto him. From what he could tell keeping his ear to the ground, the police were content to lay the blame on the dead boyfriend. Poor sap. Not that he was complaining about *that*. The sooner they signed off on the case, the happier he'd be.

He and his 'special friends' made a habit of being very discreet indeed, but it would still be a relief when he could be sure that the whole May Queen murder fiasco was finally put to bed. He'd broken out in a cold sweat every time he saw a newspaper reporter slouching through the village, snuffling for titbits. But so far, they'd found nothing to cause him any real alarm.

But that could change in an instant.

He hung up, then redialled the Welshman's number. Still no answer. Damn! He sighed. He'd have to keep trying. He listened to the unanswered burring in his ear, and stared out at the darkening garden, his thoughts on Iris Carmody and the last time he'd seen her. What a body that girl had. A face like a Victorian rose and no more morals than …

Realising where his thoughts were leading him, he broke off abruptly with a dry laugh. Who was he to criticise anyone else's morals? One thing he wasn't, was a hypocrite.

He sighed heavily.

Poor Iris. Poor greedy little Iris …

Mortimer Crowley was not the only one watching the sun set. Walking alongside a field of green, happily growing barley, Ronnie Dewberry paused to watch a pair of linnets busy nesting in the blackthorn hedges. Off somewhere in the distance, some peewits were calling plaintively. Yellow brimstone butterflies sought out their last sip of nectar of the day from the dandelions growing in the grass verges, whilst the sky slowly turned pink all around them.

Not that his mind was focused on the beauty of the natural world all around him. Instead his thoughts, as ever, were on Iris and David.

He was worried about the old man and that pretty assistant of his, who'd been around the village, asking so many questions. He didn't really understand why the coroner was still poking around. Surely, now that the verdict had been handed down, his role was over?

And yet, clearly, it wasn't. So what was going on? Did they suspect something? What did they know that he and the rest of the village didn't? Was it possible … He paused, swallowing hard. Was it possible that they knew more than he thought they possibly could?

Not that he could see how. As far as he was aware, nobody knew how much he had hated Iris Carmody – or why. But if they were to find out …

Would he be arrested?

And if he was, how could he possibly defend himself?

For a moment, in that beautiful field, surrounded by that beautiful sky, Ronnie Dewberry felt cold, and scared, and utterly alone. His heart beat painfully in his chest, making him feel sick.

Ever since he'd been a kid, he'd sometimes 'felt' things. His grandmother had said he was a bit 'fey' like her own mother had been. He'd scoffed at her, of course, but still … There had been

173

that time he'd felt so odd all day, and coming home from school had been told that his favourite uncle had just died.

Then, too, that time he'd wanted Bunty to sleep on his bed, holding her close and rubbing her black-and-white fur and feeling so weepy. And then she'd been killed by a kick in the head from a particularly nasty ewe.

And right now, he was feeling that same sense of foreboding – as if something massive and dark was looming ever closer. And he was afraid that he knew what that something might be.

That he could end up hanging by the neck until he was dead, just as his best friend had.

Chapter 27

Duncan Gillingham smiled at the waitress and ordered coffee and toast for both of them. Trudy, who wasn't allowed to leave the house any morning without two boiled eggs and some bread and butter inside her, opened her mouth to object, and then shrugged.

If her dad and brother were anything to go by, Duncan would have no trouble eating her portion as well!

She glanced a little nervously at her watch. It was still early, and she had plenty of time before she had to report to the station; even so she felt rather uneasy. Not that anyone she knew – either from work or from her neighbourhood – was likely to see her in the smart little café off St Giles.

'You look just as good out of uniform as you do in it, by the way,' Duncan said cheekily, eyeing her rather pedestrian, pale blue skirt and white blouse and darker-blue cardigan ensemble with mock appreciation.

Trudy sighed. 'Don't play the fool, Duncan,' she said. The clothes she was wearing were at least three years old. 'I don't have all day to sit and spar with you, you know.'

Duncan held out his hands in a pacifying gesture. 'Fine! I really did want to clear the air between us.' He leaned forward across the table and his dark hair fell forward across his forehead, making Trudy want to reach out and push it back.

The thought made her feel silly and a little breathless at the same time. What was it about this man that got under her skin so much? Yes, he was handsome, and yes, he could be charming and funny. But she knew it was all calculated. He wanted something from her and she knew it. But instead of all that putting her off, it only intrigued her.

'Look, I really am sorry things became awkward between us the last time. That wasn't what I wanted.'

'I'm sure it wasn't,' Trudy said dryly. 'You wanted me to remain in blissful ignorance of your fiancée so that you could lead me on and use me as a source in the police for your articles.'

She reached for her teacup and took a sip. She was rather pleased with the cool but slightly amused tone of her voice. She sounded, even to her own ears, rather sophisticated. Like Audrey Hepburn in *Breakfast at Tiffany's*.

She thought she saw a spark of surprise mixed with admiration in the look he gave her, and felt even more pleased with herself.

'That might have been true at the beginning,' Duncan admitted with a shame-faced smile. 'But that wasn't true for very long. I really do admire you, you know. Joining the police, doing the job you do. It can't be easy.'

Trudy shrugged. 'They say that nothing worthwhile is ever easy. So, why don't we change the subject? I accept your apology, no hard feelings and all of that. Now, I really must go.'

Yesterday had been a bit of a nightmarish sort of day. It had taken her a while to realise that Dr Ryder had been right to insist that she make a full disclosure to her superior officer, and after giving DI Jennings a full report, she'd been glad to get home. Not that she'd slept much last night.

Needless to say, the Inspector had somewhat grudgingly praised her diligence, but for once, pleasing her taciturn boss had given her no sense of accomplishment. Now she just wanted to get back into the case and try and make some real progress.

Duncan rose as she stood up, and held out his hand. He knew better than to try and persuade her to stay. Instead, he merely said laconically, 'Well, be seeing you then. Good luck. Have a nice weekend,' he added, making Trudy pause for a moment. Then she remembered – of course, it was Saturday tomorrow and her day off. Not that she'd probably take it, with so much going on!

They shook hands like strangers, and Trudy nodded and walked away, feeling on the whole as if she'd acquitted herself rather well.

She might not have been feeling quite so satisfied, though, if she'd been able to read Duncan Gillingham's mind as he watched her go.

For after letting her get a good head start, Duncan started out after her. She might not become his willing source of information, but he was convinced that wherever she went, a story was bound to follow. And he wouldn't rest until he'd found out what she and the old vulture were up to in the village of Middle Fenton. Most of his fellow hacks thought that the Iris Carmody case was all but done and dusted, with the suicide verdict of the dead girl's boyfriend and the coppers all but vacating the village. But Duncan's nose told him differently, and he was willing to spend some time and effort in proving his hunches right. And he'd be very surprised indeed if little Miss pure-of-heart didn't lead him to a very nice and exclusive scoop that would warm the cockles of even his editor's arctic heart.

For the next few days at least, he was going to keep close. And if he could also think up a way of getting back in her good books … well, even better! He wasn't prepared to admit that Trudy Loveday was actually managing to get under his skin, mind, but there was no denying that she challenged, annoyed, intrigued and aggravated him in a way that no other woman had yet done.

*

Angela Baines kept casting looks of pleasure and satisfaction at her daughter over her morning bowl of cornflakes, but her relief was tempered by a persistent sense of unease.

When Janet had finally come home last evening, apologetic and intent on appeasing her with a tale of being waylaid by an old school friend in dire need of succour and a sympathetic ear, she'd been so relieved that she hadn't really questioned it much.

Now, seeing the dark circles under her daughter's eyes, and the quick, slightly jerky movements of her hands as she pushed her cereal around her bowl without actually eating any of it, she felt yet more twinges of alarm.

'Did you sleep all right, love?' Angela began softly.

'Yes, fine Mum,' Janet lied; her voice distracted and almost mechanical.

'Only you look rather pale.'

Janet forced a smile and reached for her glass of orange juice, taking the tiniest sip. She thought she might choke if she had to actually swallow anything of real substance. 'I shouldn't worry, I feel perfectly well.'

'Are you going to volunteer at the shop today then?' Angela persisted.

'Yes, I think so,' Janet again lied, her thoughts chasing each other around in her head like demented hamsters on a wheel. She wished, oh how she wished, that her mother would just stop talking …

She had spent the night thinking and thinking and thinking and still not arriving at any definite plan of action. Now she felt almost unreal, as if, instead of not catching a wink of sleep, she *had* fallen asleep after all, and was now in the midst of a dream. Nothing felt quite real, somehow, and yet she knew that it was.

And with the arrival of the dawn light, she knew she had to face the fact that, now, her life had changed irrevocably, and nothing she could do or say would allow her to go back to how things had been. She could only go forward and try to fight for her future.

For some time now, she'd felt a growing discontent with her life – the sameness of it all, the constant surveillance of her mother, the limited choices, this nosy village, the sheer boredom of her existence. How she'd envied and then hated Iris, because she was probably going to make her own silly dreams of a life as an actress or model in London come true. And now Iris was dead. Bright, full-of-life, clever, cruel, beautiful Iris. Soon they would release her body and she would be buried in the churchyard and the years would eventually pass and she'd slowly cease to matter to anyone except her parents.

And here she was, Janet Baines, feeling very much alive, scared witless and yet just a little excited too, on the edge of a precipice, trying to decide at which point to step off. Because she was going to have to do *something*.

Was she in actual *danger*?

That thought had been one of many that she had chased around in her head, over and over, during the night.

And even if she was, could she let it stop her from getting what she'd always wanted ...?

'I think it might rain,' Angela Baines said, watching her daughter's face nervously. 'I think you should stay away from the city today, and keep close to home. No point getting caught in a shower, Janet.'

Janet didn't reply. For once, she hadn't heard her mother's voice, and her mother knew it.

Chapter 28

Trudy and Clement had no trouble finding Rhys Owen at home, in a rather nice semi-detached villa in Osney Mead, although it took him rather a long while to answer the summons of his doorbell.

He wasn't a big man, but he somehow had a big presence, even when he was clearly hung-over. He had a lot of shaggy, curly hair of an indeterminate shade of brown, a pair of puppy-dog, big, brown eyes, and an oddly feminine mouth set in a jaw that reminded Trudy of Desperate Dan in the *Beano*.

'Hullo, what brings a lovely thing like you to a man's door then?' were his first words, aimed, (Clement was relieved to note) at Trudy. Had his eyes not been so blood-shot as he looked at her, she might even have felt flattered.

His sing-song accent was noticeably Welsh, but Clement had the feeling that he'd probably lived in England for longer than he'd lived in Wales.

'Mr Owen? Rhys Owen?' Clement said crisply.

With some reluctance, the man turned to regard Clement Ryder. He blinked once or twice as he did so, for he had to look some way up. His relatively short stature meant that Clement loomed over him, and both of them could almost hear the

Welshman wracking his brains as he tried to recall if they'd ever met before.

'Yes, that would be me, Mr … er …?'

'Dr Clement Ryder. I'm a city coroner.'

For some reason, Rhys Owen seemed to find this funny and burst into laughter. Perhaps he had been expecting a debt collector, or a man trying to sell him a set of encyclopaedias. Whatever had amused him, he obviously regretted it, for he changed the laughter to a groan and winced. 'Ow, I shouldn't do that when I'm feeling a little delicate,' he admitted with a wide grin that showed a lot of white and well-kept teeth.

There was something almost theatrical about him, Trudy realised, and wondered if he was a stage actor, or someone in the entertainment business. 'Won't you both come in then? I can offer you coffee, at least, since my housekeeper always keeps me supplied with a constant stream of the stuff,' he said, with yet another engaging grin.

Clement had to smile back, not at all surprised to hear this. Obviously any woman tasked with 'doing' for this man would have quickly learned that coffee, and plenty of it, was a necessity.

Their host led them through to a very nice, but extremely untidy, study-cum-library, with a large bay window overlooking a rather beautiful garden. Books lined the walls, but didn't have that much-thumbed look of a true bibliophile. Probably inherited the house from someone who liked to read, was Clement's first thought.

'Take a seat, won't you?' Rhys said, slumping into a comfortable armchair and leaning back against it. The scent of wine seemed to seep from his pores in a rather pleasant way as he regarded them amiably through heavy-lidded eyes.

He'd clearly forgotten his offer of coffee and for a moment Clement was worried he was going to fall asleep on them. His trousers and shirt had a crumpled look, and Trudy wondered if he'd just collapsed onto his bed last night fully clothed, and then had simply got up and carried on wearing them this morning.

'Mr Owen, we were hoping you could tell us something about Iris Carmody?' Clement said, deciding the man needed a nice brisk shock to wake him up a bit.

'Hmmmm?' Rhys opened one eye, then another and forced himself to sit up straight. 'Iris? Oh, *Iris,*' he said, grinning widely. 'I'll say I can tell you things about Iris! What a sport that girl was.'

Clement leaned forward amiably in his chair. 'Ah, like that, is it? And we gentlemen have good reason to be grateful for sporting girls, don't we?' he said, letting his voice become warm and suggestive. The quick glance he shot at Trudy told her that he wanted to lead this interview, since he was sure that he could get more out of their sybaritic host. Whereas Rhys would waste time merely flirting with Trudy.

Trudy, coming to the same conclusions, didn't object in the least, but settled back in her chair, content to watch and listen.

Rhys Owen gave another sudden snort of laughter as the coroner's words finally penetrated the fog in his brain. 'I'll say we do. And you can always trust good old Morty to find 'em for you.'

'Mortimer Crowley?' Clement said, just for the sake of clarification. 'Yes, he's a great friend of mine too.'

'Really. Don't remember seeing you at any of the special parties.' Rhys frowned, then shrugged and gave a sly smile. 'Bit shy, are you?' he taunted archly.

Clement felt himself tense a little, realising that here he had a great potential source of information only so long as he didn't scare him off. In his experience, men of this type could become very sober and very reticent very fast if they sensed they were treading on dangerous ground. And since he wasn't sure exactly what was 'special' about Mortimer's parties, he knew he was going to have to play this very carefully. Should the Welshman ever suspect that his visitor didn't share his particular set of peccadilloes, then things could sour very quickly. As it was, Clement needed to keep him talking before his befuddled brain had a chance to start wondering exactly why he should be answering Clement's questions at all.

'Well, a man in my position …' The coroner tailed off suggestively and shrugged.

'Quite right, say no more, say no more,' Rhys said happily. 'Lucky for me, I never had to earn my own crust, so don't have a job or any position to lose!' He almost laughed again, but remembered just in time the pain that usually followed, and contented himself with a chuckle instead. 'And I was too wily to ever tie the knot. No little woman waiting for me at home, to go all sour as vinegar and disapproving of my shenanigans,' he boasted proudly.

'Ah, a sensible man,' Clement said approvingly. 'As it happens, I *have* been to one or two of Morty's little shindigs, but I'm not sure who was there and who wasn't. I'm very discreet.' He added to the lie with a knowing wink. 'I can be blind as a bat sometimes. It's shocking!'

'That's the ticket!' Rhys said approvingly. 'Not that I give a fig what people say about me, mind. Give an old dog a bad name and … er …' His brow puckered as his befuddled brain groped for something witty to say, and then gave up the effort. 'Oh, something or other.' He waved a hand airily in the air. 'No, I don't mind being thought of as a bit of rogue. Ladies like that, don't they, my dear?' He startled Trudy somewhat by suddenly leering across at her.

Trudy, thinking of Duncan Gillingham for some reason, felt herself blush a little.

Delighted with the response, the Welshman again roared with laughter, then winced.

'I take it that Iris liked the rogues too? And the excitement of it all?' Clement said, forcing the lecherous old reprobate's attention back to himself.

'Oh yes, Iris liked it well enough, for all the fact that I can smell a gold-digger a mile off,' Rhys said, with a fond smile of remembrance. 'Girl like that, she could wrap me around her little finger. Not that I ever let her get her delightful fingers on any of my gold, mind, unlike some I could mention. I never knew a girl like her for getting you to spend your cash on her. And make you feel as if you were privileged to do so,' he laughed again. 'So, whilst I never kidded myself that I was special, Iris surely did have a way with any man. Could make even the stiffest of stuffed shirts melt like toffee in a saucepan.'

'You knew her well, did you?' Clement asked archly.

'Ah, not as well as I might have done,' he admitted, sounding rueful. 'I wasn't much into threesomes myself. I like to have a girl's attention all to myself, sport, know what I mean?' Rhys said with another knowing grin.

For a moment, Trudy didn't understand what he'd just said. Then she felt her face flame in embarrassment.

Clement was less taken aback. He was pretty sure he had it now. 'Trust good old Morty to come up with the goods.' He forced his voice to come out in a rich purr. 'I take it his London pals were always appreciative of his efforts?'

Rhys Owen yawned hugely, and again rested his head back against the back of the chair. He was clearly fighting to stay awake now. 'Oh, no doubt,' he mumbled.

'And Iris got what she wanted too?' Clement pressed.

'Oh, I can guarantee that,' the Welshman said with another snort of laughter. 'She always did all right for herself, never you fear.'

Clement wanted to ask more, like who actually paid the girls – Morty or the gentlemen in question – but realised that, since he was posing as a guest of these parties, he should be in a position to know.

Checkmated, he decided to change tack a little. 'It was really awful what happened to her, wasn't it?'

'Bloody shocking, so it was,' Rhys said sadly. 'Why tie the poor girl up to the maypole like that. That showed a nasty mind at work, if you ask me,' he opined, before giving a huge yawn.

'I think it's put the wind up Morty,' Clement said craftily.

'Huh?' The Welshman yawned again. Clearly he was soon going to fall asleep, and Clement wanted to get as much information out of him as he could before that happened. Memories of his own misspent youth told him that once you needed to sleep off a bender, nothing short of an earthquake could wake you.

'You know, he must have been scared one of the party guests might have …'

Rhys blinked, then – to his credit – looked genuinely appalled. 'No! You don't think one of us could have done that to the poor girl?'

Clement shrugged elaborately.

'No,' Rhys said again, shaking his head in growing agitation. 'I just don't believe it, man. We like to party, but it's all in good fun.'

But whilst Clement was inclined to accept that this amiable soak truly did believe what he said, he was a long way from accepting his conclusions.

To his mind, men who liked kinky sex at kinky parties were prime candidates for strangling a beautiful playmate before displaying her on the village green for all to see.

Chapter 29

Janet Baines left her house as the grandmother clock in their hall chimed six. She was feeling ever so slightly sick. Ever since Dr Ryder and that young girl had mentioned David's journal, she had been kicking herself for being so stupid. How was it that it had never once occurred to her that it could possibly be important?

And yet, the more she'd thought about it, the more it had loomed large in her mind until it was almost shrieking at her. Now, as she walked through the village that she'd lived in all her life, blind to the children playing hopscotch in the street, and the gossiping of housewives she'd been polite to for all her life, Janet forced herself to remain calm.

But it wasn't easy. She couldn't really make herself believe that she was about to do what she was about to do, so to distract herself from it, she concentrated on something else instead. And pondering the personality of David Finch seemed as good a way of doing that as any.

Right from the start, she'd been a little surprised that Iris had made a play for him. Yes, he was a good enough looking boy, and his family had more money than Iris's – but then, nearly everyone in the village did! Even so, he'd never really struck her as Iris's type, somehow. He was too unsophisticated, too clever, maybe.

Too ordinary – and most significantly of all – all but useless to her in terms of helping her to get on in life and pursue her dream of 'making it' in the big wide world.

But when it became clear that Iris really only wanted him as camouflage, someone to bring out on 'date nights' to reassure her parents and distract the village from what she was really up to, it quickly made sense.

However, what neither of them had ever really thought about was what David Finch must have thought about of all of this. Granted, Iris might have pulled the wool over his eyes to begin with, but no matter how infatuated he was by her beauty or feminine wiles, he must eventually have begun to suspect the truth of things? He was, at his core, an intelligent young man and the son of a police officer to boot. So he wasn't your average, gullible village idiot, like most of the boys she'd grown up with.

Now Janet could scream at how dense she'd been. *Of course* David wouldn't have let things rest, with Iris dead and himself standing, if not openly accused, then at least generally suspected of killing her. And with a policeman father as an example, what else could he do but try and track down her killer?

He had always been a careful, methodical sort of lad, she remembered now, from their shared days in the village school-room. The kind of boy who was interested in how things worked, and why – the type to make careful notes of everything.

Aware that she was coming to the end of the village houses now, she cast a very quick glance around, and only when she was confident that she was not being observed, did she dart off the lane, and, skirting a hedgerow, make her way stealthily across country.

Her heart was thumping in her chest, and she felt even more nauseous than ever. But she wasn't going to stop now. She couldn't. She had to be sure. Her hands felt clammy and she swallowed hard. Soon, she told herself, it would all be over. One way or another, things would be settled.

She had to hold on to that to give her courage. Iris was not the only one who could be brave and reckless when the need arose, she thought defiantly, surprised to find a smile on her face. If only her mother could see her now, she'd be shocked to her core! *Who'd have thought she had it in her*, she could almost hear the denizens of the Middle Fenton saying to themselves, if they knew just what she was doing.

But once again she shied away from contemplating just what might happen in the next hour, and turned her thoughts back to David Finch again – and his diary.

It was funny how fate could change your life in just one infinitesimal moment. Because as soon as the coroner and his pretty assistant had mentioned it, she'd been almost certain that she knew exactly where it might be hidden.

As a little girl, all the children of around the same age had played the same sorts of games, in the same sorts of places. And one of their favourite games had been hide-and-seek. And one of David's favourite hiding places had been, of all places, behind the village primary school. Whilst she herself had always been happy, as a girl, to leave that place every afternoon at a quarter to four and never look back, David had enjoyed his lessons. So perhaps the place felt comfortable to him. And behind the village school was an old sports pavilion that gave way to the village playing field. Mostly used for the storage of cricket bats and footballs, oars and tennis rackets, it had never appealed to her as a particularly edifying place to visit.

But David, like most boys, had been fond of sports. And crawling under the space behind the wooden steps leading to the only door had been one of his favourite hiding places. So much so that once, when stuck for a place to hide herself, she'd used it too. And it had been whilst she was lying there, waiting for the 'seeker' to come, that she'd noticed that one of the wooden boards that blocked off the second step was a little ajar.

Curious, she'd investigated and found that someone had

loosened one nail enough so that the board could be lifted up, like a window, revealing the space in between. And in that space she'd found a biscuit tin.

Naturally, she'd looked, and been disappointed to find no biscuits within, but only a motley collection of 'treasure' of the sort favoured by boys. A homemade catapult made out of willow and an elastic band, some colourful marbles, and a book – *Treasure Island* in this case. Inside, the name of David Finch had been written in pencil, so she'd known whose stash it was.

Funny how she hadn't thought of that in years, until now. Now that the boy who'd created the hidey-hole was dead. Along with the girl he'd so foolishly, pointlessly, loved.

But she remembered that David had always had a secretive side to his nature, so it was perhaps not so surprising that he would choose to hide his precious journal there as well, and not at his home or anywhere else where it could be easily found. Especially if it contained something he might want to keep secret from his parents. He wouldn't want to cause more worry for his mother for one thing, and perhaps had good cause to make sure that some of his more furtive activities didn't reach the ears of his policeman father!

And so, last evening, she'd waited until it was getting dark and no one could see her, and then she'd made her way to the pavilion and regarded the steps thoughtfully. She knew it was pointless to try and struggle underneath the crawl space. Although she was slim, she wasn't ten years old any longer! But, with the reach of her now-adult arms, she'd been able to grope around behind the steps, and sure enough, her questing fingers had managed to find the same plank of wood, which still swung open on its now rusty nail. And a larger, newer, airtight biscuit box had been hidden there – and within it, a small, dark leather-bound journal.

How her heart had leapt!

It had been too dark for her to read it then and there of course,

189

so she'd had to take it home and sneak it into the house so that she could read it once she and her mother had gone to bed.

And what she'd read in that book, in David Finch's neat and careful handwriting, had changed her world forever.

Of course, it would be just like David, she thought angrily now, to investigate what had happened to Iris with such a plodding, methodical obsession that it had finally led him to the truth.

Damn him! Damn him! Damn him!

Janet paused, aware that she was breathing hard now and almost sobbing.

Once again her mind went back to the moment, last night, when the village church clock had been striking eleven, and she'd read the final, momentous lines in that awful journal.

She'd read the initial pages impatiently at first, not caring about the details of who he'd talked to, and what they'd said, and how he'd pieced it all together with that bit of evidence or this bit of corroboration. What on earth did all that *matter*?

But then it had started to penetrate into her feverish, frustrated mind, where it was all going. And the conclusions the dead boy was making.

And it had made her heart almost stop in horror.

So when she'd read the final line, that concluded with his stark belief that he knew who had murdered Iris – and named the suspected killer – she knew that she might never be safe, and things could never be the same for her again.

All through the night, she'd lain, shaking and cold on her bed, trying to find a way around things. Time and time again she'd tried to work it all out – following every possible scenario, desperate to find an escape route somewhere.

But with the cold light of day she finally had to admit defeat.

There was only one thing left for her to do if she was going to have any chance at all of having a decent life of her own.

And she was going to do it now.

How Iris would laugh and laugh and laugh if she could see me now. Janet could almost hear it, the mocking, ironic, jeering tone Iris had used whenever Janet had tried to stand up for herself.

But of course, Iris would never laugh again, would she?

At this thought, Janet paused, turned aside, abruptly knelt down and was violently sick into the base of a hawthorn bush.

After that, she felt a little better.

Chapter 30

In spite of everything, Trudy did take that Saturday off, since Dr Ryder wasn't available that day either, and thoroughly enjoyed her rare day of leisure.

But she wasn't particularly surprised when her friend and mentor called her Saturday evening and asked her if she'd like to accompany him to church the following morning – at Middle Fenton's St Swithin's Church, naturally.

And so it was that Trudy found herself – literally dressed in her Sunday best – at eleven o'clock the next morning, listening to the service with only half an ear, as she gazed curiously around at the congregation.

Trudy quite liked sitting in churches. There was a peace to be had inside them that wasn't quite matched anywhere else. At school, they'd been taught all the hymns, and she liked singing, although she wasn't quite sure she had a good voice and was careful to keep her voice down to little more than a whisper.

Beside her, though, Clement Ryder was displaying a very pleasing baritone, and she noticed one or two ladies – presumably unattached – eyeing him with a speculative gleam in their eyes.

The women, Trudy noticed without any real surprise, outnumbered men roughly three to one. There was no sign of Keith Finch, for instance, or Ray Dewberry or Mortimer Crowley, although Trudy supposed, cynically, that Mortimer probably rarely set foot inside a church. But Ronnie Dewberry *was* present, she noticed, sitting next to Janet Baines, a few pews ahead of them on the other side of the church. Her mother sat on her other side and, to Trudy's eye, seemed to be a little agitated.

She whispered as much to Clement when, the hymn over, they all sat down again.

Clement glanced across the aisle and saw that Angela Baines was sitting, stiff-backed, and staring resolutely at the pulpit. Both Trudy and Clement saw when Janet Baines reached out and took Ronnie's hand in her own.

Trudy gave a mental nod. So she was right. She'd always half-believed that there might have been something going on between those two, and now it seemed as if they had finally decided to make it public. And there wasn't a much more public declaration of their stepping out together than holding hands in church of a Sunday. Already several of the more eagle-eyed worshippers had spotted the telltale gesture, and were casting each other speculative glances.

Beside her daughter, Angela Baines's lips tightened still further.

Clement found his mind wandering as the vicar's words washed over him.

After Trudy had told her superior about the real nature of Mortimer Crowley's parties, he knew that the DI would do his best to track down and interview those who had indulged their appetites for the bohemian lifestyle with the dead girl.

Superintendent Finch, not surprisingly, *had* been enthusiastic and had called the coroner to thank him. Learning that the dead girl had provided rather exotic favours for any number of unknown men had opened up a whole new field for him – and given him fresh hope of clearing his son's name.

But would it? As he shifted a little on the uncomfortable, hard wooden pew, Clement felt again a growing sense of dissatisfaction.

Unless something broke soon, he was beginning to feel as if they'd have to admit defeat on this one.

The prospect was a depressing one.

In his house, Mortimer Crowley was also feeling vaguely depressed. He was in his bedroom, hurriedly packing two large suitcases and trying to reassure himself that he was merely beating a tactical retreat, not fleeing like a scared little kid.

As he packed, moving rapidly from wardrobe to case and back again, he tried to lighten his gloom. After all, the next few months or so were bound to be much more fun spent in the south of France than in this little rural backwater. He might even move on to Tuscany later, depending on how long he needed to lay low.

Trust that drunken idiot Rhys not to keep his mouth shut. When he'd finally managed to get him on the phone, he'd been appalled to hear the stupid bastard admit that he'd been shooting his mouth off. He'd seemed to think it funny.

But a dead girl was no laughing matter – not when the police were going to be looking at you very closely, anyway. He took a deep breath, hoping that he might be being overly pessimistic. Was it possible that things might not be about to come tumbling down around his ears after all – not if they couldn't actually prove anything?

On the other hand, he'd always got by on listening to his instincts, and right now his instincts were positively screaming at him to get out whilst the going was good.

He grabbed his passport and slipped it into his inside jacket pocket, put on his most expensive watch and reached for his travelling gentlemen's vanity case, checking that all the brushes, combs and shaving lotions were in place.

Satisfied, he slammed the case shut, then closed and locked both his suitcases.

With a grunt, he hauled them off the bed and headed awkwardly for the stairs. In a few hours he'd be flying out over the channel, and Inspector bloody Jennings and his nosy, flat-footed coppers could whistle for another chance to talk to him.

As he loaded up his car – a rather fine Bentley – he cast a quick glance around. The village of Middle Fenton quietly looked back at him, unimpressed.

As he drove down his drive and out into the lane, he felt an enormous sense of relief wash over him to be leaving the place.

He passed the village green and the permanent maypole, keeping his eyes carefully averted.

Duncan Gillingham sat at the back of the church, wondering if he was wasting his time. Not that he minded following Trudy Loveday around, but he'd never liked churches. They made him feel uncomfortable, as if he was being watched and judged.

Half-hidden behind a stone pillar, he yawned widely and wondered exactly what had brought the lovely Trudy and the old vulture here of all places. One thing was for sure – as soon as the service was ended, he'd have to be quick about it and nip out and hide behind a yew tree or something before Trudy could spot him.

He hoped she'd lead him to something good soon. His editor was beginning to drop very broad hints that the Carmody story was running out of steam and Duncan shouldn't be wasting any more of his time on it. But if his hunch was right, he'd soon be able to give both the editor and his prospective daddy-in-law one in the eye when he came back with a scoop.

A bee, having bumbled its way through the open church door, droned around a flower arrangement near the entrance. Duncan fought back another yawn. He'd always hated Sundays – they were so boring and dead. Nothing ever seemed to happen on a Sunday …

As the vicar finally finished his sermon and wished them all a fine day, Angela Baines rose with the rest of the dismissed congregation. She kept a stiff, polite smile firmly on her face as she made her way in the procession to the church door, and shook hands with the vicar.

Behind her, she heard Janet murmur something about how uplifting the sermon had been, and then Ronnie Dewberry's polite acknowledgement of 'Vicar'. She pretended not to notice that the two were still holding hands as they walked down the stone path towards the black wrought-iron gates. Already she could see Thelma Collier and that awful Claire Innes woman looking at the couple and whispering gleefully.

By tomorrow, she thought furiously, the news would be all over the village.

Angela felt utterly humiliated. It was not that there was anything wrong with Ronnie Dewberry, she supposed. His father did own one of the largest farms around, and he would one day inherit. But Janet could do so much better! And why had they been keeping things a secret from her? That's what made Angela want to scream and rant with rage and frustration – the fact that her daughter had been sneaking about behind her back, *and she hadn't known about it!*

It made her wonder what else might have escaped her notice. Just how long had her daughter been sweet on the wretched boy? And why was Janet making such a public show of it now?

She just knew that something, somewhere, was very wrong. She had the feeling that her life was slipping out of control; not just her own life, but that of her daughter, too, maybe even that of the whole village. It was as if they were all beginning to cartwheel helplessly down some massive, downward slope, where it could all only end in disaster.

She turned, trying to catch Janet's eye, but her daughter refused to meet her gaze. Instead she smiled vaguely at some point over her mother's shoulder and said coolly, 'Mummy, Ronnie and I are going to have a picnic lunch together. I'll see you at tea-time.'

And before Angela could object, Janet was all but tugging

Ronnie away. He, to give him some credit, managed to give her a polite smile and a nod, but Angela felt only a cold sense of rage and dread.

The moment she got home, she went straight to her daughter's bedroom, and began frantically to search it.

Ronnie let himself be led back to the farmhouse, where Janet set about raiding the kitchen larder to make sandwiches and check for fruit, cheese and cake. All the way, she talked happily, lightly, about their future together, as if she hadn't a care in the world.

Ronnie had no idea how she did it. *He* felt as if the world had turned upside down and back-to-front, all around him.

At least his dad wasn't around to witness the spectacle, Ronnie mused gratefully. *He*, no doubt, was out and about in the fields, somewhere, getting on with the usual routine. But sooner or later Ronnie would have to confess that he and Janet were now … what?

Engaged?

He wasn't quite sure.

He wasn't quite sure what Janet wanted, exactly.

He didn't even know what he thought or felt about it all. He'd always thought Janet was one of the loveliest girls he knew, even at school. But he'd never seriously thought she'd look at him twice. And now, suddenly, everything had changed.

Last night she'd called at the farm, totally out of the blue, and asked him to go for a walk with her. Luckily Dad had been upstairs in the bath at the time, so he'd been spared any knowing or speculative looks.

And so they'd walked, and Janet had been lively and bright and lovely and, somehow … somehow, she'd let him know that he had caught her eye, and before he knew it, they'd become an item and shared their first kiss.

And, despite the confusion he'd felt about what was happening, he was sort of excited and pleased about it too, because Janet was such a catch. Everyone knew her mother had money, and she was pretty and clever and a proper lady – not like that tart Iris!

How Ronnie hated Iris.

And, although he couldn't say why or how, during their giddy few hours together last night, he had formed the impression that Janet hated her too. But that couldn't be right, could it? Everyone knew that they'd been friends.

'Is fruit cake all you have?' Janet asked, breaking into his reverie, and he looked at the mundane, shop-bought offering and shrugged apologetically. 'It's Dad's favourite,' he muttered by way of apology.

But, at the back of his mind, Ronnie felt deeply uneasy. What had brought all this on? Why did he feel as if Janet had turned into a sleek cat, and he had suddenly grown a set of mouse-whiskers and a long thin mouse-tail?

'Oh well, it'll go well with an apple and some cheese,' Janet said blithely, and smiled. But the fact was, she was feeling distinctly nervous. It was important to her plans that the whole village knew that she was with Ronnie now, which was why she'd made their pairing so public and obvious. Because it was just possible that, before the day was out, she would need the protection that gave her. Ronnie must be made to see that he couldn't possibly hurt her without bringing disaster down on himself.

Hopefully, it would be all the advantage she needed.

Angela Baines sat on her daughter's bed, a picture of misery, with her head in her hands. Around her lay the scattered proof of the frenzied nature of her search, and she wearily set about tidying everything up before her daughter got home. But all the effort had been wasted. She'd found nothing that might explain Janet's behaviour, and felt exhausted and frightened, and still clueless.

As she glanced up bleakly to look out through the window, her eyes rested on the big wooden jewellery box resting on her daughter's vanity table. Tunbridge ware, it was a beautiful thing, made of many different kinds of wood, worked into an intricate design. Janet had brought it home one day a few years ago, as a birthday present to herself.

She had already opened and rifled through it, of course, but it had contained nothing but her daughter's modest collection of tasteful jewellery.

With a sigh, she set about restoring the vanity table top to pristine order, as Janet always kept it, but something about seeing the box resting there suddenly struck a dim and distant memory of her own childhood. Hadn't her mother owned something similar … Yes, she was sure she had. And something in her memory tickled at her, making her smile almost with realising it. Something about her mother's box had been exciting and pleasing to the small girl she'd once been. What was it? Something …

With a sudden cry of remembrance, Angela Baines's hand shot out and pounced on it, for she remembered now. For her mother had called her own case a 'puzzle box'. And she had shown her fascinated and delighted daughter the 'secret'. How, by pressing and sliding certain sections of the different-coloured wood, you could find a hidden drawer, and had explained to her what it had probably once been used for.

As a child, she hadn't understood what love-letters were, or why ladies in the Victorian era would want to hide them, but, for a short while, the puzzle box had been her favourite thing, until something else had caught her attention, and she'd slowly forgotten about it.

Now Angela sat back on the bed, studying the box carefully. She removed the trays of jewellery and eyed the side of the box, trying to calculate if the trays were as deep as the carcass of the outer shell – and she realised that they weren't!

Her heart leapt. Quickly she turned the box this way and that, probing, pushing, pulling and finally finding the first piece of wood that moved. After that she spent a frustrating ten minutes twisting, pulling, tweaking and swearing viciously. Had the ladies at the church been able to hear her, they'd have blanched in shock, for who'd have thought the genteel, cool and ladylike Angela Baines would even know such words, let alone use them?

Finally she felt something inside the box go 'ping' and the invisible bottom drawer sprang open.

With a cry of triumph, Angela pulled it open, revealing the treasure. And treasure it was indeed – no less than her daughter's diary.

The little madam, Angela thought furiously. She's always said she never wanted to keep a diary!

Feverishly, she opened the first page and then paused, taken aback, for just one glance told her that the neatly written pages were not filled with her daughter's familiar, rather flowery handwriting.

Instead ...

Angela Baines's mouth went bone-dry as she realised just whose diary this was. *And what it meant.*

For a moment, she was unable to take it all in. But when her numbed mind finally unlocked, so too did a tidal wave of despair, for she knew that she was literally holding catastrophe in her hands.

What could she do? How could she fix this?

But before she could even begin to formulate an answer to that, she heard the sound of a door opening downstairs, and she quickly and guiltily thrust the diary back into its hiding place and set the puzzle box back on the table.

Why was Janet back so soon?

She stepped hastily out of her daughter's room and began to run lightly down the stairs. Once in the hall, she called out, making her way to the kitchen.

'Janet? Darling, where ...'

Angela never got the chance to finish the sentence.

Chapter 31

Trudy and Clement left the church, neither one of them in any hurry to head back to their respective homes. Since it was another lovely day, they strolled to one end of the village and then back again, taking their time. In the hedgerows the first of the dog roses were beginning to bloom, and cow parsley was frothing creamy lace umbrella-like flower-heads alongside the road verges.

From a dense hawthorn thicket, a yellowhammer called out his song of 'a little bit of bread and no cheese', claiming the desirable residence as his own.

'It's going to be really warm today,' Trudy remarked, as Clement paused to raise his Trilby hat and flick back his thick white hair with a hand that seemed to tremble slightly.

'Yes,' Clement agreed. His hat secure, he reached into his jacket pocket and pulled out a roll of strong-flavoured mints and popped one into his mouth. Trudy had noticed his fondness for these mint sweets before, and it always struck her as slightly out of character – although she couldn't really have said why.

He casually thrust his trembling hand into one of his trouser pockets, out of sight.

'I suppose we ought to call on Mrs Baines and find out why

she's so out of sorts – although I fear the answer will be obvious. But you never know, it might be significant.'

'Yes,' Trudy said at once. 'I for one think it's curious that Janet and Ronnie have decided to start advertising the fact that they're a couple, don't you?'

Clement didn't, particularly, but then he wasn't twenty years old and intrigued with youthful romance. 'I think now might be a good time to see if we can't find out,' he temporised. 'Let's go and see if Mrs Baines has any insights.'

When they got there, the front door to the Baines' house stood slightly open, and as they noticed it on their approach up the garden path, Trudy and Clement exchanged quick glances. Of course, it was already turning into a very hot day, so it was always possible that Angela had left the doors and windows open to let in some air. Nevertheless, they both felt a sense of unease as they approached the door, though neither one showed it.

At the entrance, Clement pushed door open a little further, revealing an empty hallway and called out. 'Hello? Anyone home? Mrs Baines?'

Somewhere in the back of the house there came a furtive sound of rushed movement. It immediately triggered a knee-jerk reaction in Trudy who, before Clement could stop her, pushed past him and darted into the hall. Through the open door of the first room on her left she could see a small study, and a quick glance confirmed that it was deserted. If the house was being burgled, then at least the thief hadn't ransacked the whole house yet. She moved quickly down to the open door at the end, aware that Clement was now right behind her.

Like the front door had been, the back kitchen door was also open – and just moving slowly backwards on its hinges, as if it had been pushed violently open and was now going back on itself.

Again, acting instinctively, she ran to it to look out, but just as she reached it, she heard Clement give a swift and sharp exclamation behind her. It made her hesitate and turn around. For some reason, she saw him suddenly dart off behind the large, kitchen table and bend down.

Trudy, reluctant to give up the chase, thrust her head out of the door and looked around the back garden. Had she seen a fleeing cat or dog, she would have felt very sheepish indeed, but there was no sign of anyone in the Baines' garden – animal or human.

And yet the air around her seemed almost to thrum, and although she would never have been so rash as to write her feelings down in an official report, she was sure that someone, possibly panic-stricken, had just run through the garden.

'Trudy, call an ambulance!' Clement's tense voice brought her scuttling back into the kitchen in time to see her friend bent over the prone form of Angela Baines. Her face looked slack and pale, and there was blood seeping out from under her head. As she watched, Clement bent down and put a finger to the side of her neck.

Trudy froze and held her breath as she waited for his verdict.

'Ambulance!' he repeated tersely, and Trudy, shaken from her temporary shock, ran to the hall, where she'd noticed a telephone resting on a console table as they'd passed. She quickly dialled the emergency number, asked for an ambulance and gave the address. Then she hung up and dialled her own station number. On a Sunday, she doubted that DI Jennings would be in, (rank had its privileges as she'd often been told!) but she quickly related the situation to PC Walter Swinburne, who *was* on duty, knowing she could trust him to quickly set things in motion. He might be the oldest PC there – and something of a station joke – but he could still work fast and competently when it was required.

She darted back to the kitchen doorway and paused, watching as Dr Ryder put his ear to the woman's chest. Her own heart was beating so fast in her chest she actually put up a hand to her sternum and pressed down. 'Is she going to be all right?' Trudy asked, her voice just a little tremulous.

Clement's lips thinned, but he sat back on his heels and looked at her severely. 'Her pulse is erratic, and her breathing reedy. The ambulance had better get here quickly.'

Trudy swallowed hard. 'Has she been bashed on the head?' she asked, forcing her voice to remain calm.

'She has a head wound certainly,' Clement agreed cautiously. 'She might have slipped and fallen and banged her head on the floor.'

'But you don't think so?'

Clement shrugged. 'I wouldn't like to make a guess – not without moving her head for a closer look, anyway. And I don't think that's a good idea.'

Trudy had a sudden thought. 'Where's Janet?' But before Clement could respond, she turned and checked the living room – which was also empty – then ran upstairs. She was relieved to find that all the bedrooms and bathroom were also empty.

She came back downstairs. 'Janet's not here,' she informed Clement.

Just then, Angela's eyes fluttered opened. Clement saw at once that her pupils were distended, and that she looked vague and puzzled.

'Janet?' Angela said.

'It's Dr Ryder, Mrs Baines. Everything is all right, an ambulance is on the way. Don't worry,' Clement said in his best reassuring bedside manner. But he doubted that she heard him, let alone understood him, for there was no flicker of reaction on her face.

'Janet,' she said again. And then, quite clearly, she added, 'Hit me ...'

Trudy felt the shock go through her and glanced at Clement inquiringly. But already the coroner was shaking his head in warning.

'I doubt she's aware of what she's saying,' he said quietly.

'It's all David's fault,' Angela said next, with a huge sigh. 'Why did she have his diary?'

At this, even Clement looked shaken. With a questioning look,

Trudy sank to her knees by the injured woman, and said softly, 'Where is the diary, Mrs Baines?'

Angela sighed and closed her eyes.

Patiently, Trudy and Clement kept watch. It could only have been a few minutes since she had phoned for an ambulance, but already it seemed an age. Clement, his fingers clasped around the stricken woman's wrist, kept one eye on his watch.

'Bedroom,' Angela suddenly said, about a minute later.

Trudy, more because she couldn't bear to continue to watch the woman's shallow breathing, dreadfully anticipating the moment when it might stop altogether, got to her feet and went back upstairs.

It was easy to tell which of the two bedrooms belonged to Janet by simply checking the contents of the wardrobe. Then, unknowingly mimicking the actions of Angela Baines less than ten minutes ago, Trudy set about searching Janet's wardrobe, then her chest of drawers, finding nothing that she wouldn't expect in a young woman's bedroom.

Would she really find the diary? And if she did … how had Janet come by it unless she had taken it from David Finch's dead body? Of course, there might be another explanation, but at the very least, it certainly put Janet Baines firmly mixed up in things! And what must her poor mother have thought when she'd found it? Surely she too, must have wondered if her daughter was a murderess?

But so far there was no sign of the incriminating book. Perhaps Janet kept it with her? It wasn't until she sat down at the vanity table and met her own troubled reflection in the oval mirror, that she noticed the fancy wooden box.

It had been placed hastily back onto the lace cloth runner where it must habitually have been kept, making the delicate material scrunch up untidily on itself. Since the rest of the table had been laid out very neatly and with precision – brushes, scent bottles and a little dish of potpourri – it caught her eye as being incongruous.

Trudy picked it up to examine it further and felt something push unexpectedly against her hand, almost dropping it in surprise.

She didn't know it then, but Angela, in her haste, had failed to push the hidden drawer firmly enough back for it to catch on its locking mechanism. All that Trudy knew was that the bottom segment of the box had jerked open and was now revealing a hidden compartment.

She opened the drawer out, her eyes widening and her breath catching, as she saw the dark, leather-bound book inside. As she reached to retrieve it, the sudden sound of a siren, not far away, had her head shooting up. She stood and looked out of the window, seeing a blue flashing light appear at the far end of the village.

The ambulance!

Clutching the book in her hand she ran back down the stairs and out into the garden to the gate, waiting to guide the medical personnel to the kitchen.

Clement was relieved to see the attendants deal quickly with the woman. Although he was no longer able to practise medicine, he had been able to impress on the ambulance team the urgency of the situation, and his calm and knowledgeable précis of her suspected injuries were accepted with respect and relief. Probably both of them knew him by sight, for neither one questioned him, but simply accepted his orders with quiet efficiency.

As they watched the ambulance depart in a rush of speed and noise – not going unnoticed by Angela's immediate neighbours – Trudy finally felt able to turn her attention to the journal in her hands.

'I think I might have found David Finch's journal,' she said. 'We'll have to read it quickly, before DI Jennings arrives and takes over.'

Clement needed no second bidding and right there, in the doorway of the house, they began to read.

It was a detailed and careful account of everyone that David had talked to after Iris's death, and his own thoughts and feelings, and independent researches, plus his thoughts on Iris and one particular piece of jewellery. All of which lead to his growing conviction that he knew who it was who must have murdered Iris, and culminated in the final sentence of the lined notepad.

Although I don't want to believe it, it must have been RD

'RD,' Trudy breathed. 'Ronnie Dewberry. *His best friend.*' Trudy suddenly clutched Clement's arm and looked at him with wide, frightened eyes.

'*Janet!*' she wailed. 'Janet must be with him now! *We've got to find her!* You said once before you were worried she might be in danger as well, and I think you were right.' Suddenly all her suspicions about the girl being the killer fled, and instead she saw her only as a potential third victim.

Clement agreed they had no choice but to take quick action, and they both ran pell-mell to his Rover, but his mind was racing even faster than his legs. It wasn't until they were racing towards the Dewberry farm that Trudy realised that she still had the journal clutched to her chest, and that soon DI Jennings would be arriving at the house, expecting her to be there to give him her report!

But surely he'd realise why they hadn't been able to wait for him?

Even now she felt herself watching the speedometer, willing the car to go faster.

Chapter 32

Duncan Gillingham had almost been caught napping as he'd sat in his car parked a long way down the road from the coroner's Rover. He'd been absently reading a rival Sunday newspaper when he'd glanced up, and had seen Trudy and the old vulture actually running down the road, and all but throwing themselves into the car.

His own heart racing, he'd fumbled with the ignition key and had raced away to try and catch up with them. Hell, they were driving fast! Luckily, it was only a small village and he'd just been in time to see them turn off onto the no-through road that led to the Dewberry farm.

His mouth went dry. Why were they going back there, to the scene of the suicide? And what on earth had happened to make them move with such urgent speed? His heart racing in triumphant anticipation, he made the same turn-off and put his foot down. Whatever was going on, he sure as hell didn't want to miss it!

Janet heard the car enter the cobbled courtyard and frowned. She hadn't hurried getting the picnic assembled, lingering in the kitchen and talking with Ronnie, and even getting together a Thermos of tea, but now she wished she hadn't dallied. Whoever was out there, she didn't want them interrupting things *now*.

'Is that your dad?' she asked peevishly, peering over the sink and out of the window.

'Doesn't sound like Dad's car,' Ronnie said nervously. 'And I think he's out on the farm anyway.' So saying, he walked to the window and pulled a rather dirty curtain further out of the way. He saw the familiar, white-haired figure of the coroner stepping out of his car, and the pretty girl who always seemed to be with him, just opening the passenger door.

Then movement further away caught his eye and he saw another car pulling to a stop and parking up on the edge of the farm track about two hundred yards back. He swore softly under his breath and felt his heartbeat kick up a notch.

Seeing his tension, Janet very carefully picked up a small but sharp-bladed kitchen knife and carefully and slowly moved her hand down so that it rested, all-but-hidden, against the fullness of her skirt.

'What's wrong?' she asked casually.

'It's that coroner again. The one who's handling David's case,' Ronnie growled.

Janet's lips firmed into a thin line. 'What's he doing here?' she asked, almost accusingly.

Ronnie shot her a puzzled, slightly angry look. 'How should I know? I suppose I'd better go and see what he wants.'

Janet nodded and quickly followed.

Trudy and Clement were walking towards the farmhouse when the door opened and Ronnie stepped out. Trudy almost wilted with relief when she saw Janet appear right behind him.

'She's all right!' she murmured to Clement, who merely nodded. His eyes, calm but alert, went from the lovely young girl to the tense young man beside her.

'Hello there,' Clement said calmly. 'We were hoping to find

you here, Janet,' he added amiably. With all the tension he could sense in the air, he wanted to try and calm things down a bit.

'Me?' Janet said, moving just a little closer to Ronnie, careful to keep the knife in her hand hidden. 'Why?'

'I'm afraid we have some bad news,' Clement began. 'We called in at your house after church and found your mother in her kitchen.'

Janet blinked. 'I don't quite see …' She trailed off, turning to look at Trudy, then back to the older man, her eyes questing.

'It seems she might have taken a fall,' Clement clarified, not actually lying, but by no means convinced that he was telling the truth either. 'She's hurt her head. I'm afraid her injury might be quite serious.'

'Oh no!' It was, surprisingly, Ronnie who reacted first. 'Janet!' He looked at her, seemingly genuinely appalled. 'I'll drive you to the hospital. Has she been taken to the Radcliffe Infirmary?' he shot at Clement.

Trudy shifted slightly on her feet beside her mentor, aware that she was beginning to get a very strange feeling. Things weren't happening as she thought they would. She'd come here, half-expecting something really bad to have happened. Maybe to find that Janet, too, had been attacked, or to find Ronnie in the act of hurting her? But as she looked at the two figures in front of her, she wasn't so sure anymore. Why wasn't Janet more concerned about her mother? She was acting as if she'd almost forgotten her. Instead she seemed … excited? Wary? She couldn't quite tell. But there was definitely something off about the whole atmosphere that she couldn't quite pin down; something skewed somehow.

She sensed danger, yes. But she couldn't quite understand *what* that danger was, or the source of it. Trudy glanced sideways at Clement, wondering if it was just her and could see that he too was very tense and alert.

In her chest, she felt her heart pounding.

'Yes, she'll be in the Radcliffe. If you like, Miss Baines, I can drive you,' Clement answered Ronnie's question, but kept his eyes on Janet. Trudy liked the way he sounded so normal and everyday, and she hoped he'd succeed in separating the two of them. She'd feel a lot better once they were away from this place.

Janet though, seemed in no hurry to move. Instead she looked slowly from Trudy to Clement and then at Ronnie in a calculating way that now made everyone openly uneasy.

Ronnie, perhaps last of all, also felt the unnaturalness of the situation and he took a small step away from Janet, and half-turned to look at her more closely. 'What's wrong?' he asked helplessly.

Janet gave a bleak smile. 'Wrong? What could possibly be wrong?' she asked tightly. 'Apart from the fact that you murdered my best friend, you mean? And your own, apparently?'

Ronnie went white. He took another couple of awkward steps away and gaped at her. 'What? What are you talking about?' he asked, his voice half aghast squeak and half fearful whisper.

'Don't bother denying it,' Janet said flatly, almost angrily, taking comfort from the feel of the knife handle in her hand. 'I found his diary.'

'Diary? Whose … You mean *David's*?' Ronnie shot a quick look – seeking confirmation – at Clement, who met his gaze with a level one of his own.

Ronnie felt himself begin to nod vaguely, even as his mind scurried about, trying to seek traction. So his worst nightmare was coming true after all. To his surprise it was almost a relief. For so long now he'd lived with the dread of it all coming out and fearing what would happen then. But now that it had, curiously, instead of feeling even more terrified, he felt instead as if someone had lifted off a massive, heavy, suffocating weight that had been smothering him.

'I did start to wonder,' he said wearily. 'When you first asked me about it …' He turned to look at Clement, but then turned to Janet again. 'You found it?'

'I did,' Janet said with immense satisfaction. Of them all – the astute coroner, his pretty assistant, her mother, all the villagers and even all the cops working on Iris's case, not to forget Ronnie … her Ronnie … *she* had been the only one clever enough to make the discovery. It gave her a much-needed confidence boost. 'He hid it in his favourite hiding place when we were kids,' she said simply.

Ronnie blinked, then nodded with a bleak smile of acceptance. 'Under the old pavilion? I never did like playing that game much,' he added sadly.

'I know, that's probably why you never thought of it,' Janet said. If he had, he could have found the diary himself and destroyed the evidence against him. And she couldn't help, even now, almost wishing that he had.

She was watching him closely now, like a cat at a mouse-hole, and he began to feel a coldness creep up his spine.

'Why are you looking at me like that?' he demanded.

'Because I read it,' Janet said, her voice turning hard. 'David found out. About Iris.'

'What do you mean? What about Iris?' Ronnie asked, his mouth going dry. 'What did he say?'

'Oh, he was very diligent,' Janet said almost mockingly. 'He found out all about what went on at Mortimer Crowley's parties, for instance. That must have turned his stomach.'

Ronnie shook his head, looking like a bewildered puppy. Clearly, whatever he'd expected her to say, it hadn't been that. 'What?'

'Iris told me about it,' Janet said indifferently, shrugging one shoulder. 'Oh, not right away. She knew I'd be shocked and try and talk her out of going. But when she started to buy herself nice things, and saw me noticing …' Janet sighed. 'She told me about the men who paid her to … You know …'

Ronnie swallowed hard. Absurdly he felt himself flushing red with embarrassment. 'Oh,' he mumbled. 'I never knew … I mean, I knew Iris … but not …'

'Oh yes, I daresay you knew Iris all right,' Janet said, and there was no denying the bitterness in her voice now. 'I always thought that *you*, at least, were different,' she swept on, glaring at him. 'But you weren't, were you? You were just like all the others,' she went on, her voice rising and getting louder and louder as she finally lost control. 'Panting after her, promising her the world, no doubt. Just like all the silly old duffers in the village, and Mortimer's perverted London friends, and … oh, how could you?' she all but wailed.

'But I didn't!' Ronnie said, finally prodded out of his shock and into anger of his own. 'I never liked Iris, I told David so! She was no good, anyone could see that, and I tried like hell to get him to see that! We almost fell out about her – you *know* all this.'

'I know that's what you pretended,' Janet spat bitterly. 'I know that's what you'd have us believe. But David found out!'

She moved a few steps forward towards him, and that's when Trudy spotted that she was holding something in her right hand, keeping it hidden by the side of her leg, in the folds of her skirt.

What is it? She shot a quick glance at Clement, caught his eye, then looked significantly at Janet, and surreptitiously moved her hand down to her own leg, matching Janet's stance, and tapped her leg significantly. The coroner caught on quickly, of course, and his eyes narrowed as he too, realised that Janet was probably carrying a weapon of some sort.

Clement stiffened unhappily. Things, in spite of all his attempts to keep control of them, were beginning to get dangerously out of hand.

'Found out what? What did David find out?' Ronnie challenged rashly, then went abruptly white as he realised that he shouldn't have asked that question again. After all, there might still be the slightest chance that they didn't know it all … But it had been more than he could bear to have Janet, whom he'd always liked and secretly coveted for himself, looking at him and accusing him of preferring Iris, *Iris* of all people, over her.

'About Iris's sneaky little trips here, for a start,' Janet snarled, lifting her chin to indicate their surroundings. 'And you, his best friend! The poor boy must have known all about the rumours flying around about Iris and her ways with men, but he'd have ignored them, wouldn't he? Believing Iris when she insisted that she was innocent, and it was just the jealous, spiteful gossip of the village women. Maybe in his heart he knew it wasn't true,' Janet paused to take a much-needed breath. 'And maybe he found excuses for her – that Iris needed money and power and all the things he couldn't give her. But for her to betray him with *you*, you of all people …' Janet's was almost shouting now. There were tears in her eyes, and rage and pain on her face, twisting it into an almost ugly mask. 'Is that why you killed him? Did he confront you on that last day of his life? Accuse you?'

Ronnie began to back away under the attack, shaking his head at the barrage of questions.

'What? No, I didn't kill David! I didn't kill Iris! Why are you saying all this?'

'Because David wrote it all down,' Janet said, her shoulders suddenly slumping, her voice dropping back to its normal level as the emotion seeped out of her, leaving her quiet and calm and grimly accepting.

Again Ronnie felt himself sway as fear rolled over him in great waves. 'What? What did he write exactly?' he whispered, not wanting to hear it, but knowing that he couldn't go on a moment longer without it being said.

Janet looked at him now almost with pity. 'He said you killed her. And then he hung himself in your barn. Except he didn't, did he? You killed him. Unless you really did break his heart, and he killed himself after all?'

Trudy and Clement waited to hear what Ronnie would say next.

But Ronnie seemed incapable of saying anything. Instead he was staring at her as if one of them must have gone mad.

To both Trudy and Clement, who'd been watching and listening, hardly daring to breathe, let alone move, lest they make the situation even worse and more dangerous, it seemed as if Ronnie just froze. His jaw dropped and his face went slack. His eyes widened in total surprise. He looked as if he'd just been pole-axed.

'What?' Ronnie finally managed to whisper. *'Are you saying David wrote down that I killed Iris?'*

Something of his astonishment obviously reached Janet for now she stopped advancing towards him and stopped at stared at him instead, her head cocked just a little to one side. 'Why are you looking so surprised?' she asked, sounding half accusing and half genuinely puzzled. 'He was your friend; you knew how clever he was. Did you really think he wouldn't figure it all out? That you killed her?'

'But I *didn't,*' Ronnie denied once more.

It was then that his father appeared around the corner of the house, a shotgun in his hand.

Chapter 33

'What's going on?' Ray Dewberry asked, his eyes travelling from his son to Janet, to the coroner and then back to his son again. He strolled up to them, the shotgun broken casually across the crook of one arm. 'I could hear raised voices all the way from the cowshed.'

At the sight of the older Dewberry, Trudy felt herself relax a little.

Beside her, Clement did not.

Instead he took a long, slow, breath, then moved one foot a little to the left, to make his balance more perfect. He clenched and unclenched his hands slowly, flexing his fingers and unutterably relieved to feel that neither of his hands were shaking.

He wasn't a religious man, but in that moment he nevertheless offered up a lightning-quick prayer, amounting to little more than an appeal, really, that everything would be all right.

He wasn't sure, but he thought he might die very soon.

'Dad, it's all right, it's nothing,' Ronnie said quickly, the first of them to speak.

His father looked at him, his bluff, ruddy, handsome face, frowning slightly. 'What's she doing here?' he asked mildly, nodding at Janet.

'We were going on a picnic,' Ronnie said, feeling somehow very foolish.

Ray Dewberry smiled. 'That sounds nice. A good-looking lad and pretty lass like Janet – that's just the sort of thing you both *ought* to be doing. Off you go then, enjoy yourselves.'

Clement went more than a little cold. His mind instantly started calculating the pros and cons. On the one hand, getting Janet and Ronnie out of the equation limited the potential number of victims. On the other hand, it heightened the risk to Trudy, and himself, significantly. He didn't mind so much on his own account – he was virtually an old man, and bloody Parkinson's would soon start to erode his quality of life anyway.

But Trudy was so young …

Ronnie hesitated visibly. 'Dad, I don't think …' he began to say, but didn't get the chance to finish.

'Mr Dewberry,' Janet said. 'There's something—'

'Janet, be quiet,' Ronnie said harshly, urgently.

Janet, astonished, just gaped at him. 'I will not!' she eventually huffed. 'Just who do you think *you* are to be telling *me* what to do? Besides, he'll have to know sooner or later. Shall you tell him, or will I?' she added aggressively.

Clement felt himself begin to sweat. He had to do something before it was too late. 'Janet, I think we should drive you to the hospital to see your mother,' he said quietly but firmly, glad to hear that his voice sounded calm and casual.

As he spoke, he tested his balance again. With his feet now planted firmly, it would give him the best chance of good propulsion if he had to suddenly spring forward …

Trudy looked at Ronnie, then at Clement, then at Ray, not sure what was going on. She had a slightly giddy feeling, as if she was looking down a kaleidoscope that kept twisting and turning slightly, altering reality around her. What the hell was going on here? What was she missing?

'Mother can wait,' Janet said with a shocking ruthlessness that

217

momentarily distracted them all. 'This can't. Aren't you working for the police?' she suddenly asked Clement. 'Can't you arrest him?'

'No,' Clement said. 'I'm not a police officer and I can't arrest anyone.'

Trudy, though, *was* a police officer and she *could* arrest Ronnie Dewberry anytime she chose. She took a half-step forward and felt Clement's hand curl around her wrist in a strong, almost punishing grip. Surprised, she halted at once, instinctively trusting his judgement. But much as she respected her mentor, it wouldn't stop her from doing her duty when the time came. For now, however, she was willing to follow his lead and wait for the right time.

'What are you talking about, young Janet?' Ray asked, scowling slightly at her. 'What's all this talk about arresting people?'

Clement said, 'Janet, I think …'

Janet, at the same moment, said loudly, 'I've found David's diary. He knew who killed Iris. He said so.' Her chin came up defiantly.

Ray Dewberry nodded slowly. 'Is that so?' he said quietly, and looked sadly at his son.

'Yes, and he said it was Ronnie!' Janet flashed at him.

Clement saw Ray Dewberry reach for the barrels of his shotgun and snap it back into place, arming the weapon and making it lethally viable once more. 'Did he now?' he said ominously.

Ronnie said nervously, 'Dad …'

Seeing the gun begin to turn in Janet's direction, Clement knew he had to act, and act fast. 'Actually, his diary *doesn't* say anything of the kind,' he said. His voice, mild and quiet though it was, had all the effect of a bomb going off.

'What? Yes it does,' Janet contradicted angrily.

'But it does say that,' Trudy said at the same time.

'I didn't!' Ronnie's voice added to the hub-bub simultaneously. All three turned to look at the coroner.

'No, it said that RD killed Iris,' Clement corrected them. He took a step forward and saw the shotgun begin to swing ominously his way.

As he did so, Trudy couldn't help but let out a soft moan of frustration at her own stupidity as comprehension suddenly hit her with all the stunning force of a runaway locomotive. 'Oh no! We assumed RD meant Ronnie Dewberry,' she said mournfully – or at least, all of them had except Dr Ryder.

'And yet there's more than one RD in this case,' Clement confirmed softly. 'Isn't there, Mr Dewberry?' he said, meeting Ray Dewberry's mild grey eyes. He forced himself to ignore the double-barrelled shotgun that was now levelled right at his midriff, his mind buzzing like sherbet.

Could he rely on Ronnie to shelter Janet if any shooting started? He thought so. He could at least be fairly certain that the farmer wouldn't shoot his own son … would he? Clement could step in front of Trudy at any time if he thought the killer of Iris and David was going to shoot her – but that was a double-barrelled gun. One blast would kill him … but the second blast could still be used to kill her.

Damn it, why hadn't they taken the time to update DI Jennings before rushing off? At least then he could be sure that help was on the way … He judged the distance between himself and the farmer and knew it was too far. Way too far …

Ray Dewberry sighed heavily.

Ronnie Dewberry closed his eyes and gave a soft sort of moan.

Janet, the last of them all to catch on, took a few more moments before she looked at Ronnie's father and then said, appalled, '*You? It was you who killed Iris!*'

Duncan Gillingham could not believe his luck. After leaving his car back on the track, he'd crept down the lane, bent double at the bottom of the dry ditch that ran beside the hedgerow bordering the farm track to cover his approach. He had taken up position by the entrance to the yard, just behind the low stone wall that circumnavigated the farmhouse.

He'd been in time to hear almost all of what the four of them had had to say, and he'd been gleefully scribbling it all down in his fast and accurate shorthand in his trusty notebook. Janet Baines's quotes alone had been pure solid gold!

He could almost see tomorrow's headlines, blazoned across the front page, his own by-line prominently displayed; a first-hand, eyewitness story of a young woman confronting the killer of her friend. This was his ticket to play with the big boys and no mistake! He could see almost all the big daily tabloids squabbling with themselves to get in on his scoop. And a job offer couldn't be far behind, right?

So when Ronnie Dewberry's father had turned up, he could have screamed in pure frustration, sensing that the old man would act like a wet blanket, putting paid to Janet's star turn.

And then, just like that, in no more time than it took to snap your fingers – or so it had seemed – it had all gone from pure gold, to something far, far darker. And much, much, scarier.

Moving inch by inch, desperate not to make the slightest little sound that might betray his presence, he moved forward on his knees and, mouth dry and heart pounding in his chest, risked lifting his head high enough to peek over the low stone wall.

He saw the middle-aged farmer at once, his sandy hair shining in the hot May sunshine, standing in the middle of his courtyard, a shotgun pointing straight at the old vulture. And right beside him, looking pale and tense and also right in the line of fire, was Trudy Loveday.

Duncan felt his heart give a massive lurch.

Bloody hell. Was it really true? *Had* David Finch written in his diary that RD had killed Iris Carmody? And was it true that it was *Ray* Dewberry, not his son Ronnie that he'd been referring to? And if so, would he really fire that damned gun? At that short range, the old vulture would be dead for sure. And there were two barrels to that gun.

Who would be next?

Chapter 34

Ray Dewberry looked at Clement with such a totally blank gaze that it sent chills up Trudy's spine. She'd have felt better if he'd begun ranting and raving, or crying, or trying to explain and excuse himself. Anything would be better than that blank nothingness.

'Dad, don't,' Ronnie repeated, but he sounded helpless, ineffectual.

Clement, in a bid to keep Ray Dewberry's focus firmly on himself, and not on either Janet or Trudy, stepped casually to his right, a couple of paces away from his young friend, widening the distance between them. He suspected the farmer wouldn't like it if he moved forward, trying to get closer to him, but at least he could make it harder for the man to shoot both himself and Trudy in quick succession. It might give her some sort of a chance …

'Did you know what your father had done, Ronnie?' he asked casually. 'Or did you only suspect it?'

Janet blinked at this new idea, but (rather belatedly) now kept wisely silent. She had come here to confront Ronnie, safe in the knowledge that the whole village knew she was with him, thus making it impossible for him to do anything to her unless he was willing to hang for it. But even as she'd carried out her plan, she had never really, deep inside, believed that Ronnie *was* a killer. Instead, hadn't she, deep in her heart, foolishly, stubbornly hoped that he'd be able to somehow explain away all her fears, and David Finch's naming of him in his diary? But she had never, even in her wildest imaginings, thought that he might have been covering up for his own father! Now she turned wide, wondering eyes on him. She had fought for her own identity against the cloying demands of her mother for so long, that it had never occurred to her that the man she'd always wanted for herself might also have such a threatening and damaging relationship with *his* only parent.

Ronnie shrugged helplessly. 'I wasn't sure. I thought … When Iris turned up dead … I knew … But then there were so many other men … I hoped … I mean, my *own father*… I just couldn't believe …' He trailed off into silence.

Although his answer had been all but incoherent, Trudy had followed it easily. 'You knew that your dad was another of Iris's … what shall we call them? Admirers? Victims? But you told yourself that since there were so many men in Iris's life, it could have been one of them that snapped and killed her?' she said gently.

'Yeah,' Ronnie admitted, his voice barely a mumble.

'How long had Iris been … seeing … your dad?' Trudy asked, not sure what good it would do to ask so many questions now, but thinking that the more she could keep them all talking the more time it would give her to think what to do.

'Months,' Ronnie said bitterly. 'Bloody months. She was bleeding him dry, always wanting this, asking money to buy that …'

'Shut up boy,' Ray Dewberry interrupted him, but without heat. His voice sounded as flat and expressionless as the look on his face.

'She was even nagging him to sell off some land,' Ronnie said, clearly not about to shut up at all. He'd gone from a mumbling ineffectual young lad to fired-up and almost fizzing with emotion in less than a blink of an eye. Trudy could only guess how tense and wound up he'd been the last few weeks, but now was hardly the time for him to let it all explode. They needed to calm things down, not make them even more fraught!

'Land! That's the one thing a good farmer will never let go,' Ronnie continued angrily, disgust deepening the tone of his voice now. 'But she kept on and on at him, pleading, whining, wheedling. You think I didn't know?' Ronnie shot his father a swift, venomous look. 'But I heard her, up in your room, when you thought I had gone out to the pub. "We could go to the Caribbean, Ray-Ray,"' Ronnie said, parodying a girl's sweet voice. 'It made me sick. "Wouldn't you like to see Monte Carlo, Ray-Ray? Think of it, walking into the casino and just placing one bet on the roulette wheel. Wouldn't it be fabulous?" Oh yes, I heard her,' Ronnie snarled. 'And after having her in your bed – in *Mum's* bed – you were really thinking of doing it too, weren't you?' he all but shouted now. 'Selling off an acre or two here, an acre or two there. So you could spend it on that piece of—'

'I said shut up boy,' Ray said again. Oddly enough, he said it in exactly the same tone of voice as he'd said it before. His voice hadn't risen, it hadn't got angry, or threatening. It was just the same, flat, rather tired demand for him to be silent.

Clement didn't like it. He didn't like it all.

He took another step, placing him further still away from Trudy.

Then he saw Trudy notice what it was that he was doing. Saw too the flash of anger and accusation cross her face as she realised why he was doing it. Then he saw it change to one of quiet resolution, and he felt, for the first time, truly and utterly terrified. And to his horror, he saw her take a few steps of her own – in the opposite direction. Placing them even further apart – but in a forward direction, closing the space between them and the farmer. Putting her first place in the line of fire.

He wanted to shout at her to stop it. But he knew that he couldn't – he didn't dare. He must do nothing to draw attention to her. Not when Ray Dewberry was standing there, quiet and calm, watching them all thoughtfully, the shotgun held with comfortable ease in his hand. As a farmer, he'd probably spent years using that gun and was very familiar with it …

Behind the wall, Duncan Gillingham too watched in growing horror. What the hell was Trudy thinking off? Surely she didn't think she could take on an armed man? Was she crazy? She'd get herself killed!

And he didn't want her to get killed. He couldn't just crouch here, like a coward, whilst she was killed.

But what could he do, damn it? *What could he do?*

'Do you understand now why I really and truly did hate Iris?' Ronnie said, turning to looking at Janet. 'She had her claws into my best friend and into my father. She was trying to cheat me out of my inheritance, and …' He faltered to a stop, then took a deep breath. 'At one point, I even wondered if I might hang, like David did. If the police found out that I hated her and had a motive for killing her, I thought they might arrest me. And if I was found guilty …'

'Enough!' Ray said, turning to his son, his face finally twisting into a grimacing, angry mask. 'You think I didn't hate her too, boy?' he shouted. 'You think I didn't hate *myself* for wanting her? Needing her?'

Everyone froze. Trudy a few steps forward, Duncan behind the wall, Janet and Ronnie facing off to each other, and Clement, still balancing on the balls of his feet and praying his limbs didn't get an attack of the jitters now.

'You think I didn't know what a fool I was?' Ray continued, his voice still loud, but at least not shouting anymore. 'You think I didn't want to be free of her? But she was like bloody bindweed, twining around me, tightening, tightening, with her beautiful face and her beautiful body, making me go out of my mind …'

He went silent and shook his head.

'And so you killed her,' Janet whispered, tears coming into her eyes. 'But why did you leave her tied to the maypole like that?'

Ray shrugged. 'What else was I supposed to do with her?' he asked harshly. 'I found out, you see, about those disgusting parties at that London parasite's place. I knew some other men in the village had been bragging about having her too, but I always thought that was lies. Just men bragging, like they do. Iris swore I was the only one. But then, one night, when I was coming back from the fields, I saw two fancy cars parked up in the lane and some men laughing and joking about how they were going to enjoy the party that night. And what Iris had promised to do for them ...'

Ray shook his head. 'It turned my stomach. I saw myself then, as I knew she really saw me – as just one more gullible, middle-aged, pathetic man with money. Money that she wanted to get off me. She never cared tuppence for me. Probably even laughed about me, as those men were now laughing about her. I couldn't sleep for thinking of it. Couldn't eat. It drove me mad. And still I *wanted* her – that was the bloody rub of it! The next day, when I saw her I thought that I'd feel disgusted, but I didn't. I just wanted her all the more ... And you were right boy; I had approached a land agent about selling off some land. And I knew I would too, if I couldn't get myself free. But I knew I'd never be free of her. Not as long as she lived, anyway.'

For a moment nobody spoke. Nobody knew what to say. But it didn't matter, because Ray Dewberry had only paused to take a breath. 'So I decided to kill her. That evening, before May Day, I wrote her a note asking her to dress up in her May Queen outfit, just for me, and meet me by the oak tree on the green just before it started to get light. I promised her a present – something that sparkled, that she could wear that day. Something special. I knew she wouldn't be able to resist *that*.' His lips twisted bitterly. 'And she didn't. She came, looking as lovely and fresh as something out of a painting ... and inside, she was as black and rotten as flyblown fruit.' He spat on the ground.

'I didn't wait. I didn't even let her say anything – I was scared she'd be able to talk me around if I did. I just put my hands around her throat and squeezed. She looked so surprised. And then scared. She probably fought and kicked and things, but I didn't notice. There was this loud buzzing sound in my head … And then she started to turn this funny colour and her eyes bulged and she began to look ugly. I couldn't take that, my beautiful Iris looking anything less than lovely, so I closed my eyes so that I couldn't see it happening. I didn't open them for a long time.'

Ray sighed softly.

'And when I did, she was hanging there in my hands, limp as a rag doll. The first blackbirds were beginning to sing, and the horizon was beginning to glow, and I knew I hadn't got much time before the farm hands were up and about. Where could I take her? What could I do?'

He paused, looking from one of them to the other, as if expecting them to tell him. But of course, none of them could.

He shook his head and shrugged. 'Then I saw the maypole, all set up for the dancing later on, with pretty ribbons and such. And I thought … well, why not? She'd always wanted to be Queen of the May, after all, making such a fuss of it, pleased as punch and preening about it, looking forward to making all her subjects bow before her,' he choked bitterly. 'So why not let her have her last wish? So I took her to the maypole and bound her to it with the ribbons. Only she didn't look so beautiful then, did she? All that golden perfection …'

Again, for a moment, there was utter silence.

Janet and Ronnie stared at him, appalled.

Aware of their distress, Ray scowled at them and shook his head. 'What? What else could I have done?' he demanded harshly.

'And David?' Ronnie finally plucked up the nerve to say. 'Did you kill David too?'

At this, Ray's sighed heavily. 'I had to do that,' he admitted grimly. 'I didn't want to!' he added, sounding almost indignant now. 'But he called me one night, from the phone box in the village. I wish now I'd never had the phone line put in to the old place,' he added, giving a nod towards the farmhouse. 'Not that it would have mattered, in the end, I suppose,' he said thoughtfully. 'He'd have just come in person, wouldn't he?' He cocked his head a little to one side, as if actually considering the utterly irrelevant question.

It was only then that Trudy began to wonder if Ray Dewberry was actually sane.

Clement risked a quick glance around to see if there was something lying around that he could use as a weapon. This was a farmyard, wasn't it? Where were all the sharp-pronged things – rakes, plough blades, pitchforks, *anything*…

'He said on the phone that he needed to speak to me, alone. He was so insistent that Ronnie not be there, that I knew … I just knew …' For a moment Ray shook his head. 'I didn't know how he knew about me and Iris, I just knew that he did. So I said I'd meet him at the barn the next day.'

'How did you do it?' Ronnie asked, his voice tight with pain. Although he knew, late at night and lying in his bed, that his father had killed Iris, he'd never, ever, let himself even contemplate that he had also killed David. David, he'd convinced himself, had killed himself for love of Iris. But now he could no longer hold on to even that comforting fantasy.

'I crushed up some of your mum's old pills and melted them in boiling water. Then I put some whisky in that old hip flask of your granddad's. Took it with me when I went to the barn. It was funny,' Ray said softly, his face softening as he remembered back to that evening. 'He came in and found me sitting on a bale of hay. I nodded at him, friendly-like, and took out the hip flask and pretended to drink from it. And he just asked me flat out if I was seeing his Iris.'

Ray grunted a soft laugh. '*His* Iris. The silly little pup. He was nothing more to her than a cat's paw! I wanted to rant at him

227

then and there, tell him that she'd been *mine*, damn it! *Mine*. But of course, I didn't. Instead I just looked at him, and said, "Bloody hell boy, that's a bit of an accusation," and I pretended to take another swig. Then I held out the flask to him and said, "If we're gonna have that sort of a talk, we should do it proper. Have a belt – it's the best whisky money can buy." And he took it.'

Ray again gave a soft laugh. 'I wasn't sure if he would or not. If he hadn't, I'd have just had to do it the hard way … But he took a sip, and then I nodded at the bale of hay I'd set up by mine and told him to take a pew.'

Trudy could almost picture the scene. The young man, desperate to learn the truth, but still so naïve and trusting and so unaware of the sheer ferocity and danger that could lurk in the hearts of men such as Ray Dewberry. Had he secretly not really been able to believe that a man he'd known all his life – his best friend's father, for Pete's sake – had killed the girl he loved? Had he gone to that barn more than half-hoping, maybe even half-expecting, that Ray Dewberry would be able to convince him that he hadn't?

'He told me that he'd recognised a necklace that Iris had begun to wear as one belonging to my wife,' Ray went on.

'What? You gave her Mum's jewellery?' Ronnie squawked, but his father merely ignored him, too deep in his memories, probably, to have even heard him.

'O'course, I denied it,' Ray said, almost placidly. 'Said necklaces sometimes looked alike. I asked him for the flask back, pretended to take another sip, all casual-like, then handed it back to him. Told him that he was letting his imagination run wild. He sort of nodded, like, as if he took my point, then had another swallow and said that wasn't all. Iris had been seen by several people in the village walking this way.'

Ray glanced up and around the fields. 'I told him so what? The girl was free to take a walk in the countryside, wasn't she? Then I crooked my finger, and he passed the flask back. By now

I could see he was beginning to look a bit tired. I took another pass at the flask, then handed it back. He said Iris had teased him about me – saying I was the handsomest man in the village. He was beginning to slur his words now. I laughed, and said I was flattered, but she was just trying to get his goat, and make him jealous. "Young girls are like that," I said to him. "Don't you know that, boy? Courting's a bit of a game see. Don't mean nothing." And so it went on. Chatting, all friendly like, both of us drinking from the flask – well, me just pretending, like. And then, when his head began to actually nod, I just, quietly like, got the rope that I'd already tied off to the plough and with noose already made and everything, slipped it over his head and … hauled him up.'

Ronnie made a gagging sound, turned away and was sick on the cobbles.

His father ignored him. 'It didn't take long – he wasn't really awake or aware of much of what was going on, which I was glad about. Then I set it all up to look like he'd done it himself – the ladder and what-not, then came home. Washed out the flask, had a bath, changed my clothes and put them in the tub to soak, and went to bed. What else could I do?' he appealed, looking at his white-faced son, who was now wiping his mouth with the back of his hand, then moving on to look at Janet, who couldn't meet his gaze.

'I didn't *want* to kill the boy, you understand?' he said, sounding aggrieved now, and looking wildly from Trudy to Clement and back again. 'Known him ever since he was a nipper, didn't I? He was a nice enough lad, but Iris had got her hooks into him too and … well, I knew he wouldn't stop digging until he had proof. The son of a copper … What else could I do?'

He looked at Trudy for approbation or some form of acknowledgement, but she was now literally speechless.

'Did you just attack my mother too?' Janet asked, her voice cracking a little as she bit back a sob.

The farmer sighed and shrugged. 'Now that were just rotten

luck,' he said resentfully. 'I was looking for the lad's journal, see. It was all over the village that he kept one. I knew the Finches and the coppers didn't have it, or we'd'a heard of it long since. So I knew that the lad must'a hid it for safekeeping before he came to see me.' He paused and considered the thought carefully, then nodded. 'As a bit of a safeguard, like. He was always smart, that David,' he added regretfully.

'I've been looking everywhere for it, I can tell you!' he grunted. 'The village hall, the church, even the bloody phone box. I've been in a right state! I even searched the Carmody house from top to bottom, when they were out at the undertakers, although it was hardly likely to be there, was it? And then, finally, I thought of you.' He nodded at Janet. 'You were Iris's best friend after all, and one of the few who must'a been mourning Iris, like. P'rhaps he gave it to you, asking you to keep it safe, like. I didn't know if you'd read it or not, and if you had, why you hadn't turned it over to the cops.' So saying, he looked at his son then back at Janet with an awful, knowing smile. He shrugged, 'Anyways, it was worth trying, so, I went to search your house this morning, thinking you were still at church.'

Trudy shook her head sadly. How many times had she told people – especially in small villages, to start locking their doors? But nobody hardly ever did. He'd probably just walked right in through the back door without any trouble at all.

'But your mum must'a heard me. Next thing I knew, she were coming down the stairs, calling out for you, like. I just had time to hide behind the door and when she came past me, I hit her on the head with a saucepan. She never saw me though, so I never had to hit her again. And she were still breathing when I left,' he added, watching Janet as if expecting her to thank him for his consideration.

Abruptly, he turned to Clement. 'You! Stop moving about. You think I don't know what you're at? But it's no use,' Ray said bitterly. 'The thing's got to be done. We both know that – these others, they're all youngsters, they know nothing about what's what,' he said tiredly. 'But you and me – we know what the world's like. You were in the war …'

He started to raise the shotgun, sighting it on Clement. 'No point drawing it out. Might as well get it over with, quick-like. Nobody will understand, that's the shame of it,' he added, almost as an afterthought. 'Nobody will ever understand that this is all Iris's fault.'

'You can't kill all of us,' Clement shouted, but without much hope. There was nothing in Ray Dewberry's eyes but matter-of-fact intent.

'No, not Ronnie,' Ray agreed. 'But he'll help me. He's a good boy. We'll bury your bodies up in the sedges by Trigger Pond, I reckon …'

'No Dad, I won't,' Ronnie shouted, but his father didn't even react.

Trudy heard a buzzing in her head and felt her knees go a little weak. Was this really it? Was she going to die, here and now, in this place? Although she'd been advancing in tiny steps towards Iris's killer, willing and ready to try to do her duty, now that time had come she felt only cold and numb. And frankly, disbelieving.

Janet gave a low, audible moan. This morning, when she'd thought she would confront Ronnie and make him admit to killing Iris, she had imagined it would make her feel so powerful and finally allow her to come out of Iris's shadow. She'd seen herself returning to the village the triumphant heroine, admired and respected by all, no longer overlooked or underestimated. And finally she'd have the courage to tell her mother that she wanted to move to a small flat of her own in town, leave the fashionably decorated house and the fish-bowl of a village and begin to live. To finally *live*!

And now she was sure that she was going to have to do the opposite. To die. Die, before she'd even known what it was to be alive.

'I'm sorry, really I am,' Ray Dewberry said to her, but even as he spoke he was sighting down the barrel at the coroner in a business-like manner. 'But I don't have any choice, you can see that girl, can't you? I have my name to think of, and my boy's future to protect, and the farm. The Dewberrys have worked the land here since the Normans came. It's not as if I can make people really understand! Nobody would understand about Iris, see ...'

'*But what if they did?*'

The new voice, shockingly, seemed to come out of nowhere. And instinctively, Ray swung around, seeking the source of that unknown voice, the barrel of the shotgun swinging with him.

Chapter 35

Trudy recognised the voice at once, but simply couldn't understand why she was hearing it. It sounded so out of context that for a moment she had the weird feeling you sometimes got when you found yourself wondering if you were actually dreaming, and not really awake at all.

She swivelled around to look behind her and saw that she was right, and that Duncan Gillingham was now walking towards them. He carefully had his hands out either side of him, showing that he was carrying nothing more than a notebook and a pencil in one hand.

'Who the hell are you?' Ray Dewberry snarled. He looked wild-eyed and seriously put-out.

Clement took the opportunity of his distraction to quickly move further to one side and towards the farmer, putting him still further away from Trudy but closer than her to the man with the gun. Luckily, Trudy was also looking at the newcomer, and hadn't seen what he'd done.

Ronnie gave the coroner a quick, worried look. He shot another worried glance at his father, then back at Clement, clearly torn about whether he should warn his father or not. Loyalty to him had to rank high, but how far could it be stretched? Wordlessly,

Clement nodded at Janet, looked pointedly at Ronnie, then jerked his chin towards the house. With his hands, he mimicked the motions of someone dialling a telephone.

Janet nodded, understanding immediately what he wanted, and grasped Ronnie's arm and tugged pleadingly. For one awful, heart-stopping moment, Clement thought he'd refuse to move, and he scowled at the younger man, doing his best to radiate outrage. He again looked at Janet, then pointedly at the shotgun in his father's hand, and then jerked his head imperiously towards the house, his intentions clear enough for even Ronnie to understand.

Get Janet safe! What are you thinking about, boy?

To his relief, Ronnie had the grace to flush in shame for not thinking of her first, and after shooting his father's stiff back a final, fearful gaze, began to back away, keeping Janet behind him. Luckily, the open kitchen door wasn't that far away, and his father was way too thunderstruck at the interruption to sense the movement going on behind him.

'I said, who the hell are you and what are you doing here?' Ray roared.

Trudy, her heart in her mouth, saw Duncan flinch, then force a smile onto his handsome face. 'I'm the man who can help you, Mr Dewberry,' Duncan began glibly.

Trudy groaned, wanting to throttle him! Of all the times to chance his luck like this. Did he not realise that he couldn't rely on his charm or his cheek to see him through in a situation like this? Ray Dewberry didn't care a fig for his fancy words or persuasive ways – he'd just shoot him!

'He's nobody important,' Trudy said lightly, desperately trying to think of a way to ensure that Ray Dewberry didn't see him as a threat. 'He's just a pesky reporter for the local rag.' She hoped her tone came out as casual and slightly scornful as she'd hoped.

Behind her, Clement gave a sigh of relief as he saw first Janet back into the farmhouse and disappear, and then Ronnie. He was even more pleased when he saw the kitchen door quietly close.

Surely the boy would have the sense to lock it? And bar it for good measure? Hopefully Janet was even now running for the telephone to call the police.

'A reporter!' Ray said in disgust. 'That's just what I need!' he snorted.

'But Mr Dewberry, don't you see, that *is* just what you need,' Duncan said, trying to ignore the roiling in his stomach that made him want to throw up, and the slightly light-headed feeling that made him want to sit down.

When he could no longer deny to himself that Ray was about to start killing, the idea had popped into his head like a cork out of a bottle and before he'd had time to think it through, something had compelled him to stand up. He'd then walked the few steps around the wall to enter the courtyard.

Now he just had to pull it off.

'You said just now that you had no choice, and that it was all Iris Carmody's fault,' Duncan swept on nervously, needing to lay out his pitch before the man just went totally off his rocker and started blasting. 'Isn't that right? And that nobody would understand the real truth of the matter?'

Ray continued to glare at him in silence.

Duncan swallowed hard, but tried another smile. 'Well, that's where I can help you,' he said, and risked twitching his hand with the notebook in it. 'You see, I can tell your story for you, Mr Dewberry. *You can have your say.* You can tell everyone what Iris was like, and how she drove people mad, forcing you to do what you didn't want to do. You said nobody would understand, but that's only true if they don't get the chance to. But you can *make* them understand how it all was.'

Was Ray beginning to look less, well, murderous, and more thoughtful, or was that just wishful thinking? Encouraged, he took a cautious step forward. 'Don't you *want* people to understand how and why it all happened? How it wasn't all your fault?'

Duncan risked a quick look at Trudy, a silent appeal for her

235

not to do anything rash, but let him make his play. If he could only talk the man down, they might all get out of this alive. But behind the farmer's bulky shoulder, he could see the old vulture on the move, silently padding up behind Ray and carefully closing the gap.

Duncan felt his heart begin to pound. If the silly old fool tackled him and the gun went off, it could blow him, Duncan, in half!

'And don't you think people *deserve* to know the truth?' he said loudly, desperate to think of something, *anything*, that would keep the man distracted. 'After all, there are bound to be other girls like Iris out there, right?' he asked, anxious to appease the farmer, who was, in his opinion, definitely not right in the head. And what could appeal more to a mad-man than the chance to talk about the object of his mania? 'Other beautiful but rotten girls, all set to destroy other men, unwary men like you, without a single thought. Don't you think they need to be *warned*, Mr Dewberry? Surely it's your duty to do so, and people will even thank you for it.'

Trudy finally caught on to what he was trying to do, and turned to look at the armed man, trying to see if Duncan was succeeding in reaching him. And, she thought, he actually might be.

At least the scowl was gone, and Ray was looking at him more thoughtfully now.

Duncan thought so too, for he swept on encouragingly. 'Just think of it, Mr Dewberry – everyone would read your story in the paper and all of them would understand then, wouldn't they? Your neighbours, and strangers alike. You can't be the only man taken for a ride by someone like Iris, can you? So *they'd* all know how it must have been, yes? And they wouldn't judge you for it.'

Ray nodded. 'Don't reckon they would,' he conceded slowly.

Trudy held her breath and began to hope.

Clement, although still stalking the man with the gun, slowed slightly, giving the sweet-talking young man a chance to work his magic.

And Duncan wasn't about to disoblige him! He wanted the man to put down the shotgun more than anyone, since it was aimed right at his chest. 'And girls like Iris don't really fool other *women*, have you ever noticed that Mr Dewberry?' he cajoled. 'I'd bet you any money you like that the women in the village all said that Iris was no good, didn't they?' That he knew was true, since he'd interviewed his fair share of them.

Ray again slowly nodded. 'Aye, they did. None of the women-folk liked her.'

'There you are then,' Duncan said brightly. 'If you tell your story, all the women who read it will understand. And isn't that what you really need, now, more than anything? For people to understand how all of this wasn't really your fault?' He again waved his notebook in the air. 'So why don't we just sit down somewhere quiet, and you can tell me everything, and I'll write it down, and then everyone will understand. All right?'

Ray sighed. 'It's all going to hell in a handcart, ain't it?' he conceded sadly.

'I'm afraid so, Mr Dewberry,' Clement said quietly, and when the farmer swung his way, Duncan almost felt his knees give way in relief to no longer be looking down the barrels of that shotgun.

Now that he had the elder Dewberry's attention, Clement held out his hands in a what-can-you-do gesture. 'With Mr Gillingham on the scene, there's no way you can win now, is there? Not only are you hopelessly outnumbered, but his newspaper will know where he's gone. And when he doesn't turn up … besides, your son and Janet have, by now, already called the police and told them what's happening.'

At this, Ray started and looked wildly around, only then real-ising that Ronnie and Janet were, indeed, missing.

For a moment Ray quivered, a bit like a lurcher dog spotting a rabbit, so tense and alert and ready for something to happen that he was actually trembling with the need to act.

And then, just like that, it all seeped out of him. Maybe his son's desertion was the final straw. His head lowered fractionally and the gun barrels dipped until they were pointed at the ground. Eventually he nodded.

Trudy managed to drag in some much-needed air, unaware until then that she'd actually been holding her breath.

'So I'll take the gun then, shall I?' Clement said calmly, holding out his hand, moving carefully forward. 'Whilst you and this young man get to work.' He let his gaze move sardonically over Duncan. For although he would have to acknowledge the debt they owed to him, he was under no illusion. The reporter might have helped save their lives, but he'd done it with one eye on an exclusive interview with a killer – and all the fame and kudos that would net him.

'Yes, we need to do it quickly,' Duncan agreed, having no trouble reading the old vulture's mind – and feeling resentful, as always, at his perspicacity. The old sod had never liked him! 'If the police are on their way, we won't have much time, and I need to get down all of your story.'

Over the killer's shoulder he shot the coroner a hostile look.

For another moment, Ray Dewberry wrestled with the inevitable. Finally he gave a long, forlorn look around at the place where'd he'd lived all his life – and would never see again – then sighed, and wearily broke the shotgun open and half-heartedly offered it to Clement, who moved on rubbery legs to accept it.

Trudy came to stand beside her friend. She didn't have any handcuffs on her, so making a formal arrest seemed pointless. Besides, she was sure it would go a long way to appeasing DI Jennings's wrath if she left it to him to do the honours.

Also, as she watched Duncan scribble in his notebook whilst Ray Dewberry began to unburden his soul, she knew she hadn't the heart to do anything that would stop him from getting his precious story. When all was said and done, he'd risked his life to get it. And had probably saved her life, and that of at least one of the others, in the bargain. Probably Dr Ryder's, she mused.

For she knew, if it had come down to it, and she thought Ray had been about to open fire, she'd have had to take her chance and rushed him.

And she knew that Dr Clement Ryder wouldn't have been far behind her.

The wait for the police cars to arrive seemed to Trudy to be both long and short, since she was still feeling prone to that sensation that it was all a dream. She knew she was probably in a little bit of shock, but then, weren't they all?

Were they really standing around in the sunlit farmyard whilst Janet and Ronnie sheltered in the house, and Duncan interviewed a killer? Was Clement really stood there, standing guard with the shotgun, just in case?

But then they heard the sound of the sirens, and Duncan started frantically getting in some final questions. Ray Dewberry answered them calmly, as if he was talking about the price of wheat.

Chapter 36

It was dark by the time Trudy, DI Jennings and Superintendent Finch had enough time to gather together for a short meeting in the DI's office. Ray Dewberry had been processed and everyone had given their statements.

Not surprisingly, they were all looking tired and emotionally spent.

Keith Finch alternated between euphoria that his son's memory was now secure and safe from slander, and a grim, hollow-eyed acceptance that that wouldn't bring him back from the dead.

DI Jennings, too, swung from sheer relief that he'd solved his murder case, to annoyance that, once again, it was the old vulture and his wayward female WPC that he had to thank for it.

He'd already wasted some of his breath hauling her over the coals for not waiting for him at the Baines' house and going off on what might have been a wild goose chase without reporting in. The fact that, through sheer luck and incompetence, Trudy, the old vulture and some have-a-go-hero of a reporter had managed to save Janet's life, and maybe even the Dewberry boy's, was enough to make him want to chew the wallpaper. So he still had plenty of spleen left that he wanted to vent – and he was determined to do so. When it was safe to.

Needless to say, however, with Superintendent Finch now firmly on Trudy's side (and with the rest of the top brass happily giving interviews to the press on how clever they'd been in solving not one but two highly-publicised murders) he knew that she wouldn't be facing any actual disciplinary charges. And her star, as ever, was rising high.

He supposed, grudgingly, that he had to admit that she'd acquitted herself quite well, all in all. It wasn't every green young copper who could keep their head when faced with a killer holding a shotgun.

'How is Mrs Baines doing, sir, do you know?' Trudy asked now, jerking the Inspector's mind from his inner grumbling.

'Last I heard, the doctor said she was in a coma,' he grunted and glanced at the coroner. 'Bleeding on the brain, or some such thing?'

Clement nodded in understanding. 'But they've relieved the pressure and they're hoping she'll recover. However, I think young Janet is in for the long haul. Her mother's going to need her.'

Trudy sighed. 'I hope she and Ronnie will get together. After all they've been through I think they deserve some happiness.'

Jennings grunted sceptically. In his experience, tragedies like this tended to do no good for anyone involved. For a start, young Ronnie Dewberry was probably going to be a pariah for all his life – at least in Middle Fenton, where he'd always be regarded as the son of a killer. And he couldn't see Mrs Baines, when she was fit and well again, ever letting her precious daughter marry him. Unless the pair ran off to Gretna Green and then set up a new life somewhere far away from here. And even then – what sort of a start were they going to have? Janet had admitted that she'd thought Ronnie was to blame for Iris's death, and could the boy really forgive that – even given the extenuating circumstances?

'Well, I have to get back to my family,' Keith Finch said, and held out his hand to Clement. 'Thank you, Dr Ryder, for all that you did,' he said, swallowing hard, his voice gruff.

'I wasn't on my own,' Clement pointed out, making Jennings fairly grit his teeth.

'No indeed. Constable Loveday.' Keith turned to her and shook her hand too, totally against protocol. 'I'm expecting great things of you,' he told her.

Trudy felt herself blush.

Jennings waited until his superior officer had left the office, before turning his gimlet eye on Trudy. Great things indeed!

Clement chose that moment to also rise from his chair. 'Well, I'm off home as well. It's been one hell of a day, and I need my bed.'

He looked as if he did too, Trudy thought with some concern. He looked tired and worn out and … well, for the first time since she'd known him, actually … *old*.

Clement forced himself to stride confidently to the door, but was secretly relieved to discover that his legs held him. There was no doubt about it, today had been a serious strain on him, and he could no longer fool himself that his illness wasn't beginning to make itself felt.

But, he was sure, after a good night's sleep and a solid breakfast he'd be right as rain tomorrow. He wouldn't let himself be anything else. He was not ready for the scrap heap just yet.

All he had to do now, Clement thought wryly, was get home without driving into a ditch or something.

With the departure of the old vulture, Jennings was able to finally relax, and with a slow, satisfied smile, turned his attention to the young woman who seemed determined to make herself the bane of his life.

'Right then Constable …' he began ominously.

Trudy sat up a little straighter in her chair. 'Sir,' she said flatly. At least some things, she thought – almost gratefully – could be relied on never to change.

242

Dear Reader,

Thank you so much for taking the time to read this book – we hope you enjoyed it! If you did, we'd be so appreciative if you left a review.

Here at HQ Digital we are dedicated to publishing fiction that will keep you turning the pages into the early hours. We publish a variety of genres, from heartwarming romance, to thrilling crime and sweeping historical fiction.

To find out more about our books, enter competitions and discover exclusive content, please join our community of readers by following us at:

@HQDigitalUK

facebook.com/HQDigitalUK

Are you a budding writer?
We're also looking for authors to join the HQ Digital family!
Please submit your manuscript to:

HQDigital@harpercollins.co.uk.

Hope to hear from you soon!

ONE PLACE. MANY STORIES

If you enjoyed *A Fatal Affair*,
then why not try another gripping
mystery from HQ Digital?

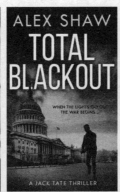

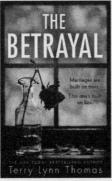